LOSS

Jane Lightbourne

Nevada Street Press

First published in 2022 in Great Britain by Nevada Street Press. www.janelightbourne.co.uk

ISBN: 978-1-8382168-3-2

Printed and bound by CPI Group (UK) Ltd, Croydon CR0 4YY

Your eyes hold a thousand tomorrows, tiny fires,
an ocean wide, calm 'neath steely skies,
but I, I look only to forest flame,
to tired trees still holding their leaves,
before change breaks them
again & again.

PROLOGUE

It was still early - the moon pale and lingering, reluctant to leave the darkest part of the sky, dawn only a silver line on the eastern edge of the horizon. I was driving, had driven the same route several times, and the petrol station with its three dilapidated pumps, the junkies slumped outside the Gothic church on the corner, the derelict houses, their windows like dark eyes, all seemed familiar. It was a bumpy ride - the road full of icy potholes.

When I came to the last of the small, tatty houses on the left I knocked, not once but three times. No one came to the door, even though through the ground floor window I glimpsed a light burning from somewhere at the back of the house.

"You sure you got the right address?" my partner asked. He hadn't been best pleased to be dragged out of bed but hadn't wanted me to travel to that neighbourhood alone at that hour. He'd exited the car behind me and was now standing by my side.

"Yes."

"I thought you no longer needed to visit. I thought the girl had been doing well. They were going to discharge her, you said."

"But she told me to come. She was gabbling on about the baby."

"What did she say?"

I shook my head. The girl hadn't made much sense at five a.m. that morning, only insisted I come at once. Her call had come through on my mobile that I left on the office voicemail in case of emergencies. "I'd better try her mum's place," I said.

I'd been assigned the case some months back, on account of question marks over the young mother's ability to cope. The nurses at the hospital had flagged up the possibility of post-natal depression, on top of previous addiction issues. I was delighted to have been given the case; as a junior this felt like the kind of situation where I could make a difference, where trust was everything. The girl's husband was friendly, helpful and polite, the mother too. I'd only visited a few times, but on the last two occasions - more than a month ago now - the girl had seemed animated, lively, happy, the baby thriving too. I hadn't felt the need to visit in person since.

Until I got the call from her at five o'clock that morning.

I was flattered enough to leave my warm bed for her.

I'd been to the girl's mother's house only once before. It backed onto the canal; now the sun was just starting to touch its oily, wavering surface and a sharp reek of rotting matter rose from its banks. As we exited the car, we heard the slap of water and the single cry of a wakeful seagull.

The girl's mother opened the door. She was wearing a stained green dress and swaying slightly in time to the swinging of a bare bulb overhead. There was a curious smell emanating from her, a slightly over-ripe, almost sickly smell, like rotting fruit.

"You shouldnae have come," she said, the moment she saw me. "Go back to bed."

"Where's your daughter?"

"Here with me now. She just needed my help with the bairn. She was struggling with the feeding. You know how 'tis."

I didn't. I hesitated. I was freezing, craving coffee, but she wasn't even going to let me in, let alone give me a drink.

I thought I could hear the sound of a baby crying upstairs.

I looked around. Dan was waiting by the car this time. I could see him passing the car keys from hand to hand. He was never a very patient person.

As I stood there, a mangy black cat came downstairs and weaved itself around the woman's ankles.

"Maybe I'll come in, check everything's ok," I said, hesitating.

"There isnae any need."

Now I could hear footsteps on the stairs, and the girl's husband appeared, holding the baby, all swaddled up. The man was so good looking - thick, messy hair, strong jawline dark with shadow, clear grey eyes - he would have made most girls swoon. But I prided myself on my professionalism.

"The bairn's fine. We've all been looking after her, haven't we?" he said, turning to the mother. "Katy's sleepin' now. Best not disturb her, if you know what's good for you."

Then he smiled at me - a big, broad, come-hither smile that made a pulse quiver in my throat, just as it sent me scuttling back towards the car.

"Tell Katy I'll try her in the week," I told him.

He nodded and raised one hand. I didn't see him smile again because by that time I was in the car. I heard the front door slam behind me though. I think the whole street did.

But by that time, we were driving away fast, along busier streets where people, intent on their own business, hurried past us, eyes averted, pale faces lifted to the sun. And after that, the day took over with its myriad set of demands, and I didn't give the young mother, or her baby, another thought.

JAMIE

Three years later

It was the exact same shocking sound a body makes when it hits a car screen. I knew the sound, remembered it well. I started, heart pounding - but it was only the thud of the girl's fist on the glass, her knuckles pressed white against it, the blood-red of her blouse squashed against the window. For a brief instant our eyes met, and then the light turned green. I hesitated; for a few fatal seconds I hesitated, my foot hovering over the gas pedal. The car slowed for an instant; then I pressed my foot down.

But she didn't give up. She trailed the moving car, still banging at the window. When that didn't work, she ran faster, looping round in front of the bonnet. That's when I started pulling over to the left. She didn't give me much choice - if I'd carried on moving, I would have made her as flat as a pancake.

I was a very careful driver these days.

It was half past five on a Saturday morning. There were few other cars on the Holloway Road at that godforsaken hour - I was amazed anyone was around at all. But there she was, in amongst the pigeon shit and the dead leaves, the only spot of colour on an otherwise sullen street, her heart-shaped face oddly familiar, her bloody blouse billowing about her.

As I slowed, I saw the sign she was holding. 'INVERNESS' it read, in big scarlet letters. The paper was torn and dirty and streaked with rain.

Adrenalin made me nervy and angry. I swore as I wound the passenger window down, winced as the rain hit my face.

The girl leaned in, so close I could see raindrops tangled in her hair, I could have reached out and touched them.

"You got a death wish or something?"

She smiled at me. "I might do," she said. "Does it matter to you?"

Her voice was low and cloudy, shot through with smoke. There was a curious lilt to it, an accent that I couldn't quite place. Up close her eyes were grey and luminous, the centres flecked with gold. Their pupils didn't look quite right. They were large, dark pools, but they weren't calm. They were the opposite of calm.

I sighed. Who was she, anyway? Just another drugged-up, going-nowhere girl. What did I care, right?

"I don't give a shit," I told her. "Just keep me out of it, all right?"

A creepy sense of déjà-vu crept over me. The girl's face faded, replaced by another, more familiar, just as I'd seen it for the last time - bloodless, broken, eyes vacant and sorry. My heart caught in my chest, trapping my breath in my lungs.

With an effort, I turned my attention back to this girl, the one in front of me. Her nails were chipped and broken, bitten down to the quick. Her hair was tousled and dirty. When she pushed her sleeves up, I saw small bruises at the tops of her arms. How had they happened, those bruises? She seemed not to notice them, or even care.

"Where're you going, then, in your flashy car?" she asked me. She spoke fast, passing one hand nervously through her dark blonde hair, while with the other she stroked my car's bonnet - long, sensuous strokes, as if she were stroking a cat.

It was raining even harder now, and my windscreen had clouded over; I could just see the deserted road ahead fork into two, before both roads vanished in the watery mist. As I watched the strange girl a pulse quickened inside me. At the same time, I felt a sudden pull - as if my body were trying to curve towards hers, as if it were trying to respond to her question with a question of its own. When I spoke again, I knew I'd made a kind of unconscious decision.

"Get in, before you get even more wet."

She grabbed the small navy suitcase she'd dropped at her feet, opened the door and settled into the passenger seat. I saw a sudden blaze of bare flesh, before she pulled her skirt down to cover it.

"Shouldn't you be wearing a bit more? It's freezing."

She smiled, crossed her legs, pulled her skirt even further down. "I'm burning up," she said.

I looked at her again, as if she were a slide beneath a microscope: her hair that fell around her face in a long cloudy mass, her make-up smudged slightly at the corners of her eyes, a mole on her left cheek, a pulse beating ever so faintly in her neck, a small pool at the base of her throat where the raindrops had collected... in the hollow at the base of her throat...

I swallowed with difficulty, passed one hand over my eyes. She moved closer, and beneath the complicated perfume she was wearing, I could detect the faintest trace of fresh sweat, laced with something feral and considerably more potent.

Our eyes met, and I saw in hers something of the hunted, of the creature living in the shadow of the steel trap.

"What's wrong?" I asked her.

"Nothing," she said. "Can I smoke in here?"

"I'd rather you didn't."

Quickly, I looked away. I breathed in, sensing my mind expand with her nearness, and then contract. My hands rested for a second on the steering wheel, like birds poised for flight. I looked out at the street, at the bleak and shuttered shops, the pigeons scurrying like rats on the road. I closed my eyes.

"Where are you going?" she asked again.

I didn't answer her.

"Wherever it is, will you take me with you?"

"You don't know where I'm going yet."

"Take me just the same."

"I could be a lunatic. A rapist or worse."

"I've met them all. And I could be the lunatic," she said.

I swallowed again, turning this possibility over in my mind before discounting it. No - she was just some girl at a low ebb, probably looking to trade sex for shelter, food, reassurance, cash.

"Look - whatever you've got to give me, I'm not interested. OK?" As I spoke, the maddening, muffled itch of sexual frustration tightened my balls, its insidious pressure making them pound, and I almost regretted speaking at all.

"Do I look like a prostitute?"

"I didn't say that."

"You didn't have to," she said.

"Well, are you?"

"What do you think?"

"I wouldn't know."

She laughed. "Look at you, Mr High and Mighty," she said. "Never even been tempted?"

I ignored her. "I'm going to the Highlands," I said stiffly. "To visit my brother."

"I knew you were going to the Highlands."

"How could you possibly know that?"

"I don't know. You could say I have…a…sixth sense about things. I get stuff about people without their having to tell me. It gives me a kind of…hold over them, if you like."

"Should I be scared?" I asked her.

Her eyes rested on my face. She smiled, said nothing.

"Is that why you stopped me?" I went on. "You knew where I was going?"

She laughed. "That, and…I liked your face," she said. She pressed both hands together, clutching them tightly in her lap. Her pupils were dark and wide. "Take me with you," she murmured.

I caught the smell of sweat again; stronger, more acidic this time.

"All the way to the Highlands?"

"Yes, definitely the Highlands."

When I didn't reply, not at first, she asked "What? Don't want me to meet your brother? Is he your keeper or something?"

"Hardly," I snorted.

"Well then."

"Well what?"

"Shall we go?" she said.

I didn't have to drive her anywhere at all. Of course I didn't. I could have pushed her back out onto the street, driven off and left her to walk home in the rain. I had a choice. It just didn't seem like that at the time. I could feel that pulse beat inside my head, the dark thud of blood pushing me forward, as if it had a life and purpose of its own. The long journey up to the Highlands lay lonely and undriven before me. Solitude had never held much appeal; yet to share my space with some random stranger - well, that was unthinkable. Wasn't it? I released the handbrake, edged my foot towards the gas.

The girl held out her hand. "I'm Katy, by the way."

I held her hand briefly, feeling the heat radiate from it. The luminous golden flecks in her grey irises now bloomed with life, a warmth and fire that drew me in.

I moved away. My mind was playing tricks with me again. Every night I woke, reaching for a face I knew was real; a familiar face, angelic, haunting, surrounded by raven-coloured hair. But as soon as I put out my hands, the face would vanish into the darkness and my fingers would close on nothing but empty space. Daylight brought only brief respite; the next night, the face would appear again, mock me once more. The face itself never changed, only the background from which it appeared: sometimes land, sometimes water; once, the bed beside me, my own crumpled sheets. That incident had been most frightening of all. And every time I woke, semiconscious in the half-light, I tried to recollect the detail of the landscape so that I might track the face down to a particular patch of land, or water, city, or a river. So far, no joy.

"You okay?" Katy asked me.

I started. "I'm fine."

If I focused on her face - her real face - for long enough, perhaps that other face would finally cease to haunt me.

Swayed by this, I pressed my foot down on the clutch.

"You didn't tell me your name," my new companion said.

"It's Jamie." I put the car into gear. "Scotland's a long way away. Shall we drive for a bit and see how far we get?"

She nodded happily. "You can throw me out if you get sick of me."

"Don't tempt me," I said.

I pressed my foot down on the gas and the car leapt forward. Within seconds, we had left the Holloway Road behind and were heading up past Archway to the A1.

KATY

I went into some sort of trance sitting in that
fancy car, saying nothing, just enjoying the silence
and the feel of silky leather on my back. For the
first time in a long time I felt calm, and the calm
wasn't accompanied by the woozy high coming
off some sort of drug, but then I closed my eyes
and all I could hear was my mother's voice, all
I could see was her face beneath my lids, eyes
bloodshot, staring at some random space, while
she hissed

- Give her back! Give her to me!

And then she vanished, and there was Steve's
puggish face, puce with fury, jabbing at my chest
with one meaty finger

- What you playing at, Katy? Prancing up to
Scotland! What are you hoping will happen?

And I shivered as the pain of his grip on my
arms came flooding back, blunt and dirty nails
digging into my flesh.

But I'd asked for it - I'd needled him, knowing
that in the end he'd do just what he did, which
was to turf me out onto that lonely, rat-infested,
rain-ridden street...

- You alright? my driver asked, cutting into my
thoughts.

I looked over at his face, with its faraway eyes and hair falling into it, so desperate for a cut.

- I was thinking about my boyfriend, I said.

- You've a boyfriend? Then how did you come to be standing all alone, in the wet?

- We had a row. I wanted him to take me to Scotland, but he kicked me out instead.

- Why did you want to go to Scotland?

But I couldn't tell how I wanted to get my daughter back; I just sat, nursing my plan, as I would a baby at my breast. The voices, those angry, hungry voices that came and went, that wouldn't let me sleep or eat, that made me do things that afterwards I might regret, had now dulled to a low murmur, and I could pretend that they didn't exist. So when he asked me that, I just clammed up, muttered something about a friend, hoping he would get the message and drop it, which in the end he did.

After we'd driven for a while with no sound, only the beating of the rain upon the roof, I asked him what his wife thought about his trip.

- How do you know I have a wife? he asked.

- It's a dead giveaway - that look of misery on your face.

He winced and I saw spots of colour stain his cheeks.

- I'm just tired, he said. I'm a lawyer. I've been

working late.

- Where do you work? I asked, and he told me the name of the firm and then looked like he regretted it.

- How long have you been married?

- What's it to you? he said.

- Just passing time, I told him. It's a long journey up to Scotland, I know that much, I said.

He was quiet for a bit.

- I've been married three years. But I've been with her since I was twenty-six. His mouth turned up as he said it, but his eyes seemed to die a little bit.

I already had an image of his wife in my head - humourless, and wound up, always working, smartly dressed, no time for sex. I wanted to ask him about her, see if I was right, but I hesitated, and he asked me what I did instead.

- I've been working over a year now for some pampered media type, I told him.

- How's that?

- Well, I've been working long hours, but getting decent money for it.

- Decent money? As opposed to - what?

- Being on the streets.

He coloured up again, and I thought *Screw him. Who is he to judge?* I flared with anger, thought I might open the car door and that would be an end to it, but he was driving over eighty at that point, and I thought *I don't want to die just yet, not until we've had a fuck.*

I wanted to tell him then how happy I'd been to get my job, to escape that crazy cocktail of shame and drugs, the shaking and the sweating and the horrible weight loss. How much better that was than the jobs I'd had when I'd first got to London - waiting on tables at grubby caffs, cleaning out loos in Charing Cross. How I'd often have to take a few days off, when I was too wired to put on a social face, but Marcus, my boss, whom I'd met at some club, who'd wanted a pretty piece to do his PA work, he was generous with that. He never cared if I was a little flaky - I had 'skills', he said. He didn't want me to bugger off.

But I couldn't tell this man any of that.

- I came to London three years ago, was all I told him. From Scotland, I said.

- Why did you move?

- To escape.

The words had slipped out and now I shook my head. I'd fled after my kid went - I was so scared they'd all come after me, asking me loads of questions, torturing me any chance they could. So in the end, I didn't have a choice - I had to put a stop to it. A mate of mine who'd left for London some years back, Nancy her name was, we'd kept in touch, and she'd said she'd help, gave me some bullshit story about how I could get rich quick.

I just had to go to London, she said. But once I got there she'd just set me up with a load of no-hopers who'd got me hooked on Angel Dust.

It was Donna in the end who'd helped me out. I'd been so lucky to meet her through one of my shitty jobs. She was the one who forced me into rehab, who held me while I cried and slept and sweated out the drugs...

- Donna, I told him. She helped.
- Who's she? he asked me.
- My guardian angel, I said.

After that, silence stretched between us, and the voices were once again deafening inside my head, their roar loud as that of an approaching train. Idiot! they hissed. *How is he going to help?* But then Jamie flicked the stereo on, and the Sisters of Mercy came and filled the space, and the voices receded and I thought *More* was a pretty good song anyhow, and just now it was near perfect, the right song at the right time in the right place.

As I listened to the rain on the windscreen and the push of the wipers, I felt my head pulse with the music, and I heard the soft pump of blood inside the chambers of my chest. My stomach still seethed, but for once the menace was like the distant rumble of thunder, too far off to catch. In the great grubby city we'd just left people drank and farted and shat and stank - but at last I was leaving, moving so fast the ground fell away beneath my feet, my head buzzing with the thoughts bursting out of it...

Then Jamie burst in, and said - What are you thinking, Katy? And it was as if he'd thrown a blanket over my head - all my fire, my energy, my ideas, snuffed out.

And of course I wouldn't tell him. I couldn't tell him anything. Not just yet. Not for a while. I needed to see how things played out.

- I need a cigarette, was all I said.
- I told you - you can't smoke in here.
- Don't you want one? I asked him.
- I don't smoke, he said.
- I had you for a smoker, I told him.
- I've given up, he said.
- Can we stop? I asked him.
- Not just yet, he said.

And then a little later I asked again.

- In a bit, he said.

And all the while I was desperate for that cigarette, until at last he indicated left to leave the motorway and I was glad, because I wanted to sit and talk to him, not sideways on but face-to-face, and I was just filled with wanting, wanting that and the cigarette.

JAMIE

We stood at the entrance to the service station café, barely sheltered from the rain, my fists thrust deep into the pockets of my jacket, Katy with her arms wrapped around her, cigarette dangling from the two fingers of one hand. Watching her smoke was somehow mesmerising: the slow rise of her fingers to her mouth, the slight flick of her wrist as she deposited the ash. Each time she pulled on that cigarette; I felt a corresponding tightening in my guts. Despite the cold, I could have watched her forever.

"You're left-handed." *Like my sister*, I thought. *Like Sarah.*

"All the best people are," she said. She smiled, and it was like the slow opening of a secret door. I smiled back, took a step towards her.

Katy offered me the pack of cigarettes. "Want one?"

The smell made my stomach spiral, brought back the heady freedoms of halcyon days. I'd smoked for years - when I first met Rachel she'd ignored the cigarettes, eventually expressing mild disapproval, which became ever more insistent, until finally I quit. I started again after my sister went missing, cigarettes my only solace through those sleepless nights following her disappearance. Rachel struggled to conceal her irritation, even then. I remembered midnight forays through my wardrobe, my wife's aquiline nose quivering like a sniffer dog's. Once, she descended on me, brandishing a packet of fags like a weapon. That last incident had killed my longing pretty fast.

"I can't," I said.

Katy stopped smiling and that door slammed shut in my face. "What, the wife won't let you?"

"Shall we go in? I need coffee," I said.

As I said it, I felt my body scream for caffeine - a poor alternative to that cigarette, it seemed now, but it would have to do. The morning's lack of coffee perhaps explained my pounding headache; that, or the altercation I'd had with Rachel before setting off.

I'd found my wife up painfully early, her back to me in the kitchen as she bent over the sink, elbows moving vigorously.

"Come back to bed," I'd said, reaching out one hand to touch her stiff shoulders. I'd softened my voice, seeking to persuade her, and she'd misread me. She'd turned to stare at me.

"Why would I want *that*? After what just happened?"

"I only want you to rest."

"Well, I wouldn't be able to sleep; not after what I've been through."

That made me consider yet again what she had been through: the twisting pain, the bloody sheets, a brutal end to budding hopes, and then the emptiness, final and complete, like the curtain coming down on the show.

Guilty, impotent, I reached out a hand to her, touched her pale, frail face. "Rachel..." I murmured.

I'd felt her soften. "Don't go to Scotland, Jamie."

"I have to. My mother, she wants me to."

She turned back to the sink. "Do you have to do what she wants all the bloody time? Ever since the accident she's wound you around your little finger."

"But she isn't well."

"She's in remission, Jamie."

That was true. My mother had had a cancer scare some years back, but now, finally, she seemed to have beaten it. I'd visited a lot at the time, less so of late. My family home was in Norfolk, a big rambling farmhouse that I got lost in as a child, sometimes deliberately. But now its low ceilings and smoke-blackened timbers depressed me. I still loved the garden though, overgrown, neglected for many years, the once well-tended lawn now wild with wet grass, and stems of hollyhock and foxglove that grew against the rotting timbers of abandoned sheds...

"Jamie?"

"Sorry," I murmured. "Just thinking about mother."

I concentrated now on my wife: ever-present, pragmatic, highly organised, the motivated daughter of a clergyman and his wife, both award-winning golfers, both still going strong after a recent move from Cheshire to a mock-Tudor house in the Cotswolds. (I didn't like going there either, but for different reasons.)

"I need to see Peter," I told her.

"Damn Peter. He'll never forgive you either."

"Is that a reason not to try?"

"If you want to go on banging your head against that particular wall. How long has it been now?"

"Four years."

"Precisely."

I flushed. "You told me you needed some space."

"I did," my wife admitted.

It was true that Rachel seemed to relish her own company, spending many hours working at her laptop in her office in the basement - I was astonished that she was so unaffected by the lack of natural light there - or rearranging kitchen cupboards or writing lists. (Rachel loved lists.) She seemed not to care if I was around or not. When she was out, working usually, or at the gym, I was prone to restlessness, conscious that something was missing from our unusually tidy, some would say pristine, house.

And what was that thing? A baby perhaps, as one particularly nosy neighbour had suggested. Well, we were trying.

"Well, then. I'm giving you what you want, Rachel. I'm giving you space."

But she'd put her back to me again to hide her face

and banged a pot on the side to conceal the sob in her throat.

"Just go, Jamie. Leave. I can't stop you."

That was the thing with Rachel. There was no point in fighting. She would never let me win.

"Something the matter?" Katy asked innocently, stubbing out her cigarette. "You were miles away."

I shook my head, shaking Rachel out of it. "I just need coffee," I said.

After we'd stepped into the café, Katy excused herself to go to the bathroom, and I picked up a coffee for each of us and sat down on a bright orange seat. The coffee smelled of plastic and tasted of tar. Sipping at it gingerly, I took out my phone. I sent a conciliatory message to Rachel, as I usually did after any altercation. Always I was the one to say I was sorry - Rachel never did. Words were cheap, as my wife was so fond of saying to me. But not worthless, I thought.

Katy came and sat opposite me, her pupils wilder and more dilated than they had been. I looked away quickly. What did I care what she'd been up to in the loos? I was under no obligation to stop her from snorting her life up her nose if she wanted. I didn't have to bring her to her senses, or live with my failure to do so, every goddam day. No - with this girl, I didn't have to even try. I could sense a weight shift from my shoulders with that realisation…but still, I couldn't deny it; what I suspected she'd been doing in the loos irritated me just the same.

My companion looked away from me and started to trace a line around her saucer with a spoon. Her left hand was shaking ever so slightly. When she saw I'd seen this, she put the right hand over the left.

"It's not what you think. I'm not using," she told me. "Not anymore."

"Of course."

"The Angel Dust, it gave me nightmares in the end. Made me hallucinate too. I saw all kinds of things in those days."

"What things?" I asked before I could stop myself. "I don't care what you do or did," I said quickly.

"Oh, but I think you do."

I took a large swallow of my coffee to conceal my annoyance, cursing when the black liquid scorched my throat.

"You need a haircut," she told me. She smiled, and that door opened up again with her smile.

I swallowed quickly. "So my wife tells me," I told her. "But I like it long."

"It doesn't suit you. Hides your face."

I shook my hair over my face, in mock hippy stance.

"I like to hide, sometimes."

Katy laughed. "I like to hide too."

When I looked at her again, her lopsided smile, her

laughing grey eyes, I was overcome by a sudden crazy urge to kiss her. "Can I have a cigarette?" I asked her.

"Can't smoke in here."

I looked around. Our part of the café was empty, save for one lone figure, sweeping the floor. "Go on, give me one anyway," I said to her.

"Look at you! A lawyer, breaking the law. Must be my influence." She handed me the pack.

I lit a cigarette and inhaled. The smoke made the knot in my stomach relax a little - I sighed, smiling with pleasure.

"See how good it can be, to smoke with me?"

I laughed. I hadn't felt this relaxed for a while.

"You missed it then?"

"Too much."

"You look tired."

"I *am* tired."

"I'm too wired to sleep. What's your excuse? Work?"

"I wish it were."

Work wasn't big enough to keep me awake at nights. After all, what was I? Just a senior, some would say too senior, assistant in a small - a very small - City law firm; the same firm I'd entered as a trainee thirteen years ago. And yet, night after night, I'd wake - sometimes at one, sometimes later, but never when I was supposed to. Shaking and sweating in the darkness, knowing I'd lost someone infinitely precious, and that I would have to go on searching, searching, until finally I dropped from guilt and sheer exhaustion.

Rachel had for an appropriate length of time been quite sympathetic about this, for she was acutely aware solace was part of her job description. But she had tired of my grief over my sister a while ago, when she'd felt it had reached its statute of limitations. How could she understand grief has no limits, when she couldn't grasp anything she could not see or touch through her five senses? Anxiety, insomnia, irrationality, these things Rachel had no time for. So now, if she knew I was lying awake, she usually mumbled something and turned away. Unless it was her Time, of course; those two days every month when she turned towards me and turned me on with her hot breath and her hot tongue…

I started. Katy was talking. Her speech was fast and frenzied, and I'd missed half of it.

"You tried pills?" she asked me.

"The legal ones don't work."

"What about the illegal ones?"

"I thought you'd given up."

She shrugged her shoulders. "Occasionally I have a little dabble."

I stiffened. "Too much fun for me, I'm afraid. I'd lose the plot completely. I'm risk-averse, I'm told."

"Boring, you mean."

"Never."

"Scared you might like it, or just scared?"

A sudden memory hit me: a casino in Monte Carlo

at Peter's stag do years ago – I, high on the coloured light, spending, spending…

Peter had had to drag me away in the end. I'd have spent every last penny I had.

"I'm just the addictive type, that's all," I told her.

I knew I'd succumb after just one hit, just one - go under, my organised, carefully created, *civilised* life unravelling, ripping along the seams…

"We'd be dangerous together then. Give Sid and Nancy a run for their money."

I laughed.

Katy was tapping her knee against the table. She moved continually. I wondered what it would take to keep her still. Without thinking, I reached out and touched her hand. I felt her flinch, as though my fingers had burnt hers.

"You OK?" I asked her.

She stared at me. Her eyes were dark pools of liquid fire. "I'm fine," she said.

I sighed. High people wore me out. Complicated people wore me out. This woman was both. I removed my hand quickly, pushed it into my pocket, feeling a pulse running through my fingers.

She leaned into me. "It's not what you think," she whispered. "I'm high, but not in that way. I'm excited, Jamie. I'm full of plans."

"What sort of plans?"

"I can't tell you. Not yet. Just need to get up to the Highlands, like I said."

"Who's in the Highlands?"

"I already told you. A friend," she said. "So...tell me about you, instead."

I blinked. "What do you want to know?"

"Bit of a dark horse, aren't you? I can't tell what you're thinking. Usually I can, you know. I can read men like books."

Looking into those large, rather unnerving eyes, for a second I believed her. "Well, I'm sorry to disappoint."

Her grey eyes flicked onto me and flicked away again. "You don't disappoint," she said.

I felt slightly unsteady when she told me that, as if I'd taken one of those illicit pills she'd been on about. I was relieved when I felt a tap on my shoulder, followed by a polite but firm request from a disaffected attendant to put out my cigarette.

"Where does your brother live?" Katy asked, when the offending butt had been extinguished.

"In Cromarty. You know it? It's very...charming." I tried to keep my voice even, free from sarcasm, envy, anything at all.

"What's he like?"

"He's..." I searched around for an epithet to describe Peter. "He's very tall," I said at last. "And he's got a perfect fucking haircut. And a wife who's perfectly dressed and two perfect kids."

She laughed. "No vices at all?"

"Oh, plenty of vices. Stuffed full of them, in fact."

"You don't like him?"

"It's complicated."

"I'm listening."

"I don't want to get into it. Not now."

Katy shrugged. "You got any kids?"

"No. Why, do I look like I have?"

"No. You look tired, but not *that* tired... Do you want kids?"

"My wife does."

"And you don't? Or just not as much as she does?"

I shifted uncomfortably.

"What's with the third degree?"

"Can't I ask questions?"

"Not all the questions, no."

A silence fell between us. I thought of the smug brother whose company I was actively seeking for the first time in four years. I remembered the last time I'd seen Peter - his furious face yelling at me; the pain in my jaw where he'd smashed his fist, my head slamming the floor; the panic when my throat constricted and I couldn't swallow, the taste of blood coating it, blocking it...

I shut my eyes. I didn't want to think about Peter, let alone see him. Still, if my mother hadn't been begging me to do so, if I didn't feel I ought to resolve the situation, I wouldn't be here now, sitting opposite this rather alluring girl.

"Are you going to tell me why you really want to go to Scotland?" I asked at last.

Her eyes clouded, and she started to twist a single strand of hair around one finger. Round and round the finger, like a guilty child.

"This friend I want to see - I haven't seen him in ages."

"And where does this person live?"

"In Lochalsh," she said vaguely.

"Where in Lochalsh?"

"Nowhere you know."

"Is this friend a boyfriend, perhaps?"

"I told you, I have a boyfriend." She smiled. "Or rather, I had one. I don't suppose he'll be too keen now."

"Do you care?"

"He was holding me back. I need to find my friend. He will help me find..." Her voice tailed off.

"Find what?"

"Find what I lost."

"And what did you lose?"

She shook her head. "Anyways, Steve was just a filler."

"You do that, do you?"

"Do what?"

"Use men to fill time?"

Her eyes widened in shock. "I don't use men." She paused in her winding, the tip of her finger now as pale and bloodless as that of a corpse. "What about your wife?"

"What about her?"

"Tell me about her."

"There's little to tell."

"Like…how did you meet?"

I thought back to the occasion - almost nine years ago now - when, as assistants at different firms, Rachel and I had both happened to attend the same fairly tedious legal seminar. I couldn't concentrate on the lecture - I'd been too busy admiring this woman's sheet of sleek, dark, almost unnaturally smooth hair in front of me. I'd wanted to go on admiring it, so I'd had coffee with its owner, then another coffee, and then dinner, in and around the demands of Rachel's tyrannical diary. And now, with a somewhat stiff wedding in between, here we were, trying with increasing desperation (on my wife's part, at least) for a baby that never seemed to happen.

And so it laid itself out in front of me, my married life, in all its glory, its comforts and tedium, its bitter bouts of squabbling and inevitable disappointments. I hated it. But I loved to hate it. That was the problem. My marriage, my law firm, my malignant brother - these were the forces I needed to pit myself against. Without them, I suspected I would feel utterly lost.

I suppressed the sudden urge to confide all of this to my new companion, as I did most untidy, unwelcome desires.

"We met at work."

"Where do you live?"

"In London."

"London's a big place."

I shifted uncomfortably. "North London."

"Nice house?"

I thought of our house: small, only three bedrooms, but yes, nice. In the best part of Canonbury. And immaculate, thanks to Rachel's hard work. My wife had an appetite for building work, managing wayward builders tirelessly and with some success.

"Very." *The house was a golden cage,* I thought. *A very golden cage.*

"How long you been together?"

"Almost nine years," I told her. I held my breath and then let it out carefully so that it didn't resemble a sigh. Then I stood up, rather abruptly, scraping my chair on the floor. "We'd best get going. Don't want to spend the night on the A1 if we can help it."

Katy opened up her mouth as if to say something and shut it up again. I seemed to have successfully prevented further questioning, and I was acutely aware of my companion's silence at my side as we made our way back through the driving rain to the warmth and comfort of my car.

KATY

I didn't want to fall asleep; I was scared to do so, these days. Night time brought all sorts of horrors. Even stopping the drugs hadn't made those horrors go away. But I couldn't help it; the motion of Jamie's car was so soothing that eventually I slept.

As I slept I dreamt I was running, clutching onto a bundle, that precious bundle that I had to keep by me at all times, that I had to *make safe*. I was running fast, and the path ahead was shrouded in mist, but I could just make out a figure standing in the street ahead of me. The figure was wearing a hooded jacket and I couldn't see the face beneath. I couldn't stop, so I was going to run right into whomever it was, and he or she seemed to want that, because these arms were opened out...

I was woken by a shuddering and a voice muttering Fuck! Fuck! I opened my eyes to see Jamie - pale, shaking, staring straight ahead. The car wasn't moving - he'd taken his hands off the wheel.

- It was a hare, he said. I think I hit it - bugger, I'm sure I did. I'll get out. Take a look.

- I'll go, I said.

I stepped out and saw what was left of the hare; all mangled up, barely recognisable as such, and my stomach churned as I walked back. Jamie looked at me and I nodded. He was still shaking, his face all broken up. He sat a while with his hands on the wheel, and then put them up to his head.

I reached out and touched his arm, and after that the seconds seemed to stretch, and I felt his trembling slow and then stop.

"Do you want me to drive?" I asked him.

He turned to me and smiled. "I'm not as bad as all that!"

He put his hand out to touch my arm and I heard him murmur something I couldn't quite catch, felt a moment's hesitation, a miniature struggle and then he said

- We must get on if I'm going to get to Cromarty tonight.

I knew then that I could make him say and do what I would like - I knew it - the way I knew stars come out at night or the sun burns when it is hot. When I spoke again, I spoke so soft he had to lean into me to hear it, and as he did, I moved my body closer, feeling the hairs along my arm brush against his.

- What if we finished the drive tomorrow? I asked him. What if we stayed near Glasgow, found somewhere to stay the night? It'll be so late by the time you get to Cromarty, and I know a place where we could stop. Somewhere we could have dinner, somewhere we could talk, I said.

He looked at me, and his eyes lost that faraway look and came close.

- No, Katy...

When he said my name, it was soft, with nothing after it, just empty space.

- We can just talk, I whispered. And sleep. Nothing else.

- I'm so tired...

- Then let's stop, I said.

When I saw him nod, I felt triumph flood through my head, and it was just as sweet as the effect of any drug. And at the same time, I knew that I had the power to make the sweetness stop; I could do it - but I knew too that I would not.

He drove fast after that, but it didn't frighten me, I just sat back and listened to the radio, to Johnny Cash, his voice like honey melting in my mouth. I watched Cumbria shift and pass, the sharp staggered hills, the rocks sticking out like gravestones from the grass, and I thought about the Highlands - the skies vast and empty, the clouds forming and reforming in a million different patterns overhead. I tried to think about how beautiful that land was, and not of the terrible darkness at its heart; or what had happened three years ago, the circumstances in which I'd left.

After a while we stopped at another service station, and Jamie got out, to make a call, he said. After a minute I could hear him shouting into his phone, though I couldn't catch what he was saying. When he stepped back into the car, he was swearing beneath his breath.

- Your brother?
- Yes.
- He wants to see you tonight, I guessed.
- It's his way or no way. Fuck him, he said.

Eventually we drove through the streets of Glasgow, now grainy with dusk, until we came to a tiny village just to the north of it and stepped out into air that was full of the sound of horses, birds, the bleating of sheep.

The woman at the desk of the bed and breakfast I'd been told about had sullen eyes that flicked suspiciously from Jamie to me and back again.

- We've only the one room left, she said.
- We'll take that then, I told her, and I stood close to Jamie as he booked in.

- Do you want to go up now? the woman asked, a grim smile turning up the corners of her mouth. She dangled the key to the room in front of us.

I felt Jamie hesitate.

- Let's eat first, I said.

We sat next to each other at a table Jamie had found facing the bar, our knees almost touching but not quite, and in the air between us I could feel a pulse, like the ticking of a clock.

Jamie went to the bar and came back with a bottle of red, and I saw his hand shake as he poured the wine out. And as I drank, the wine moved down me in a gentle stream, and I closed my eyes and smiled and thought *This is how freedom feels.* It had been so long; I'd completely forgotten what it was like.

- I woke up this morning next to Steve, I told him. And he was on at me about Scotland, and I was scared, no idea how the day would turn out.

- What was he saying?

- You don't want to know, I said.

My head was quiet now as the wine loosened each of the knots in my stomach with slow, gentle fingers, forcing them to relax.

- So what do you do when you're through with work? I asked him.

- It feels like I'm never through, he said.

- But how do you relax?

- I don't have much time for hobbies. Rachel, she's so organised - she fits in the gym three times a week, and she's always learning different skills - how to play the violin or chess.

- How impressive, I said, though really I

thought it was rather tedious.

And he started talking about how they filled their weekends: tennis with other couples, but he didn't play so well, his wife said; dinner parties in, but his wife didn't cook so it was a lot of work; dinners out, with friends, but Rachel only liked high-end places, while he was happy anywhere as long as the food was good, he said. As he talked, very gently with my fingertips I made a circle on his wrist.

- It's your turn to talk, he whispered.
- What do you want me to talk about?
- Tell me who else is in Scotland first.
- Apart from my friend?
- Yes.
- Well…my mother, for a start.
- What's she like?

Now I remembered my mother but from way back - I remembered her singing when I was a kid, the soft, slow lullabies she used to sing to get me to sleep, and the way her hands would trace soft soothing circles on my head.

- She was OK once. But then she changed, I said.

When did I start having to persuade her to get out of bed? To bring her the weak, sugared tea she said always helped get her moving? Was I six - or a little older - when dad started going out all night, and I'd get up before either of them and hide her bottles, before he could come into the kitchen and go mad with the stink of all the drink?

Except once I forgot.

But that wasn't what made him move out.

The drink wasn't the only thing he couldn't forgive.

- She was so high at times. You couldn't stop her talking. She was excited, full of plans. She'd stay up all night, and once she painted a mural on the kitchen walls while we slept. But other times she'd lie in bed, doing nothing, not talking for days on end...

He was forcing me back now, to think about how things were, how good it made me feel, knowing she was happy, and how desperate I felt when I realised she wouldn't stay that way, no matter what I did. How I always wanted good to come from her, and that was like waiting for the sun to come out - I had to wait forever, but when it did I could bask in its warmth and light, like a cat.

- And your dad?

I thought of dad - how tall and dark he was, with thick hair and a strong jaw and a nose which was broken, but who gave a fuck? How when he was happy he threw his head back and laughed a laugh that bounced like a hard ball about the place, and when he was mad his eyes were mean, and his tongue lashed like a whip…

- He left when I was eight.
- Why was that?
- It was something that happened. But I can't…I can't talk about it, I said.
- What happened, then, to your dad?
- He died. Or so I heard.
- You didn't keep in touch?
- No, I said. No. It hurt too much to see him after that.

I waited and then at last I took one of Jamie's hands in mine, sliding my fingers over his, as though I were wrapping a gift. Heat burned through my fingers and through my chest.
- What was that you said? I whispered.
He smiled.
- Only if you wanted something to eat.
I didn't like to tell him I never felt like eating; I just let him choose for me - some chicken dish - and he chose one of those large pies that would have filled me up for a week.
- My dad died too, he said, after he'd given our order in.
- When was that?
- When I was at university. His heart gave out while he was at work. They called me, in the middle of the hottest day of the year. I was playing cricket at the time. The lawn was so

green, and I was so relaxed. I felt so guilty that it happened while I was doing that.

He blinked.

- Mum thinks it was all the pressure on him that did it - the strain of making cash, schooling the three of us. Then losing his house in the recession and having to start all over again. That was the final blow. Maybe she's right. That's why I want to do things differently, he said.

- Is that why you don't want kids?

- I never said I didn't want them, he said.

- You have another brother?

- I had a sister. But I…I lost her. Four years back. She…she just disappeared, he said.

- Did someone take her?

- I think so.

- Didn't the police look?

- We all looked. Everywhere, he said.

- And now?

- I…I haven't given up, he said.

I was conscious of a burning at the base of my throat and behind my nose. When the food came I had to force myself to eat, although I felt nothing but hunger inside, as if I were being possessed; but it was a hunger that food could never fill or cut or kill or satisfy.

Finally, I stopped trying to eat and stared down at the remaining food on my plate.

- I lost my dad once, I told him. I was in a

market. He let go of my hand. I remember running through the market, searching all over for him. In the end, some stranger took me to the police station, and my dad was there, I said.

The sound and colour of the market receded, and the thumping in my chest subsided. I could no longer see or feel my frightened seven-year-old self, only Jamie sitting in front of me.

- I was so lost, I blurted out.
- You were lucky - you were found, he told me.
- I was so happy then, I said.
He took hold of my hand.
- And now? You don't seem happy now.
- Right now, with you, I'm good, I told him.
- I'm glad.
- But I can't talk any more.
- Then let's go upstairs, he said.

I came towards him before we could take in the room, and I felt his kiss upon my neck before even our mouths met. The catch on my skirt snagged; I struggled with it, finally letting the skirt drop down my legs as he pulled my shirt up over my head. I arched my back, tilting my breasts up to him. He moved his tongue over them, then sank down so that he was kneeling in front of me, and I could feel him on me, slow at first and then pressing into me. Then his fingers were inside me, pushing deeper as I clung on to him. When I pulled him back towards the bed, undressing him as I did, our kissing was like a dialogue - the easy, natural dialogue we couldn't have.

As he fell away from me, I could see the golden ring glowing on his finger and I could feel his wife inside his head. We lay then in silence, save for his ragged breathing and the slow return of reality, like the drip, drip, drip of a tap. Then he got up and I heard the sound of running water and the toilet flush.

Afterwards, he came and sat opposite me, in a chair by the bed, but he didn't look at me, only beyond me, and his face was blank. I could see his wife now - so tall, so smartly dressed, just how I imagined her to be - she was standing by him, staring straight at me. I shut my eyes to block the image out.
  - It'll be ok, I told him.
  - It's not ok, he said.
  - Come back to bed.
  - I'll stay here, I think.
But he stood up, passed a hand over his face.
  - Maybe I'll drive up to Cromarty tonight.
  - Don't, I said.

The bed seemed vast and empty and smelled

of sex, but I must have slept for a bit. When I opened my eyes, Jamie was still in the chair, and he was asleep.

I got up and stood by the window and lit a cigarette, letting the breeze fan my face. I stood there for a long time, trying to think, and finally I went to my bag and opened it. Inside was the knife I'd bought from a mate of Steve's. The moon shone dully on the metal as I placed one finger against the sharp edge. I thought of the man who'd sold me the knife, and the skinny dog at his feet and the scar that pulled his left eye down so that it was just a slit. I put the knife back and lay down again on the bed. This man, I thought, this man can help. I pressed my fingers to my head; but instead of thought there was only feeling, an empty aching feeling that seemed like it would never stop. Then, once again, I slept.

This time I dreamt I was following the dance of a wavering light along the ground - looking for something, or someone. I could feel wiry heather scratching my bare legs, and, where my torch touched bracken, there came eerie flashes of fire through the darkness. Then my torch hit a larger black space and I moved towards it. The hole was illuminated now - I could see its dark walls and the tree roots, like spiky hairs, that lined them. I crept closer, silently, but then I heard a branch crack beneath my feet, and suddenly a figure rose from the hole and started moving towards me.

I screamed and screamed, and then I felt Jamie beside me, wrapping his arms around me, pressing his body up against mine.

- Katy, Katy, he whispered, kissing my hair, my face. What was it? Or who?

I shook my head.

- I'm just scared, I told him.

- Of what?

- Only of the dark, I said.

- You're safe with me, he said.

He held me until my breathing settled. I moved my face to his. In his kisses I found infinite possibilities, tenderness without limit. The room was filled with silver glowing light. I could see the open curtain stir, hear a lonely owl call through the night. I thought of my cramped basement flat and shivered. I could feel the emptiness that filled me spill out, as if it had its own voice and was calling out.

Jamie pulled me closer towards him.

- I want to make you come this time, he whispered.

- I already did, I said.

- Don't lie. Don't ever lie to me, he said.

And this time it was slow and sweet between us, until the sweetness flooded my body, came flooding through me, and I cried out and pushed

into him and cried out again; and then the cries
subsided, and all the sweetness faded, and my
world went dark.

JAMIE

I woke at six with a sick feeling in my stomach and what felt like a pitchfork pressing at my head. I took in the room for the first time: the shabby curtain masking a single small window, the gloomy oversized wardrobe in one corner, the mould running over the paintwork on the ceiling. The bed next to me was empty, the bathroom too. I was alone. Quickly, guiltily, I checked my wallet - intact. I winced as I remembered the night before, my mouth on the girl's, how driven I'd been to consume her. I pictured her standing on the Holloway Road in the rain, looking so helpless, pleading, with those big lost eyes. I sighed. A pro, no doubt about it…and I'd fallen for her lines, every last one of them. And yet - I wasn't sure. She seemed vulnerable and rather mysterious. I wasn't sure she fitted the bill.

Peter would know, of course. Though the chances of Peter meeting her were a million to one.

I sat up, raking one hand through my rumpled hair. I hadn't fucked like that for years. All thoughts of Doing the Right Thing had vanished out the car window at her suggestion we stop for the night. *I*, who prided myself on my loyalty to Rachel, on my honesty. *I* who, up until now, had never even been tempted, not even to create opportunity, and if I had had those opportunities, a couple times at the odd raucous office party, I'd walked away. Easily, it seemed. And now, well, I was in the gutter for sure.

I couldn't even think - I could only remember how it felt, being inside her, like nothing I'd ever felt before... But I'd only just picked her up the morning before. I was a bastard - a randy, selfish bastard! I wasn't worthy of licking my wife's smart boots.

I staggered to the bathroom and examined myself in the mirror. My chin was covered in stubble, my eyes shot through with red. Guilt surged through me like a radioactive current. As I stood there, an image of Katy's naked body flashed before my eyes. Soft and full of shadows, more compelling for its imperfections: the bruise on the right thigh, the crimson scar on the left leg, the slightly tilting breasts with their dark, almost purple nipples... I felt my erection stir, a dull ache rise in my balls. Jesus. I wanted nothing more than to get her back into bed as quickly as possible, and to fuck her again and again.

I splashed cold water over my eyes. I had to pull myself together. Get back in control. I was thirty-five years old, for Christ's sake. I knew Katy's type: unhinged, just not right. I'd heard stories about women like her, read about them, watched films about them. And she was still a complete stranger to me. I was pretty confident I could excise her from memory, if I had to.

I started to shave, but my hand was shaking so, I could barely apply the foam. I remembered the slippery silk of Katy's inside, how I'd wanted to press my mouth to her until she ran dry...

I dropped my razor and threw the window open, gulping down the fresh air. In front of me, pale sunshine washed over green fields where horses grazed. If I gazed at them long enough, I could even imagine last night had never happened. After a while I lost my erection and, feeling calmer, picked up my mobile to call my wife.

Unable to reach Rachel, I left a lame message, telling her I'd call her later, and headed downstairs.

Katy's breakfast lay in front of her, virtually untouched. I hadn't much appetite myself, but I sat down opposite her and helped myself to coffee and toast. She looked well, I thought. Her cheeks were flushed, her hair tumbled over her shoulders in a fine soft mass. I wanted to reach out and touch her. I wanted to pull her to me and kiss her. I drank my coffee with a shaking hand.

"You washed your hair," I said to her.

"Yes."

"You look good."

"Thank you." She struck a pose and I laughed. She finished her coffee.

Abruptly, I asked her: "Why did you flag me down?"

"I knew you were going to Scotland, and I had to get there," she said.

"Who's in Scotland?"

"I already told you."

"Not properly."

"You'd hate me if you knew."

"Would you care if I hated you?"

"Are you sorry we met?" she asked me. She looked like she cared, really cared about my answer.

I felt strange, light-headed, as though my tongue wasn't a part of me, as though I had no control at all over what it said. "No," I whispered. Now I was well and truly fucked. "But I *am* sorry I behaved as I did."

She leaned in to me, no longer smelling of sex or of sweat, but of something more subtle and sane: soap, shampoo. "I'm not," she whispered. "I'd do it again in a heartbeat."

The sunshine hit her hair and her eyes, and she shone with it.

"Jesus, Katy, I'm *married*." I closed my eyes, as a sudden memory came over me, of burying my face in her flesh, of her sweetness spilling into my mouth. I was losing my grip, I thought. I passed one hand over my face.

"You do that a lot."

"What?"

She mimicked my gesture.

"When you're stressed."

"Yes, I suppose so."

"But you're rested, now. Right?"

I hadn't thought about it before, but she was right - for the first time in ages, I'd slept like a dead man. "I pretty much passed out."

"Me too," she said. She picked up the cigarettes on the table and started playing with them.

"Katy…?"

"Yes?"

"You remind me of someone," I told her.

"Who?"

My sister's face swam before my eyes. "Never mind. It's not important."

I watched her open the pack, fiddle with her lighter. It was cheap, pink plastic, somehow out of place in the sober room where we were sitting. She put it down and picked up a piece of toast, only to put that down too. "My toast has gone cold," she said.

"I'll ask for some more."

"I won't be able to eat it."

"I'll ask anyway."

"Where did you last see your brother?"

Her voice seemed to come from far away, perhaps another planet.

"What was that?"

She repeated the question.

I sighed. "In Newcastle. At Sarah's last known address," I said.

I remembered standing next to Peter and opposite our mother in the grimy, dilapidated Tyneside kitchen, one bare bulb swinging over our heads, listening to the singing of an ancient kettle and the distant rumble of a train, trying to make sense of what the policeman was asking us. Sarah had already been missing for two weeks by then. My mother was barely able to answer his questions - she was distraught, wild-eyed, unslept.

Minutes after the policeman had left, Peter had knocked me out. I'd felt the pain from that blow, the panic and breathlessness that accompanied it, every day since.

"My brother hates my guts," I told her.

"Why?"

"He thinks my sister's gone forever. And that it was my fault she disappeared in the first place."

"And was it?"

"No. Yes." I sighed. "There was an accident," I said.

"What sort of an accident?"

I shook my head. I couldn't talk about the accident. "The fact is, Peter and I, we've never been a great match. We're too different. He winds me up. We fight, we always did. When I was a kid, he stole my sweets; when I was a teenager he stole my girlfriends; now I'm an adult, he patronises me all the time."

"Why are you going to see him then?"

I sighed. I thought of the Highlands now, the silver lochs in the dark elbows of the hills, the vast skies, the silence so profound it impregnated the very air one breathed. I used to go there all the time on fishing trips with my father, but I hadn't been back for years. I wanted to lose myself there again. But beyond that, deeper still, there was the primeval pull of blood. "He's my brother," I told her. "And my mother wants me to."

I was sure Peter would hate me till my dying days, but I'd never stop trying to bring him around. I'd try forever. That's just the way it was.

"Do you always do what your mother wants you to do?"

"Don't most men?"

"*I* wouldn't. I can't stand mine. Not now." Abruptly, she changed the subject. "I had a brother once, but he died."

"How did he die?"

She looked at me, then away. "He just died. He was a baby," she said. "There were rumours…"

"What sort of rumours?"

"About my dad, my mum, me…"

"*You?*"

"It was no one's fault," she added quickly. "Sudden infant death syndrome," they call it."

"How old was he?"

"Six months."

"And this happened in Scotland?"

"In Scotland, yes." Her grey eyes clouded over, and I was drawn to them, as if by the tug of a tide. "Bad things happened to me in Scotland."

"And yet you want to go back?"

"I have to."

"Why?"

"Would you help me, if I asked you to?"

"That would depend."

"On what?"

"On what you wanted me to do."

"What if... What if I wanted you to kill someone for me?"

My eyes flew open in shock. She smiled guiltily. "I was joking," she said. She finished her toast, quickly this time. "We had sex, that's all. You don't have to pretend to care."

"But I do." I searched helplessly for the right words. "I want to know you."

Katy had retreated into herself. Her eyes had a glazed look. I seized one of her hands in my own, crushing the fingers, and as I did so, I felt them cringe, move away from mine. I saw her as she'd appeared last night - her body bathed in moonlight; I felt her legs shake beneath mine, heard the murmur from her throat as she came...

She was pale and her lower lip was trembling. "Well you can't," she whispered.

I foundered. It was as if she'd dropped a noose around my neck and then just walked away. One night gave us no claim over each other. She had a story in her somewhere, like we all did, but it was one I had no right to read.

I stood up, pushing my chair back, suddenly keen

to be driving somewhere, anywhere, just away from that table and the half-finished conversation that hung in the air.

"Let's go," I said.

I settled the bill, and we stepped out into the hazy morning sunshine.

KATY

We drove pretty much in silence, until the
Highlands came tumbling back: withered
bracken, brown-backed streams, barren hills
dotted with stunted sheep, and with them came
the memories I thought I had suppressed, and the
emptiness - more constant than any companion
I'd ever had, more frightening than any I'd ever
left. Now, reflected in the car window, I saw my
mother's younger face, felt her smile, and felt
myself smile back. Then that face faded, replaced
by the sad and bitter face of now; hers was the
laugh I heard, hers the voice that whispered

- *You fool - coming back! They'll find out, and
they'll lock you up because of what you did!*

- *I didn't do it, mum,* I said.

- *Yes. Yes you did.*

Then came another face, darker, leaner, meaner
still, and I put one hand over my mouth to stop
the screams coming out.

I knew Jamie had seen me because soon after
that he brought the car to a halt. At once I pulled
the door open and stepped out. I tripped, almost
fell, but then recovered and started to walk. As I
walked, I could hear Jamie calling after me, but I
started to run, till I couldn't hear him any longer.

The air was heavy and sullen, the silence almost deafening. The wind was hitting and slapping and turning my hands to ice. The land smelled of damp, rotting matter, of iron and rust.

In front of me there was a wooden bridge that ran across a stream choked with rocks. Moving down, I parted the reeds, cupped the freezing water in my hands and drank. Then I stood up, my head clearer, walked back up to the bridge and leaned over it.

I felt Jamie before I saw him, felt the warmth of his hands on my shoulders.

- They're coming after me, I told him.

Very gently, he turned me round to look at him.

- Who, Katy? Tell me, he said.

There were tears streaming down my face. I rummaged in my bag for a tissue, and as I did so I dropped the bag and my knife fell out.

Jamie looked at me and he looked at the knife. He bent down to pick it up, but I leaned over and pulled it away from him and as the knife slid from his fingers I heard him cry out.

Quickly I hid the knife and took some tissues out. I held the tissues to his finger to stop the blood.

- I'm sorry, I mumbled.

- It's only a scratch, he told me. Though it hurts like fuck.

I moved as if to leave then, but with his other

hand he held me back.

- Why have you got a knife?

- I need it, I said.

- Why?

- Because they're after me, like I said.

- Who?

- People with questions, and people with answers, I said.

I put my hands up to my face.

- I'm scared, I told him. I'm scared of so many things, I said.

He held his good hand out to me.

- Don't be scared. Not with me, he said.

I leaned into him, and we were kissing, but then I pushed him away. When I missed his kisses, I thought *They're right about me, Mike and my mother; I am a stupid, crazy bitch.*

I turned my back on him then, started walking back; but he caught up with me and caught my hand and held it as we walked.

We drove in silence after that, until we hit the outskirts of Inverness.

- Where can I drop you? he asked.

- I'm going to a town in Lochalsh.

- Which one?

He looked at me when he asked that, and the car swerved, and I don't know why, but I told him the name of the town, the real name, I didn't lie, nor did I pretend.

- I'll drop you there, he said.

I panicked.

- No - just take me to Inverness.

The land had changed, become flatter, more dreary, and it had begun to rain. As we came closer, I thought I remembered landmarks: a petrol station with broken pumps, a white house with no windows, a small wood they said was haunted, a derelict church. But then I looked again and there was nothing - only empty space.

At last we came to the train station, and Jamie stopped the car. But when I tried to get out, he locked the doors and pulled me to him, both hands on my arms; gentle, slow. I could feel the heat moving through me as he came close.

- Don't, he said, his breath hot against my neck. Don't run off, not just yet.

- I have to, I said.

- Let's just talk a bit.

- We've talked enough.

- But you haven't told me anything, he said.

I felt something tight inside me snap.

- I lost my kid. I've come to Scotland to find her, I said.

- How did you lose her?

- Someone took her, I said. I moved away from him. Now unlock the door, I told him, and let me get out.

- But I don't want you to go, he said. Not while you're in this state. I just want you to be safe, he murmured. I want to make you safe.

I felt desire bloom inside me like the opening of a thousand flowers, and then the fear came, and all the flowers shut their petals up.

- You *can't*, I said.

He came towards me and tried to hold me again, and I felt his arms shake.

- What have I done to you? I whispered. A pause, and then, Whatever it was, I'm not sorry - I'd do the same again, I said.

At last we stepped out and the air was cold, the wind lifting up our clothes. He put one hand to my face.

- I'm glad we met.

- Why are you, when it ends like this?

He hesitated.

- Take my coat, he said, and he wrapped his coat around me.

- And some cash.

He pushed a wad of notes into my hand.

Then he moved back and into his car.

But I wouldn't have it end like that. I ran up to his car and banged the window, my fist smacking the glass until he had no choice but to open up.

- I don't want your cash, I yelled at him.

- What *do* you want, Katy?

I stood there a second, thinking he was all I wanted, and then the moment passed and there was so much more I wanted, all things I couldn't have.

- You take your fucking money back! I yelled at him, and I flung the cash at him, thinking at the same time that I was a crazy fool, because I certainly could have used that cash and all I could have got with it. But I wasn't going to let him know that.

He revved the engine up and drove off. I saw the notes flying around his head, and I stood there hating him - hating his fancy car, hating what he thought of me, hating that I couldn't control anything he did or said. As I stood, I counted the seconds off, ten, nine, eight, but he didn't stop, seven, six, five, and I could still see the car, just about, four, three, two, one, and then he was gone, and we were over, so over, though we'd barely just begun.

JAMIE

"You look fucking freezing," were my brother's first words to me. "What happened to your coat? This is Scotland, not the bloody Bahamas."

Peter stood in the porch of his mansion, towering, as usual, over his wife, his figure silhouetted against the yellow light from the hall, his dark shadow dominating the sweeping gravel drive. At his feet I could just make out the shape of a large dog; a Labrador, I thought.

I felt a sharp cramp in my left leg as I moved towards him, and realised I was completely exhausted.

"It's a long story."

"A good one, I'll bet."

He strode towards me. Instinctively I took a step back, but he merely embraced me, typically expansive. The dog, as if encouraged by its owner's display, came over and tentatively licked my hand.

I felt my body relax. Perhaps this was going to be easier than I'd thought.

"Who's this?" I asked my brother, patting the dog.

"That's Lucy. I got her a couple of years ago. She's a rescue case, so still a bit nervous around the boys. Loves me to distraction though."

Emmeline came forward and pecked me on both

cheeks. Her kisses were small and dry, like a bird's.

Peter turned to her. "We were expecting you last night, weren't we, Emmy? I'm afraid I ate the steak intended for you."

"That must have been hard."

"I polished off the fine wine, too." He chuckled, clapped one hand on my shoulder. "Come in now and make up for it."

I swallowed as I followed Peter and his wife into their handsome Georgian pile, my brother's affluence making me veer, as ever, between envy and disgust.

"Emmy's been decorating, haven't you, darling? Or, rather, re-decorating." Peter rolled his eyes.

I looked around obediently. The house's fine proportions were swamped in a welter of wallpaper, curtains and cushions. "Nice," I murmured.

Peter rummaged in a capacious drawer, cursing under his breath as he did so. "Can't find a damn thing in this house," he muttered. "Kids' shit everywhere. Emmy, where's the bloody corkscrew?"

Emmeline glanced in the drawer, located the corkscrew with ease and handed it to her husband. "Anyone would think it was me you couldn't live without, Peter, and not Lucy," she told him.

Peter opened the wine swiftly and poured out two glasses. "Drink!" he ordered, handing a glass to me. "I'm sorry about giving you a hard time on the phone."

"No you're not."

My brother grinned. "How was the rest of the drive?"

After leaving Katy, I'd felt as if someone had severed one of my limbs. I'd driven like a maniac all the way to Cromarty, reliving her kisses as I did so.

"Uneventful," I said.

Peter's sharp eyes scanned me. "You look like shit. And what the hell's happened to your hand?"

I looked down at my finger. The blood had dried around the cut, which was fortunately shallower than I had originally thought. "Oh, that? The cat scratched me." I was surprised at how easily the lie tripped off my tongue.

"I thought Rachel hated cats."

"She changed her mind."

"I didn't know your wife could be so...*flexible*, Jamie."

"There's a lot you don't know about Rachel. Or about me, for that matter."

"You're not as mysterious as you think, Jamie."

To distract him, I asked after the kids, and as he began talking, I felt the wine warm my throat and weigh down my eyelids. I watched Emmeline move with ease and efficiency around the kitchen, wearing a pair of very high heels. She seemed somehow familiar to me, as if I'd come home - women like her weren't going to chain-smoke or pull knives on me at a moment's notice. Nor would they... I tried to imagine Emmeline's perfectly made-up lips delicately pulling back my foreskin. No. And yet I was used to women like her - women who were perfectly in control and concentrated all their energies on staying that way. Women who were attractive and yet not attractive at the same time.

I put my drink down. "I have to call my wife," I said. My phone had sounded several times during the drive over. I was convinced the calls were Rachel's.

"So soon? Finish your drink first."

"I should call now."

Peter turned to his wife. "Take Jamie somewhere quiet," he said.

Emmeline led me to a study lined with pristine books and left. Quickly, I took out my mobile and called home.

But the voice that answered had far too much gravel in it to be my wife's. I was torn between relief and disappointment.

"Angela? How are you? You're staying with us?"

"Only until tomorrow," my mother-in-law told me. "Then I have to get back to Charles - we've a golf tournament near Banbury. I've been trying to get hold of you, Jamie. I wanted to cook some soup for Rachel. You know; that lovely chicken soup you make..."

As I rattled off the recipe, I thought of my wife - gaunt, ashen-faced, scarcely eating after the latest drama. I swallowed guiltily. "I can look after her, Angela."

"Why aren't you then?"

"I had to be here. It's complicated."

"It always is with you, Jamie."

"Can I speak to her?"

"She's at work. I tried to stop her, but she *would* go. She needed the distraction, she said. It's so hard for her, you know." Angela's voice dropped to a whisper. "This business of Getting Pregnant. It's grim, isn't it? Just *gut-wrenching*…"

I winced. I hated the fact that my mother-in-law had access to this most private part of our lives; but then my wife insisted on involving her in detail. "It's hard for both of us, Angela."

I waited until she ran out of steam, which took a while, and then returned to my brother, who was lying spread-eagled on the sofa in a room adjoining the kitchen. Lucy was lying alongside him, her head on his knee. She opened one eye as her owner called out to me.

"What's up with you, o brother?" he asked, having seen the gloom on my face.

"My mother-in-law, if you must know."

"Hmm. Emmy won't let her mother talk to me. I've upset her too many times, she says. So, why didn't you pitch up last night? Come on - spill."

"I got tired, that's all."

"I don't believe you. You're lucky Rachel didn't call - I don't know what I'd have said to her."

"I'm sure you'd have managed."

Peter's eyes narrowed suspiciously. "How *is* the lovely Rachel, anyway?"

"As if you care."

"How is that blue-eyed beauty?"

"Admit it, Peter. You don't like her."

"You're being paranoid."

"You yelled at her on the phone last time I tried to call you."

"She was playing peacemaker. I told her to let you do your own dirty work. You're good at that."

"Well, she's working, actually."

"On a *Sunday*? Is the woman *insane*?"

"Some of us have to work, Peter."

"Now, now. I've no interest in your petty jealousies. How do you think I managed to buy this house?"

"I have no idea. You don't work very hard, as far as I can tell."

He ignored me. "I mean, seriously, Jamie, she's one of these wom..." he had the grace to look sheepish "...people who can't cope with a big job. Can't handle stress, that's the problem. They're better off at ho-"

"*Seriously*, Peter?"

Emmeline appeared at this point with a plate of pitted olives, which she placed in front of her husband, as Peter appealed to her. "The kids, the house - it's a full-time job, isn't it, Emmy?"

"It is if there's one person doing it."

"Oh, come on - I help out."

"You've not touched the washing machine in six months."

Peter flashed her a look full of malignant fire.

"As for the dishwasher - Jamie, he's never even switched it on. *Never.*"

"I do so, switch it on. Don't tend to empty it, admittedly."

"We can't all earn a packet the size of yours, Peter." I tried to keep the bitterness out of my voice.

"You don't have to live in Central London, do you? Emmeline and I paid peanuts for this place."

I doubted it, but this time I kept quiet.

Peter pretended to think, as he was so fond of doing, when really very little went on in that brain of his. He was all drive, and aggression. And guts - I'd give him that.

"Another mistake," he said at last. "Marry a woman with a better brain than you have and you'll live to regret it. Mind you, you do regret very well, Jamie. You live and breathe it, as far as I can see. *And so you should.*"

Those last words were *sotto voce*, but I was clearly meant to hear them. I looked up, shocked, my adrenalin spiking. Silence fell between us.

"Shouldn't we help Emmeline?" I asked at last.

"What with?"

"Supper."

"Leave her to it," my brother said. "Have some more wine."

I watched Peter turn the glass in his hand. His mood had changed - suddenly. He was now genial, relaxed. "I have a little dream rolling around in my head, Jamie. One of these days, I'm going to buy a vineyard in the South of France and live out my days there. All on my lonesome, except for Lucy. But I might let you join me - if you ever climb down from that high horse of yours. That fucking high, Trojan horse..."

I felt a sudden stab of jealousy and yearning - though God knew where it came from. Being stuck with Peter anywhere, even the South of France, would kill me. Except if Peter weren't there, and Katy... Katy...

I could barely hear what my brother was saying.

"Do you know, Jamie, this wine is forty years old - exactly the same age as me? But there, sadly, the comparison ends. Would that I had as much substance, body, depth -"

"You seem pretty pleased with yourself, Peter."

"And why not?"

I studied my brother now, as he bent his head to light a cigarette: he was over six feet tall, his auburn hair thick and glossy, his skin glowing with health; though my features were more regular, he seemed to carry off his crooked nose well, making it somehow rakish and appealing. Would he be surprised if he knew what I'd been up to? Would he hate me for it? Or be delighted to have a partner in crime? The latter, probably. My halo was already tarnished as far as Peter was concerned - in a different way, but irreparably.

He looked over at me now, shaking the cigarette packet. "You've quit, presumably?" I nodded. "Rachel made you, I suppose." He curled his lower lip derisively. "I don't know how you put up with it."

"Why don't you concentrate on your own marriage and leave me to focus on mine?"

"Happily, dear brother."

"How are you and Emmeline anyway?"

"Fine."

"She still has no idea about your little dalliances?"

"Nor will she. I know you never can, but keep your trap shut, if that's possible. OK?"

"Sure."

"How's work? Gruelling, I should imagine."

I swallowed bitterly. "So so."

"Ah, well. London life. Glad I got out of it."

Peter had moved to Scotland shortly after he'd met Emmeline (just over twelve years ago now), and his decision to set up his own fund management business, with just one other partner, had made him very comfortable indeed. His first marriage hadn't worked out, it was true (he'd got caught out with one of his friends' wives), but he hadn't let that trouble him unduly. From this, his only failure, he had learned one thing: to conduct any extra-marital affairs with discretion. In other words, "Do anything you like, as long as you don't get caught doing it." He and Emmeline seemed to live harmoniously enough.

My brother wasn't fond, loving, indulgent, as our mother could sometimes be, though he had a high dose of her selfish gene. Nor (unlike Sarah and I) had he inherited our father's demons - a tendency to self-loathing, overthinking, insomnia. His self-esteem was an impossibly smooth sea.

I envied him. Even worse, at times I hated him.

"How's Rachel?" Emmeline asked me later, at dinner, ladling potatoes onto my plate with a silver spoon.

There was no love lost between Emmeline and my wife, either. Rachel envied Emmeline her children but pitied her for being married to my brother. Emmeline envied Rachel her brain and her independence but pitied her childless state.

"She's fine," I told Emmeline, finishing a mouthful of rather dry pork.

"Anything...new with her?" Her myopic eyes, fish-like between heavily mascaraed lashes, blinked innocently into mine.

I hesitated. "Well, she's hoping to make partner this year."

"She means is she pregnant yet?" my brother cut in bluntly, feeding a large piece of meat to Lucy. "Didn't you, darling?"

Emmeline dabbed daintily at her mouth with her

napkin and shot her husband a look of silent fury.

I looked down. "She…well…no."

"Tell you what it is," said my brother, sawing with his knife. "It's this fucked up generation of females. So obsessed with their careers, they've left it far too late to have kids. Haven't they, my love?"

"I do feel *terribly* sorry for her," said Emmeline. "And for any woman in her situation…"

"Well, you needn't," I cut in. "Rachel's fine. Happy."

Peter, unpredictable as ever, swung round to my side. "Yes, Emmy, not everyone wants to be kept up all night by a brood of howling brats. At least Rachel's escaped that. She and Jamie can enjoy long lazy Sundays together, doing fuck all. Isn't that right, Jamie?"

"Absolutely." Though it had to be said, our Sundays were usually quite frantic - certainly not given over to languid lovemaking.

Emmeline was not to be side-tracked, however. "Hasn't she taken the test yet? The one that calculates your ovarian reserve?" I looked confused. "The Menopause," she whispered, darkly. "Creeps up on some women unawares, apparently."

I placed my knife and fork deliberately on my plate. "I'd rather not talk about it."

"I read an article about it just recently…"

"He told you, he doesn't want to talk about it! Leave him alone!"

My brother's temper-flashes were always sudden and violent. This one subsided quickly, but not before Emmeline had left the table "to fetch the desert." I caught a glimpse of her face as she left, her pretty but bland features all crumpled up.

"Why are you such a shit, Peter?"

"Treat 'em mean…"

"You can't believe that."

Peter pushed all his hair back from his head, a childhood gesture I remembered well, and we both sat listening to the ticking of the grandfather clock behind us until Emmeline returned to the table, her composure restored.

"Did mum call you as well?" I asked him after a while, the wine loosening my tongue somewhat.

"She might have done."

"What did she say?"

"She told me to be nice to you, if you must know." Peter raised his glass to his mouth with a steady hand. "As she always has, if you remember. "Stop stealing Jamie's sweets, Peter," or, "Quit flattening his sandcastles, you beast." Ha! It's all coming back to me now. You were always mummy's little pet, weren't you? That's why she's forgiven you this whole sorry mess."

I wasn't sure she had. Our mother was religious enough to embrace the notion of forgiveness, but the ice in her eyes at times belied her position. At others, when talking to me about an inconsequential matter, unrelated to Sarah, a sharp note entered her voice. That was partly why I avoided the family home, that and the sight of my sister's room that lay untouched, exactly as she left it at sixteen, when she had left home suddenly, after a particularly heated row with my mother. Now, whenever I drove up the long lane towards the place, stems of cow parsley brushing my car, its tires sinking slightly in the mud, Rachel's nose wrinkling at the smell of manure, a sense of gloom would descend on me.

I felt it now.

"I wasn't her pet," I told my brother.

"Don't lie. Unless you want me to hate you more. Anyway, mum told me she doesn't want us fighting over her coffin."

"That's rather morbid of her, seeing as she's been doing so well."

Peter muttered something indecipherable under his breath.

"What was that?"

"I repeat, Jamie - give me one good reason why I should be nice to you now, after what you did."

I closed my eyes briefly, but couldn't stop the scene flashing through my head, like a sequence in a horror film. A road coated in black ice, lit only by fog lights. A car spinning out of control, and finally flipping over, like a fish in a dark sea of tarmac. The sound of Sarah's head slamming the windscreen, then drawn-out screams, until they stopped, the silence worse than the sound, replaced at last by the long wail of a police siren. My sister, slumped unconscious next to me, a single line of red moving from her hairline down the centre of her forehead…

I'd been driving, of course. And Sarah hadn't been wearing a seatbelt. I should have made her wear one. Fuck that - I shouldn't have been on the road at all.

Peter was staring at me, jaw set. He had little imagination, but I knew he was picturing the same scene. He'd been waiting for his moment to strike, like a charismatic puppeteer controlling a show. Now he emptied his glass again while I concentrated on steadily loading my cutlery. My nerves were jangled up, every sense reeling.

Suddenly Peter slammed his fist on the table.

"For fuck's sake, Jamie!"

"The breathalyser…"

"I don't give a fuck about the reading. It was taken an age after the event anyway."

"The police didn't pursue it, Peter."

"Fools. You can't hold your booze and you know it. You're lucky that man wasn't killed."

"He walked right out in front of me. He was off his face."

"Makes two of you. Only Sarah was sober, for once."

"You know how terrible I feel about the whole thing."

"I don't give a fuck about your feelings."

Abruptly, I stood up. "I'm going to bed. Yell at me some more tomorrow, why don't you?"

Emmeline, eyeing her husband warily, barely acknowledged my thanks for dinner. I made for the stairs, feeling like a child as I did so, running away from my belligerent brother through the old Norfolk farmhouse, wanting to bury myself in one of its warm safe spaces…

I looked back to see Peter stand up, scraping his chair back as he did so. He headed after me, Lucy at his heels. I fought the instinct to break into a run.

At the top of the staircase, Peter grasped my arm so hard it hurt. I gasped and turned to face his fury and was astonished when suddenly he smiled, one of his rare, winning smiles that once made our female acquaintances melt. "Let's grab some fresh air tomorrow, Jamie. Go for a hike. Weather's meant to be OK."

I stared at him, unable to speak.

"And then we'll open a bottle of Scotch and sit up late. There's a lot to talk about, isn't there? It'll be just like old times."

The earnest note of supplication in his voice touched me against my will. I hated Scotch, but I nodded. "Can't wait," I lied.

He smiled again, before dismissing me with a wave as I made my way to my bed.

My room was little used - everything in it was so smart and new I could have been in a hotel. I lay down on the bed, fully clothed, my head spinning from the drink. I thought of Katy. As I did so, my insides flipped over. I missed her already, though I didn't know whom or what I was missing. It didn't make any sense.

I got up and drew the heavy curtains back, opened the window and leant out. The cold air cleared my head. I could just catch a glimpse of the North Sea, of the glance and glitter of the waves in the moonlight. A solitary gull wheeled overhead. I lingered a while, breathing in the fresh air, grateful for it. At last I stepped back, drew the curtains together and switched off the light.

KATY

I waited until his car had disappeared and then I wrapped his coat about me and thrust my hands deep into its pockets, letting the cashmere warm my fingers up. I listened to the rumble of a train coming in and the silence thickening as it went out. Then I went into the station and bought a ticket for the town where I used to live.

On the train, as the darkening land sped past, I explored the pockets of Jamie's coat, and found a penny, a pen and a tatty business card. I flipped the card over. On it was Jamie's name and his mail address. Jamie Kinsella.

Kinsella. It spoke to me of better things.

I transferred the card to my bag.

The smell of the train brought it all back: fleeing Scotland after my kid disappeared; hiding from my mother, from Mike, from everyone I knew, from the questions, the accusations I knew they all had.

I'd done nothing wrong. I'd only done what any mother would have - *tried to make my child safe.*

But I'd failed. That was the worst of it.

I must have slept, for when I woke, there was the sign for my hometown, 'KOLCAN', glowing through the dark.

I jumped out just as the doors were closing, felt them grip the coat like a set of teeth. I pulled hard, heard the tear as the lining ripped.

Then I started walking. I walked past rows of dishevelled houses, bins outside overflowing, through streets that were familiar, plumped full of memories, through air that was dank and wet and smelled of smoke. And the cold followed me everywhere I went, pressed against my cheek like the blade of a knife.

Finally I reached the main square or what passed for it. I stopped, while all around me the world went dark, and the cars sped past and the wet from their wheels went down my legs. In front of me stood the statue, the man on the horse all covered in pigeon shit. And the other shops: the chemist, the cobbler's, the caff - I counted them all off. The shops were shuttered and black - the only light and life came from the inns; two very different places, one upmarket, even smart for the place, which might explain why it was always empty, the other the draw for all the lowlife scum for miles around, but for all that the only proper place to drink.

I came to the second inn, to the heat and light that hit the street, and I told myself to go in. But I remembered the last time I'd seen the place, and I hesitated. I felt faint, confused, as if I wasn't standing, but lying down, cheeks sticky with my own blood, forehead bruised, right arm twisted, almost passing out from the pain of it. I could even hear the screaming from bodies crowded around me, blocking the air out with their breath. Or perhaps I was the one screaming, as I cowered in the dark, to get away from the dark body standing tall over me...

I smelled him first, and then I felt a hand on my back. I tried to move but I couldn't. I could barely raise my head.

- Katy! Katy, what the fuck?

I shivered, hearing his voice. No, he was not Mike - but even so my stomach twisted over and then back.

- Mac, I said.

Mac the Knife, a gutter-talking, heavy-drinking layabout, one-time dealer, always in trouble with the police. He'd had a soft spot for me once, though he'd gone quiet after I met Mike.

- Holy fuck, it *is* you, he said. Ach, you've got guts coming back here after what you did!

- I did nothing, I said.

- That's not what they all said.

- And you believe them? You think that?

- Me and everyone else. Fuck knows what you did to that kid, Katy. Last time I saw you you were bleedin' right here in the street. I remember thinking *She must have done something pretty bad to deserve that.*

\- And what about Mike?

\- What aboot him?

\- You know what he's capable of.

\- Why then are you back?

\- Actually, I was looking for you, Mac. I've missed you, I said.

His thick face flushing, he swiped his red hair back from his head and reached out to touch the necklace around my neck (the one my mate Donna had given me before I left.)

\- Aye, I missed you too, lassie. My God, I felt that bad for not going after you, after the fight - but you have to understand how it is… *There's none here can mess with Mike.*

He dropped his voice, whispered those last words.

\- Let's gan somewhere quiet where we can talk, he said. It's no good going in there, not now. You'll get yerself messed up again pretty quick.

I let him lead me down the street. As we passed a streetlight, I saw his face was mottled with the drink and that he walked with a limp - each time he put his weight on his bad leg he gasped and held his breath. I remembered the talk - that a car had hit him when he was drunk, that if he'd been sober the shock would've killed him, people said.

We were walking down one of the streets that fanned from the square out to the right. I thought I could see faces in the houses, looking out, white against the windows, their mouths great dark Os, voices hissing as we walked past. Soon I picked up the metallic smell of the river, sliding past us through the dark like some great oily beast. When we drew close to the water, we stopped, and Mac's yellow stubby fingers closed around my wrist.

- Come here, Katy, he said. It's been a while since I feasted my eyes on that bonny face.

He dragged me towards a light.

- You've not changed a bit since you were seventeen, he said.

I thought back to when we first met, when I was so young, my body wired to the demands of his drugs, and no, I hadn't wanted him, but I hadn't the strength to fight him off. I hadn't hated him, not enough. When he'd finally pushed himself inside me it hurt, and when the pain was replaced with something nearer to pleasure, though not quite the same, that was just the point at which he'd stopped. I remembered it now, how afterwards I went home and stuffed a sock in my pants to soak up the blood, another in my mouth to block my sobs, because I didn't want my mum to know what was up. But she knew the minute she saw my face - and days later, when I told her what had happened, she said

- That's the thing about the first time - you can never take it back.

And that was worse than if she hadn't said a thing.

And then a year later I met Mike.

Now, very gently, I pushed Mac back.

- Let's wait. Till we get to your place.

Mac lived in a small, grimy flat in a desolate part of town, on a street that wasn't even lit. He let me in, then poured me a whisky, waited while its golden bite warmed me up. I watched his thick yellow fingers roll up a joint and shivered, recalling those fingers deep inside my flesh.

- Where's your wife? I asked him. I remembered her well - a woman with a droopy face and a long list of complaints.

- She upped and left. Took the kids. Which means I'm single at long last, he said. So it's a good thing you came back.

I made my eyes, my body go all soft, and then I went over, put my hands on his legs, and rested my head on his shoulders, my breath hot against his neck. He drew my face towards his for a kiss, but I pulled back.

- I came to find Mike, I whispered.

- What the fuck? After what you did? The mess he made of you. *Why?*

- Why do you think?

- Because you're a lunatic, just like they all said.

- Tell me where he is, and I'll stay the night...

- Sweet Jesus, Katy, you really are a crazy bitch. You'll stay anyway, if that's what I decide.

He gripped my wrists, started unbuttoning my shirt.

- Mac, I murmured, tell me first.

I'd lost him, though, I knew it. So when I felt his teeth against my neck, I brought my knee up - and with all my strength, I slammed it in his crotch.

Mac staggered back, coughing, doubled over.

- Fuck! he cursed, wiping the phlegm from his mouth.

He came for me, but I picked up my glass.

- Take one step closer and I'll use this, swear to God. I'll do it, unless you tell me where he is.

Mac turned away. With two hands, he gripped the sink, leaning over it, breathing hard.

- You're a hoor, he said.

- He's got something that I want. You know what that is.

- He ain't got your kid.

- He knows where she is.

- That's not what people round here said.

- And you listened to them?

- Aye, cos they were likely right.

- Just tell me where Mike is.

- He fucked oaf, Mac muttered. Just after you, in fact.

- And my mother? I asked, after a bit.

- Yer maw?

- I'll bet she knows where Mike is. They was always thick as thieves. Is she still in the same place?

- The house by the canal? Yes. Now get oot, you've caused me enough grief.

- Gladly, I told him. You know how many times I wish we'd never met.

- Aye, well then, fuck oaf why don't yer, he said.

I stood up then and I ran out of that house as fast as I could, slamming the door behind me. And the dark came from the streets to swallow me up and with it came more of my mother's words and they spun around my head like a thick fog that wouldn't lift, and I couldn't escape what they said: *Nothing consumes a person like Regret.*

JAMIE

There was a girl sitting by my bed, a girl with long dark hair. She was winding a white handkerchief around her fingers, tighter and tighter, until the tips were paler than the handkerchief, so pale, they glowed through the dark.

"Sarah!" I whispered, reaching out one hand to touch the girl's face.

But her glassy eyes remained open, unblinking. The skin on her cheeks froze my fingers.

"Sarah!"

She stood up and took a step towards me, her eyes unseeing.

"I'm sorry. Sarah, I'm…"

She reached out both hands to me, as if she were going to place them around my neck. *I deserve this,* I thought. I waited, heart racing. But suddenly her face faded, and another took its place - this one heart-shaped with luminous eyes. And then that face fell away from me too and I was falling, falling with it, until I woke with a start, my mind cloudy with confusion and disappointment.

I sat bolt upright, shivering as the sweat dried cold on my back. I looked towards the window, expecting to see the orange glare of London lights through the curtains, but there was only more darkness behind. I listened out for the hum of traffic, but I heard only the slow hoot of an owl, calling to its mate through the night.

I was late for breakfast. Peter and his two boys were already at the table. The younger boy, Andrew, seemed taciturn and tired; the older, William, was indomitably cheerful, cracking constant jokes and hoovering up vast quantities of toast. I thought William charming until I spotted him surreptitiously pinching his brother's arm. Thereafter I felt heartily sorry for Andrew - I sympathised with his predicament entirely.

"Morning," my brother muttered through a mouthful of toast. "Sleep well?" he asked, then snapped at his elder son "Don't talk when you're eating!" before I'd had a chance to respond.

I had barely started dissecting my kippers (which, as everyone knows, take infinite skill and patience to eat) before Peter said "Time's up. Got to get up a mountain and be back in time for tea."

"It's only nine o'clock."

"You never know. We might hit traffic." He grinned at me. "Let's go."

Pink Floyd's *Breathe* was playing on the radio as we backed out of his drive, a track in tune with the brooding landscape but at odds with Peter's determined jocularity. The skies over Cromarty were steely, pregnant with rain, and my brother's driving was unfocused and rather erratic. Some of the puddles on the road he skirted carefully; others he drove through with childish glee. Once he braked sharply at a double bend, almost throwing us off the road, grinning when I yelled at him. "Don't dare lecture *me* on my driving, Jamie."

We passed few cars, only sheep, standing sodden and lonely by the side of the road. All around the sombre land lay silent, watching us.

A track fringed with golden bracken and gorse bushes led to the loch. At last, it opened out in front of us, a vast expanse of water, flanked by low-lying hills. Directly behind it, our destination, the tallest of the hills, reared its head. It looked distinctly unappealing - I could barely see the summit through its grey shroud of rain.

We started tramping over sodden ground, our boots sinking into the iridescent mud. Lucy bounded around, sniffing at clumps of rabbit pellets, burying her snout in the wet turf.

Finally we began to climb. Peter strode ahead through the dead heather, oblivious to his surroundings, his natural pace outstripping mine. Lucy stuck close to him, and I followed on behind, bending to touch a greasy skein of wool left by a passing sheep, startling at the scream of a seagull.

Higher up, the world seemed to empty out; walking became easier, and my mind opened up. Thoughts of Katy flitted through my head, small physical details, like the way the rain had clung to her hair or the cluster of freckles I'd kissed at the top of her shoulder. I struggled to recall a clear image of her face. I tried to picture the town she'd told me she was heading to. Was it as grim and hopeless as I feared? What if it didn't exist at all? The name of the town was all I had to go on; the only real thing I knew about her.

"Peter?" I asked, as we skirted a large lichen-coated boulder.

My brother pulled the hood from his face. "What?"

"Do you know a place called Kolcan?"

"Over on the other side? Near Inverness?"

"Yes. What's it like?"

"Dunno. I've never been."

I sighed again. At least it existed.

"What's up with you?"

"Nothing."

"Want to stop? Had enough?"

I turned back to face the way we'd come. The loch lay beneath us, a silver puddle between the dark hills. Above the summit a single raptor swung in slow, lazy circles.

"Let's stop at the top."

We walked a further forty minutes before we reached the summit. Peter sat down immediately, taking out a silver package from his small backpack.

"Sandwiches." He gestured to the rock on which he was sitting. "Sit."

We shared the sandwiches. Lucy ate our crusts

gratefully, breaking off at one point to chase a rabbit that appeared out of nowhere, its white tail bobbing through the undergrowth. The air was thin and fresh, the sky cut through with blue.

Peter sighed. "These taste like shit. She should have saved herself the bother."

"If it winds you up that much, why don't you try cooking?"

"Me? You must be joking."

"You're a good cook, I seem to remember."

Peter had often cooked on Sundays when he was a teenager, in a flamboyant, messy way which had aggravated our mother no end. Afterwards, while my mother and I cleared up after him, he lounged in the room next door with Sarah, listening to The Cure or The Doors or Siouxsie and the Banshees, or whatever Sarah was into at the time.

"Hmm. Sarah thought so, I suppose. If she was around, maybe I'd cook still." My brother crushed the remainder of his sandwich in his fist, jaw tensing. "What about your lovely wife? She started to cook?"

"Not yet. But *I* enjoy it."

"That's what I admire about you, Jamie. You won't say a word against her. You're unwaveringly loyal, and you'll be that way till the bitter, the very bitter end. It's a rare quality these days."

"You say it like it's an insult."

"You're being paranoid."

I hesitated. "I'm not so loyal," I told him.

Peter turned to me, raised an eyebrow. "Have you got something to tell me, brother?"

I opened my mouth to speak. Suddenly a frantic yelping came from the undergrowth - then a sharp, awful squeal. I turned to my brother, startled, as Lucy came bounding out of the bracken, the limp body of a rabbit hanging from her mouth. I watched as Peter carefully extracted the rabbit from Lucy's jaws. Incredibly, it was still alive; its eyes rounded and globular, aglow with fear.

Peter laughed at my consternation, dispatched the rabbit with a quick twist of one wrist and threw its body into the heather.

"You and your squeamishness, Jamie. Always spoiling our fun. Come on - let's go."

We started down towards the car, walking in silence. By the time we reached the boggier ground at the bottom of the hill the sky had darkened with more rain, and the silver waters of the loch had begun to fade to grey. The land brooded, sullen, full of latent menace. Shadows that had lurked in the undergrowth earlier now moved steadily towards us. Fanciful as it sounds, I felt a distinct sense of threat, and I was relieved when at last we reached the car.

On the drive home, I watched the encroaching darkness suck out all colour from the sky, until there remained only a single bright band of gold on the far western horizon. I kept that glowing line in sight all the way back, as if by doing so, I could bottle up its brightness, lock its golden band inside my mind.

After a brief stop at a girlfriend's on the way home (I waited in the car), the change in Peter's humour was palpable - he was genial, expansive, like my dad had been after his first drink, and I allowed myself to hope for the evening ahead. But after a stiff gin and tonic, he carried on drinking steadily through dinner. Following dinner he left the table, only to return swinging a bottle of Scotch as if it were a weapon. Emmeline tried to remonstrate with him, with little success. She made her excuses pretty swiftly after that. I would have given the whole world to have left the table with her.

I attempted to escape twenty minutes later, citing my dislike of Scotch, but in vain.

"You *will* sit down," Peter told me. "And you *will* drink. You're in Scotland. Scotch it is. And this is a fine one."

After just a couple of glasses I sensed control slip from me, the weight of my tongue sitting sluggish in my mouth. Another glass and I was getting perilously close to drunk. I sat swirling the ice round at the bottom of my drink, contemplating the darkness that swam up out of it.

Peter stopped bitching about his business partner long enough to fix his belligerent gaze on me.

"What's up with you, Jamie?"

"Nothing."

"You look knackered. What's the matter? Conscience troubling you?"

"I had such a vivid dream last night. She was *there*, Peter, sitting by my bed. She was so close to me, and she was *alive*."

"That is simply not possible," my brother retorted.

"If you really believe Sarah's dead, Peter, why don't you tell them to call off the search?"

He flushed but didn't answer me.

"Hasn't this hatred gone on long enough? *I* wasn't the bastard who took her, Peter. If someone did take her."

My brother refilled his glass. "Oh, we know somebody took her." His hands were shaking. "We just don't know what they did with her. But we know what *you* did, my dear brother. You caused the accident that sent her nuts, Jamie. The one that eventually drove her into that bastard's arms. She was just sitting beside you, not doing anything, no big mistakes - except *fucking trusting* you…"

I ran my hand over my eyes, drained my drink and stood up.

"Peter, you're not being rational. The crash didn't kill her. It happened over a year before she disappeared. You know that."

"The accident mangled her brain though, didn't it? Scrambled her synapses nicely. They said she'd made a miraculous recovery given the damage to the frontal lobe - horseshit. The slightest thing would send her into a rage. Her memory was shot to pieces. She even *stole* from me, Jamie. That's right; stole from her own brother to buy smack. If the accident hadn't fucked her up, if she hadn't started running around with the wrong crowd the moment she got back on her feet, she'd still be here. And that accident was *all your fault.*"

It was true. After the accident Sarah was all edges, nervy as a cat about to take a leap. She'd started to use drugs, left her advertising job suddenly and moved from Norwich to Newcastle. None of us knew why, only that she'd got another job (we had no idea what that was), and that she was living with new friends in the Byker area.

Shortly before she'd disappeared, Peter had visited her and established she was using heroin. He'd called me up about it.

I should have done something then. But we were all treading carefully, too scared to weigh in, conscious that a careless act, a single word, might tip her over the edge of the precipice on which she was walking.

I shook my head. If the crash had never happened, if she hadn't hurt her head, would she have plunged so deep into the darkness, until the devil himself threw his bloody cloak over her head? We - I - would never know.

Peter cut into my thoughts. "Remember that time

she had to have her stomach pumped? Remember that? And that bloke she got so friendly with just after she moved - the psycho in that Satanic cult? The one who watched her lacerate herself, harvested her blood? She'd never have let him near her if she'd been in her right mind - would she, Jamie?"

"Stop!" I whispered. I covered my ears. He was advancing towards me now, glass in hand. "It's not my fault she's gone. I *loved* her, for fuck's sake!" I looked up at him as he stood over me, hating him for his money, his self-righteousness, the sneer on his fine face. "I loved her," I protested weakly.

"You fucked her up, Jamie."

"No - *you* did that. Growing up with you was no fun. You tormented both of us. You're nothing but a bully, Peter. A big, fucking…"

I didn't finish my sentence. Before I knew it I was on my back, contemplating Peter's intricate Georgian cornicing.

Finally I sat up, nursing my jaw. Lucy was sitting by me now, panting sympathetically as blood dripped from my nose on to Peter's pristine carpet. I felt as if I were nine years old again to his eleven, with our father nowhere to be seen and only Sarah around to make things better.

Except she wasn't around now.

"You *bastard.*"

I tried to get up, without success.

"Here, take this," Peter said, holding out a silk

handkerchief, and eventually moving forward to help me to my feet.

I held the handkerchief to my nose. After a while, the bleeding stopped.

"I hate you," I said to him.

"No, you don't."

Peter led me to the drawing room, deposited me on the sofa, and poured both of us fresh drinks, before sitting down on the coffee table in front of me. Lucy at once put her head on his left knee.

"I'm making a bad situation worse, I realise that" my brother told me.

For all his attempts to be conciliatory, the brutality was evident on his face. I swallowed, my nose throbbing, then stood up, swaying slightly.

"What's up with you anyway, Jamie?" he asked after a while. "Sit down. You're a bag of nerves."

"I'm fine."

"Hardly. Is it Rachel?"

"Leave her out of it."

"Why didn't you get here Saturday?" He paused, shrewd eyes assessing me. "Don't tell me," he said. "You were screwing some beauty in a seedy roadside joint, hmm?"

I watched as his laughter died, replaced by a priceless look of complete incredulity. "You're joking, right? Mr Pious, Mr Monogamous, off on a little frolic?"

I was silent.

"Where did you find her? By the side of the road?"

I flushed. "She was…hitchhiking. On the Holloway Road." I hesitated. "She reminded me of Sarah."

Peter made a half-laughing, half-choking sound. "You picked up a girl who reminded you of our little *sister*? And you *fucked* her? Jesus, Jamie, are you twisted or what?" He whistled, a long low whistle. Then he drained his drink, lit a cigarette. "Christ, I think you've lost it. I'm surprised she didn't clean you out. And she reminded you of *Sarah*? *Why*?"

I hesitated. Sarah's eyes were brown, her hair almost black, while Katy was fair…yet they both seemed to have a quality that drew others to them, something more powerful than charm or beauty, and more difficult to define. With a shock I realised what it was. Like my brother, they'd both been blessed with charisma; and yet, unlike Peter, beneath it, they both seemed utterly and completely lost. They had a vulnerability that would make some men want to crush them to bits, while others…others would give up their lives to help them…

"Where did you stay?" my brother asked me.

"Near Glasgow."

He continued to scrutinise me as he smoked, staring at me as if he were seeing me properly for the first time. "I'm at a loss for words."

I couldn't help but smile at that.

"Oh, wipe that smirk off your face." He poured himself another drink. "So - what now? Are you going to see her again?"

"I didn't take her number."

"Your ability to torture yourself is legendary. Why not take her number and be done with it?"

"Because I can't use it. I can't just pick people up and put them down again."

"Bollocks, it's perfectly possible. Unless you've fallen for her." He looked at me quizzically. "No. *Please* tell me no, Jamie. Expand on the sex, if you must, but spare me the sentiment."

I lapsed into miserable silence.

"She's *special*? She *bewitched* you?" Peter's coarse laughter grated on my ears. "You idiot. You've got a decent job, a nice house and a wife who…well, she's *there,* at least…and you'd fuck all that up for some random shag? Rachel would have your guts for garters." He paused. "What was she like, anyhow? Must have been something bloody special to make you break your precious vows."

An image of Katy burst like a flare in my mind. I snuffed it out immediately.

"You fool."

"Fuck off, Peter, why don't you?"

"Oh come on, brother. We all fail sometimes. This makes me like you a little more, Jamie."

I stood up, swaying.

"Where you going?"

"To bed."

"Have a nightcap."

I sat down again, put my head in my hands.

"I've had ten nightcaps."

"Have another one. And take my advice: forget this girl. Sleep with the next one, if there is a next one, then forget her too. Focus on Rachel. Poor Rachel. Wants to get pregnant - can't get pregnant. Poor girl."

"Cut it out."

Peter grinned suddenly. "Do you actually *want* your wife to get pregnant, Jamie?" He leaned back. "You can tell me anything, you know. Seeing as we're having a little heart-to-heart."

"Peter, why would we have been trying for three years - three fucking years! - if I didn't bloody well want her to get pregnant?"

"You tell me."

"I'm just nervous."

"No, I suspect there's a little more than that going on. *I* was never nervous."

"But you're perfect, Peter. We all know that."

"And you're a jealous wanker." He paused. "So what is it? Mum? Dad?"

"No. But having kids certainly made them miserable."

"They made each other miserable too." He paused. "Well, it's true that if you're not fucking like rabbits and foolishly happy before kids, you can forget about any amity, joy, lust; whatever. Even Emmy and I had our moments before the kids came along. My advice: if it's not great now, get out."

"I didn't say it wasn't great."

"You didn't have to." He sighed, crushing his cigarette. "Do what you like, then. You always do. But you won't win any prizes for misery. Dad never did."

Certainly miserable now, I drained my drink and stood up again.

"In any event," Peter went on "try not to get too distracted by this girl - what's her name - Katy. Pointless waste of time."

I was suddenly sorry I'd told my brother her name. I put my glass down. "I have to go to bed."

"Just one more thing."

"What is it?"

My brother had been rummaging around in his pockets. Now he drew out a bunch of keys. "I'm going to give you something," he said. "In case you need it." His voice was slurring slightly, and it occurred to me that he was at last, quite drunk. He removed one key from the rest and dangled it in front of my nose.

"What's that?"

"What do you think it is, you half-wit? It's a key."

"I know it's a key. What's it for?"

He tapped the side of his nose. "I have a secret bolt-hole in London, near the Angel." He told me the address, then repeated it. "I go there when I've had enough of this desolate place - and Emmy, for that matter. That's where I fled when she got pregnant for the first time."

"I thought you took to the hills."

"Only metaphorically speaking. I went to town, Jamie. Got my fun where I could before she sucked it all out of me. I still go to the flat on occasion. She doesn't know about it."

"You want me to have it?"

"I'm not giving the place to you, you moron. I want you to stay there, if this whole bloody thing blows up in your face. And my guess is it's only a matter of time before it does. You, Jamie, are a bomb waiting to blow."

"What do you mean?"

"I mean you're going to lose control. Spectacularly. As only you know how to do. I've seen it before, remember?" I hesitated. "Take it," Peter went on.

"Why are you being so generous, all of a sudden?"

He waved me away. "Call it payback. For how bloody awful I've been to you for four years. Take it quick, before I change my mind. And fuck off, before I beat you up again."

And so I pocketed the key, backed away from Peter and started walking up the stairs, somewhat heavily. I turned only once, to take a last look at my brother's prostrate form, before, slowly and somewhat unsteadily, I made my way to my room.

KATY

I ran until I couldn't hear Mac's footsteps
following me, until I could no longer hear my
mother's voice inside my head. I ran until I
couldn't run any more, and then I doubled over
and threw up.

The houses in the street around me seemed
misshapen, crooked and curved, or perhaps it was
the drink I'd had at Mac's, the hours now of no
sleep. And then it started to rain, and the sheen
on the bricks seemed to turn to slime that dripped
down onto the pavement and trickled slowly
towards my feet.

I headed back towards the square and found
the hostel where I had remembered it, small and
fortunately empty with no one minded to judge
a girl dishevelled and dirty and so tired she was
almost dead.

Inside, I drew the curtains of the room I'd been
allocated (which fortunately was empty) and
opened the window up. I could hear police sirens
and car horns, drunks laughing in the street. I
leaned out over a windowsill that was washed
white with the light of the moon that rested on it.
Eventually the riot of voices in my head subsided,
until not one was left, save for the voice of the

man, the stranger with whom I'd shared the start of my trip. At last that one voice, sweet as a caress, grew so strong that it alone filled me; and then I lay down on my bunk bed, closed my eyes and slept.

Bad things happened to me in Scotland, I'd told Jamie. But that night I dreamed about how it was before the bad things started, back to a time when childhood dripped its undiluted sweetness like wild honey running to my mouth. I dreamed of my old friend, Caitlin, of how we first met that first day of school. What a fun, feisty thing she was back then, always charming her way out of trouble, golden pigtails down her back. I dreamed of my mother, as she once was, before she started the booze, and before she had my baby brother, and lost her mind after it, before her baby died, and my dad left, and she finally broke apart. I dreamed of the burnt-biscuit smell of her hair when she lifted me up, of the perfume and the cream she used to take her make-up off. I dreamed of the dance of dust motes in sunshine as I listened to her singing. Then of my dad, of his face that shone like a god's, and his eyes that dripped fire, and how my parents were together, how happy they once were before the baby came and went. And all these pictures bloomed bright in my head; but then they began to spin, before disappearing into the darkness, vanishing.

The room was pitch black when I woke up. I leaned over with a shaking hand and turned on the light. Opposite, the houses were in darkness, but as I smoked a cigarette the first light came to colour the concrete pink, and then there came the start-up sounds of the street, the buzz of early traffic, a driver's radio, the sound of seagulls - it had been a while since I'd heard that. I wondered if my mother knew where Mike was, and if she didn't, how the hell I was going to find out.

When it was light, I made my way to the other side of the canal, to the bit of town most forgot, the part already claimed by the lonely land surrounding it, where banks of heather ran wild in gardens, bracken clung to walls and moss papered over cracks and coated in virulent green the roofs of the small and grubby homes.

Years ago, my mother had kept her house immaculate, forever tidying what was already tidied up, making sure taps were tight and locks were locked, a thousand times she did that, and she got worse with that after her baby went, as if by achieving pristine order she could stop herself unravelling, seeing and hearing what wasn't there, stop the stares, the jabbing fingers, the rumours flying about. But after dad went wild with grief,

built a fire and burned all the baby stuff, my
mother just gave up; locked herself inside, glued
to her seat, with the same dirty cup sat in front of
her, each time with a different drink, no energy
left to even wash that out. Then after he left, she
exploded, started throwing stuff about, breaking
plates and glass, destroying everything of his he'd
left, before she went back to sitting, mouth slack,
not bothering to clear any of the mess.

And now as I walked up the steps of that
place, I saw the same dishevelment, and I knew
then that nothing had changed. I thought about
my little baby brother, his tiny bandy legs, the
sweetness of his skin, his hair and breath. I
remembered how, long after he died, and all the
officious people left, when my mother got really
mad, she'd tell me that I was the one who did it;
I'd rocked him too much or made his milk bad
or maybe even my breath had poisoned him,
she said. No baby was safe around me; that was
the truth of it. And now, as I raised my hand,
I thought of my own baby, and my fire came
flooding back and I knocked, three times, so loud
I made the whole door shake.
  She came soon enough, make-up like a mask,
eyes heavy with clogged mascara, lipstick
bleeding into the wrinkled corners of her mouth.
Her eyes registered nothing on seeing me; she

simply blocked the door so I couldn't pass. I saw bald patches amongst the thinning hair on her head, brown spots upon her arms and beneath the stink of booze I smelled a smell that was sour, medicinal; the smell of old age she couldn't be bothered to fight off. I forced myself to look her in the eyes, and saw how creased her skin was, each line carved by Time's knife deep into her face.

She was wearing a green dress with long sleeves that I recognised.

- I remember that dress, I said.

- Aye, it's the same one I wore the day your dad left. Over twenty years ago that was, she said. See? It's falling to bits. And she held up both fraying sleeves.

- Let me inside, I told her, but she pushed me back.

In my mind's eye I could see the kitchen, the pictures I'd drawn hanging up, the table, covered with the scars and scribbles I'd left as a kid, the same teacup sitting on it.

- Not pleased to see me, mum?

As I spoke my mother's cat appeared, a mangy black thing with startling green eyes. It weaved its way around my ankles, its purr a low thrum.

- Inky is, she said.

I bent down to stroke the cat's bony back.

- How old is he now?

- Thirteen, she said. Her eyes narrowed. I didnae expect you back. Why are you here? What do you want, Katy?

- I don't want a thing from you, I never did.

- That's a lie, and you know it is. You're always wanting, always after what you can get.

I watched her fingers twisting over, twisting over, twisting back.

- What you been up to? I asked.

- Nothing, she said.

- That's right. Doing Nothing is like some disease that you can't shake.

- How long since I saw you last?

- Three years, and you know it is.

- It's more than that, lassie. I barely saw you when you were with Mike. I'd wait for you to come, just like I waited for your da. I could have died and rotted waiting, for all either of you gave a fuck. Your da was too busy fucking around, and you were too busy fucking up, isn't that right, Katy? Being led about by the nose? Ignoring your own mother and your tiny kid?

I was used to how she was, but I hadn't expected her to launch in so quick. I blinked back tears, took a breath.

- Things are different now. I have a job. It's not much, but it gives me my own cash.

- You, a job? I cannae imagine that.

- There's a lot you don't know about me, mum.

She pressed her lips together, a bloody line in her face.

- People don't ever change, she said.

- You know, mum, I'm not surprised dad left.

Her eyes flew open at that.

- You have no idea about your da.

- I know he couldn't take it any longer, I said. After what happened to the baby, and your craziness before and after it. I'm not shocked at what he did.

- Do you ever think about what *you* did, Katy?

- I didn't. I did not!

- That's not what they all said. And I know. I know what you're capable of. I'd be surprised if you can sleep at night.

The pain was like a slow squeeze around my throat.

- If my baby's gone, it was something you did. You or Mike. I just wanted to make her safe.

- Aye, that's your version of it. Leaving her out to freeze at best, to be eaten by foxes or by rats.

- I bet she's here, I whispered. You're hiding her.

- Your mind's playing tricks, like it always did. Seeing things that aren't right.

- You know where she is.

- No, Katy, only you ken that. She would have been better off without you. She was at risk. But we didnae take her. We didnae get a chance. Think about what you did, lassie. Go look at yourself hard in the mirror.

- You had it in for me. You wanted my blood, I whispered, tears burning. You and Mike.

- You're cuckoo if that's what you think.

- I want to find Mike, mum. Help me find him. Tell me where he lives.

I forced myself to come close to her, so close I could smell the faint trace of the warm biscuit smell that clung to her, beneath the burn of the booze. And I stroked one of her hands, just once, felt its fine veins hum and pulse.

- Please, mum? I whispered, as she looked at me and shook her head. *Please?*

She held my arm, scanning my face as if it were a book.

- What drugs you on now, Katy? she asked.

- None, I swear to God.

- And do you still hear them voices?

- You heard voices, mum. After the baby, remember?

- I don't want to talk about it.

- I went to see the doctor. I'm better, I promise. Ever since I got this job, I've got myself together. That's why I've come back - to find her, I said.

I saw her hesitate.

- I couldn't stand for more bad to happen, she said.

- I just want to speak to Mike.

I saw her face soften just for a second, saw its creases start to iron out.

- Ach, wait one minute, she told me, and I waited,

long, tortuous seconds for her to come back.

She came at last, holding a scrap of paper in one fist.

- Here's Mike's address, she said. Around ten miles from here. We keep in touch, so I ken that's where he is.

I took the paper and stuffed it in my pocket.

- Thanks.

I wanted to go then, but it was as if some very fine thread were drawing me in.

- I'd best go now, mum, I said at last.

Her colour rose beneath the make-up she'd slathered on.

- Aye, that's right, Katy. Walk back into my life, get what you want from me, then chuck me away, like you always did, as if I were an empty case or some such shit.

And she pushed me, only a small push, but enough to unbalance me. I stumbled backwards down the steps, banging one knee and grazing my right hand.

I put my stinging hand to my mouth and looked up and back. There she was, still standing there at the top of the steps, staring down at me, utterly unrepentant, a frail and lonely figure in her tatty green dress.

JAMIE

Peter didn't even bother to see me out when I left his place early the following morning. He was sleeping off his hangover, no doubt, and for that, I was grateful, for I couldn't quite face his recalcitrance. It seemed that my visit had only worsened our relations, and it was with a familiar feeling of failure that I finally got into my car.

Sunlight brightened the decrepitude of the few solitary houses on the moors, but somewhere after Inverness the wind started up, and at several points, heavy rain virtually obliterated the road. The return journey seemed long and lonely. I'd hoped to be back in London by early evening, but the traffic on the A1 was heavy, and it was dark when I finally found myself driving past the point at which Katy and I had first met on the Holloway Road. But for the anxious knot in the pit of my stomach, I could have believed we had never met at all.

It was eleven o'clock when at last I opened my front door, to find the house displaying the pristine order that my wife coveted, and only managed to achieve while I was away. My ready meal was, as Rachel's curt note informed me, in the fridge, ready for the microwave. Warmed up, it tasted of plastic.

I sat at the little-used dining table that smelled

of French polish and ate staring at the intricate reproduction fireplace with its empty grate. On the mantelpiece were photographs of my brother and Emmeline and their two kids, taken when they were babies, of Rachel and I, as younger, pasty-faced lawyers on a firm bonding weekend in Wales, of the holiday we'd taken one April in Tuscany (where it had rained non-stop and I'd finally proposed in a waterlogged Italian garden, after consuming the best part of a bottle of Chianti), and finally a wedding photograph, taken on the steps outside the registry office in Islington on a stifling June day. Rachel and I were standing inches apart but facing each other, posed and poised, like silent film stars. Rachel was wearing a high-necked white dress, a line of buttons running down along the neck from her chin. I remembered keeping my eyes fixed on those buttons, terrified I'd forget my marriage lines. And now other details of our wedding day came back to me: the rather stiff ceremony at the registry, held without music (Rachel and I couldn't agree on a particular piece we both enjoyed), the champagne, sour and dry, the congratulations of our acquaintances, and the overdressed hotel bed we sank into at the end of it, too tired to make love. I remembered turning to my new wife and asking her if she'd enjoyed the day, knowing she hadn't, yet still oddly disappointed when she'd smiled apologetically and said it had been 'a bit of a trial.' Rachel, always so unflinching, so honest, and I, once so relieved she was built that way - why had I wanted her to lie? Were wedding days always a let-down, I wondered now, and did it matter? The wedding wasn't the point, was it? It was only the start of the journey.

I shifted uncomfortably on the chair on which I was sitting (a cushion-less designer thing Rachel had bought from a shop on Upper Street), my head still reeling with the long drive. I finished my food, rinsed my plate and placed it in an empty dishwasher. I looked at the calendar on the fridge. Rachel was starting Mandarin classes near Regent's Park Wednesday. She had a Pilates session before work at 8 a.m. on Thursday. Then that evening we had dinner with Ivan and Cathy, work colleagues of Rachel's. My wife had reserved a table at Moro's for 7.30 pm. Wasn't 7.30 too early to eat dinner? I wondered. Shouldn't we still be sipping long indulgent cocktails at that hour, congratulating ourselves on another day done? But Rachel didn't do cocktails. She barely drank anything at all, save for the occasional white wine spritzer.

I studied the long 'To Do' list my wife had left out on the counter, separate columns for each of us. Rachel's enthusiasm for lists increased when she was unhappy. And if my wife *was* less than perfectly happy, how could that be her fault? She was so ordered, so successful at managing her time at and out of work. And if not hers, whose fault was it, if not my own? I crept up the stairs, shame-faced, exhausted.

Rachel was sleeping. I wouldn't have to face her until the morning, when we'd go our separate ways to work shortly after breakfast (egg on toast for me, and low sugar granola over low-fat yoghurt for Rachel). It wasn't as if my wrong doing were written on my forehead, I reasoned, as I slipped between the sheets. With any luck, my wife, at times impervious to the emotional turmoil of others, wouldn't be able to tell anything was the matter.

The sheets were as cold as I, but I settled down to sleep straight away.

A few seconds later, white overhead light flooded the room, and I was staring into Rachel's taut, tired face.

It was as if centuries had passed since I'd last seen my wife. I'd forgotten how fragile her face looked without make-up. Dark circles ringed her eyes, lines scored her high forehead. How different she'd seemed even a few years ago. Rachel didn't do enthusiasm, but she'd seemed fresher, livelier, then.

Pity and guilt overwhelmed me as I looked at her, infecting the air around us, making it close and heavy.

"How are you feeling?" I whispered.

"What happened?" Rachel asked, without answering my question. "Peter wouldn't let you go?"

"He was foul. You were right. I'm only late because

of the M1," I mumbled, stretching across to give her a kiss. She smelled of expensive face cream, and her cheek was colder than the sheets. "You tired?" She nodded. "What did you have for supper?" I asked, before I could stop myself.

Rachel rolled away from me and pulled the duvet up. "Oh, don't start. I had sea bass over samphire, if you must know."

"Did you cook?"

"No. I ate out."

"Did you have potato with it?"

"Jamie! What is this obsession with potato?"

"I like it," I protested.

"And *I* don't. So, why was Peter impossible?"

"It was ever so."

Rachel chuckled, a sound I seldom heard, and always enjoyed. "Wasted trip?"

"Sort of," I said, evasively.

"I told you so."

"How's work?"

"Late, the last few nights." I sighed. "What, Jamie? The deal doesn't sleep. And the assistant who's working on it is so incompetent it drives me nuts."

"You're so harsh."

"I know. But I'm hard on myself too."

"And on everyone else. Why don't you delegate, as I do?"

"You're lazy." She smiled a little, to soften the insult, and then yawned, stretching out both arms in front of her.

"Charming." I bent my head into the hollow between her shoulder and neck and kissed it. "Sleep," I whispered.

Rachel put her hand on my arm, moved it up over my shoulder and down my chest. "Help me to sleep, Jamie." Her fingers moved downwards. I was tired and guilty, but even so I felt the first stirring of an erection. There was an irresistible sweetness in our familiarity, surely, even if it was just a little cloying? Weren't we in a safe space - to fight, to fuck up and make up without any terrible consequences? Yes, I respected Rachel, knew her inside out, admired her forcefulness, and she, she tolerated my foibles, accepted my vulnerabilities. All was as it should be... except...

I moved my wife towards me decisively, pulling her on top of me, placing my hands on her thighs. She bent over to touch my mouth. Her mouth was dry and tasted of salt. I worked my fingers gently, as she arched her back, gripped my shoulders.

She pushed her hands against me to stop me moving, as she moved up and back and over me, pressing her breasts against my mouth. Her breasts were small, the areolae perfect circles, the nipples hard and erect.

I had to work hard with Rachel, perform properly. Stay focused, not let my mind wander. She sensed immediately if I did, in or out of bed. But I'd had years of practice. I continued using my fingers, trying not to thrust into her, until she whimpered softly, and with a single exhale, I could let go at last, letting the darkness crash around me as I came.

When my breathing had returned to normal, I let one finger play gently up and down Rachel's arm. I wanted to say something to make her laugh, but I never could make Rachel laugh. A familiar feeling of impotence washed over me. My wife remained on her side of the bed, her breathing regular. I reached up and touched her cheek. Her skin was cool and dry.

"Better?" I asked.

"A little."

"You didn't miss me too much?"

"You've only been away a few days."

"You came?" I whispered.

Rachel put out one hand towards mine. "Couldn't you tell?"

"Yes."

"Why did you ask then?"

I was drifting into sleep when I heard her whisper, "Jamie?"

I turned towards her. She was a dark shadow amongst the ghostly bed linen. "What?"

"I made a decision while you were away. I decided I want to start the treatment."

"But Rachel, we talked about this. Because they haven't found anything wrong, as such, so next time it might work - might…stick. So we should wait a bit, right? Right?"

I sensed her stiffen in the darkness. "Each time…is worse than the last. I feel…" She hesitated. "Empty. I feel empty."

Of course she did. It made sense. I swallowed hard. "Come here," I said.

She moved over towards me, and I put an arm around her.

"I'm not going to put it off any longer, Jamie."

"I thought we'd agreed…"

"I've waited long enough." Rachel drew in her breath. "Honestly, Jamie, what's wrong with you?

Panic set in. *Something* was wrong, surely? *Everyone* wanted this.

"I talked to mum when she was here…"

"Of course you did. And what did Angela the fertility expert say?" I cut in, before I could stop myself.

"She said we're fools if we leave it much longer. Because of my age."

Angela always had a view. And she always made that view known.

"You're only thirty-four, for fuck's sake. Hardly past it."

"Well, I feel it." She moved away from me.

"Rachel…"

"You're full of shit, Jamie. I don't believe you really want me to get pregnant."

I winced. "That's rubbish," I said hastily. "I'm just thinking we need to…to enjoy each other a little more, before we can enjoy a child. Will a child bring joy into our lives, if there's no joy already?"

"Joy? *Joy?*" My wife, suddenly passionate, spat the words out into the darkness. "What are you on about, Jamie? Anyway, Mum found a new clinic while you were away. They're good, apparently. They've got a cancellation tomorrow at two o'clock. Mum's a magician to have got us that appointment."

"But I've got to go to work," I protested. "I can't just up and leave…"

"Will you be there?"

I closed my eyes. Unpleasant images ran through my mind: endless hospital appointments, needles, drugs, drugs, more drugs. And after that? Disappointment, probably. Or, just possibly, no disappointment. Just possibly, joy…

What did that even feel like? I couldn't remember.

Of course I couldn't refuse her. I owed her this. I'd let her walk down the aisle in that white dress. I'd promised her the whole fucking fairy tale, even if it hadn't quite materialised.

"I know what's going on with you, Jamie. I *know* you."

I sighed. "You say it like it's a threat."

Her veins glimmered blue in the half light of the room. "I know what you're thinking."

"What am I thinking?"

"You don't want a baby at all, not really. Certainly not with me."

"Jesus, Rachel, that's not fair! I...I'm just...it's a lot to take in, that's all."

I sighed. The effort of making my voice heard with Rachel exhausted me. Sometimes, I felt I had no voice.

"I don't know why," she went on. "Maybe there's something wrong with your wiring, or maybe it's just me. Or maybe you need to just grow up, Jamie."

"Let's talk Friday."

"My deal closes Friday."

"I don't want to row. I hate rowing with you."

"Then do what I want."

"And what about what *I* want?"

She turned to me. "What do you want, Jamie? I *know* what I want. Do you?"

Panic washed over me. My chest contracted painfully, and I closed my eyes. "Can we talk about this another time?" I said at last. "*Please?* I've just driven for twelve hours straight. I need to sleep."

"You've perfected the art of absence in presence, Jamie. Even when you're having sex, you aren't *there*. And you never want to talk."

"And you never want to listen. You don't *listen*, Rachel."

"I *do*."

It was an argument so familiar we were bored by arguing it; by mutual agreement, in this, if in nothing else, we both fell silent.

Rachel turned over her pillow, smacking it with her hand. I lay awake for some time, feeling her anxiety pulse through the room, like an electric current. At last I drifted into an uneasy sleep. In the morning, the bed beside me was empty. She was gone.

KATY

I woke thinking of Mike; not of the man that
at last I left, but the man before that - how he
was at first, how I was at eighteen, so young
and gorgeous and full of it, and he like nothing
I'd ever met, the big bad love I'd spent my life
looking for, that rubbished everything before it,
that made my mother sick. With him I couldn't
give enough, couldn't get enough, I'd be awake all
night and forget to eat and drink and shit. That's
what being with him was like.

I was with my old school friend Caitlin that
night we met, tearaways the pair of us, all eyes
and tits, always out and causing trouble, breaking
hearts and giving nothing back.

After a few drinks, Caitlin pointed Mike out.

- That guy over there - he looks a week bit like
your dad, she said.

When I saw the way he stood and held himself,
as if he were the centre of his own world and of
others', I knew then that she was right. And I
was sure from that moment that this man was all
I wanted, that we'd walk off into the sunset on
paths of glass. Caitlin and I, we both stood staring
at him (I know Caitlin was hoping he'd ask her
out - I could tell by the way she was standing,

chest pushing out, lips in a pout), but when at last he came over, it was me he singled out.

He bought us both a drink - Caitlin was talking at him but it was as if for him she didn't exist; it was *my* arm he took hold of, it was *me* he pulled out into the darkness that came at us as we kissed. And then he led me back inside and went to get us more drinks, leaving me standing next to Caitlin's sour face and thinking *How could I have lived so long and not known this?*

After that, Caitlin and I, we fell out - she started with the little barbed comments, like poisoned darts, and soon she became an outright bitch - couldn't keep a lid on it. And to be fair, I never called to find out how she was doing - always I'd be out with Mike, and we'd go back to his place, usually, when his mates were out, as my mum clearly didn't want us in the house.

One night Mike drove me to one of the hills outside Kolcan. It was a hot summer night, the air outside the town breathing out the scent of heather, the moon making the moorland rocks glow white, and when we sat in his car looking down at all the lights, it was as if the stars had spread themselves beneath our feet. And then we were kissing and he said

- I love you, Katy, I'll love you always, come live with me, be my wife. And before I had a chance to speak we were more than kissing and before I could draw breath we were driving back.

That's how it always was with Mike: moving fast, too fast, like a star falling, that burns too bright, burns too quick, and you falling after it, too fast to think, falling at last through total darkness when all light cuts out.

I remembered the non-stop fucking, each loving everything the other did, like my mum and dad in the beginning, like Adam and Eve before the serpent came and they were forced out. And the row with my mother when I announced I was moving out - that spiteful look upon her face. (Though things changed once I did, she calmed down, and she couldn't get enough of Mike by the end - he'd help her around the house, charm her right when he felt like it.) And then the turning point with Mike, several months after I'd moved in, the row over nothing that started it, when he drank some milk I'd left too long in the fridge, spat it out and hit me in the face. And that one rough touch was all it took for those strings of coloured lights that had been swinging through my head, making it look so pretty, like a fairy's place, for all of them to just burn out.

Now I thought of the darkness that came after, how I stumbled, how I tripped, how freely towards the end Mike used his fists, his feet, his teeth. How once I'd turned up sobbing on my mother's doorstep, having left her alone a fair few weeks, and her telling me I couldn't just turn up when I felt like it.

- You made your bed, now go lie in it.

I remembered the calls to Caitlin that went unanswered, the whispers behind my back.

- What was it this time, love? Did you walk into a wall - another one? the women said.

But they were all of them scared of Mike. Except for Caitlin, who was a jealous bitch.

Only one bright moment stands out: the jolt of joy when I first found out I was pregnant, when I saw those two lines on the stick, before fear burned through my guts as I stood in front of Mike, waiting to tell him what I'd found out.

Now, as I made myself up, I tried to forget the hell that came with Mike, until I could get my strength up, could feel tough enough to make him talk. At last, I was ready to step out, looking as if I were wearing an immaculate mask, and I picked up my bag, felt inside for my knife, clasped one hand around it and pressed, until pain stilled the riot inside my head.

At the station I bought a ticket for Mordon, where my mother had told me Mike now lived. I waited on the icy platform for some time, warming myself with cigarettes, until at last a train came, and spewed me out on another freezing platform, where I stood stamping my feet, summoning up the courage to ask for directions to Mike's place.

I didn't have long to wait. The first man I asked was only too happy to help, to walk me most of the way there, in fact. But as I came to the address, I cursed to find the house shuttered up, with no sign of life. With no particular plan in mind, for now at least, I wandered the desolate streets until I found an inn, where I resolved upon just one drink.

I found a seat near the meagre fire and there I stayed, nursing my glass of whisky mixed with ginger, sweet and tart. Then I stood up, and, ignoring the eyes that were on me, the whispers behind my back, I walked over to get another drink.

I saw him as I came up to the bar, just when it was too late to stop, to shrink back into the shadow near my seat. I couldn't miss him, the great handsome bulk of him: dark hair, still thick and full, chin shaded with stubble, eyes the colour of stormy skies, nose much straighter than my dad's. He was standing on his own at the bar - it seemed people couldn't stand to be too close to him. And when I saw him I froze, unable to speak, or to move, to turn around and go back.

He didn't recognise me, not at first. He smiled,

but it wasn't the smile he used to use on me; it was the smile he'd give a stranger, a charming, come-on smile. I knew, though, that soon he would find me out. He would smell me, the feral smell I couldn't hide under perfume, just like his own, something part way between sweet and rotten, that I would smell when I closed my eyes and breathed in Mike.

- Remember me, Mike? I said to him, and I smiled as I said it, even as I prayed: don't step back, don't hit me, don't do anything but smile back, please God, smile back. And I blinked and smiled again, and he lost his smile - but he did offer me a drink.

He came close to me with my drink, and as he did so his smell washed over me, that smell of stale tobacco and tree sap, and I remembered how it was between us at first, when that was enough to get me into bed, when I was convinced Mike was my ticket out of the miserable home where I still lived.

And when I remembered that, our first nights together, my fear went, and I could sit near him, talk to him, and when he leaned close to me and said

- You fucked me over.

I could answer without fear, without shrinking back.

- Yes, and I'm sorry now that I did.

And when he whispered

- You ken how much I hated you for that?

I could forget limping home after his last attack,
then sitting in our flat, unable to eat or sleep,
deciding then that I would flee, throw myself and
my stuff out onto the streets. I could blank all that
out, lean into him, whisper

- Mike, do you remember what we were like?

And when at last he smiled and breathed out

- Yes.

I could say to him, and mean it a thousand times
over

- I want us to be again like that.

I could come up close to him, and watch his eyes
close, as he whispered

- I've missed you, lassie.

And when he traced one calloused finger down
my throat, I craved his touch as if I were thirsty,
craving drink, and I knew then I was back in
time, that my transformation was complete.

- Come on, he said at last. Let's get out of this
place.

He tipped my drink to my mouth, forcing me
to drink the last of it, so a little spilled down my
neck. As he took my arm, he squeezed so hard I
could feel the bruises springing up. I looked down
at the tattoo on his wrist. I could just make out
the letters faded on it. 'CARA' they read.

He dropped my arm, and waved his wrist in

front of my face, before jabbing with one finger at my chest. I swallowed hard, tears hot behind my eyes.

- She's still here, Katy, he said. Our kid. Still with me all the time. In spite of everything that you did.

We walked out and to his car, the cold air like a fist in my face. As he opened the door for me, he bent towards me and I thought he was going to hit me but he kissed me instead, and after a while of that I forgot about everything else, and I was kissing the Mike I first met, not the Mike in every bad dream I'd had since; the owner of the voice who told me I was worthless, of the hands that rained blows upon my head. I was out of my head's prison, free of it, for a glorious minute, as if I were on drugs, until I realised how dangerous this all was, that I had to make him stop.

- Let's take our time, Mike, I told him. Let's go back to your place.

He drove fast, his hands barely touching the wheel, moving all over me instead, and he drove down ill-lit empty streets, until we reached the darkness at the town's very edge. When I saw where we were I panicked, clammy fingers seeking out my knife.

- Don't you live on Regent Street?

Mike braked so suddenly the tyres screeched on

the icy street.

- How in the name of fuck do you ken where I live? Who blabbed? Was it Mac? Caitlin? That little bitch.

I shrank back.

- No. I promise - no! We've not been in touch.

He placed his fingers upon my throat and pressed, and pressed harder, till I felt my breath squeezed out. I managed to shake my head, putting up both hands to fight his fingers off.

- You fuckin' fibber, Katy.

- It was my mum, I gasped at last. Mike, it was my mum.

He dropped his hands, and I almost sobbed with relief.

- Can we go now? I rasped. Back to your place?

- Let's stop here a wee while, he said. That way I ken you won't bolt. The street's empty - you can make as much noise as you like.

Now he rested one hand on the base of my neck, pressing one finger into it, before working all his fingers down towards my chest. Then he smiled, a smile that made the sweat prickle on my back and pool between my thighs, gluing them to the seat.

I looked around. He was right - there was no one about. There was a streetlight up ahead, where the road ran over a bridge, but we were outside its silver circle of light.

I closed my eyes. I could barely hear Mike

breathe for the rush of blood in my head. I leaned over and kissed his neck, felt the sharpness of his Adam's apple that tugged beneath my lips. I forced myself to move slow but sure, kissing until I knew I could make him do anything I wanted, and then I helped him to undress.

I bent towards him, still wearing my dress, so he could place his hands inside, up on my breasts. I could feel the leather of the car's steering wheel at my back, warm where his hands had rested on it. He put one hand on my thigh while with the other he spread my legs, pushing one finger inside me. I shut my eyes and moved back to the passenger seat.

- Katy, come back! he laughed. I've missed your fucking gorgeous cunt!

I felt beneath me for my bag, opened it, put one hand inside.

- Close your eyes, Mike, I told him. I've got you a treat.

- Fuck that, he said. I'm too far gone. Come back!

- Close your eyes, Mike, I said, and at last he did, and I sat over him again, my lips on his throat. Again I smelled him, and my head was rammed full of it and all that it brought back.

- I cannae last with your doing this, I heard him whisper, and I closed my eyes.

This is the worst of it, I thought, when I felt him

inside me, and I heard myself cry out, not from pain but from the shock that I was wet. And I knew that some part of me had wanted him, had wanted all that came before, not just the end of it. *That was the worst of it*, I thought, *and now it's over*, as I brought up the knife and I pressed it against the soft skin of his throat.

- Don't move, Mike, I whispered. Else you'll get hurt.

His eyes flew open, and their whites widened in surprise.

- You wouldn't dare, he laughed nervously.
- Try me, I said.
- What do you want?
- I think you know.

I could smell his sweat now, like fear and rust.

- You're a crazy bitch.
- Tell me where my baby is.
- Ach, she's gone, and there's no other you can blame for it! You hid her too well, he said.
- You found her!
- I found nothing. I told you that. But you were so out of it, you wouldn't listen - you just went crazy, as you always did. You went to bits the minute she was born, and long before that you weren't right.
- You wanted to kill her. I saw you put stuff in her bottle.
- It was for her teeth!

- I wanted to keep her safe.

- Ach, you bitch. Look what happened to your wee brother - we all know that was no accident. Everyone knows it, except for the polis!

He reached out and pulled my head back, and I cried out, and my hand trembled, and the knife shivered, the blade breaking at last into his skin. Moving through my fingers and down along my wrists, I could feel the warm wet stickiness of his blood.

It happened so quick, all that came next. I heard him mutter under his breath as he sank his teeth into my hand and pushed me to the passenger side. I cried out and dropped the knife. My head slammed back against the window as he came at me and butted my cheek. Then I saw him lean down and pick up the knife.

The metallic smell of blood filled the car. I opened the door, scrambling from him and stumbling onto the street. I could hear him yelling as I started to run, then the car door slam, and footsteps moving behind me. My head was pounding, my hand throbbing, but I carried on running, until I at last could hear the steps fading, and I knew I'd left him behind. I ran until I reached the centre of town, and the station platform, where I doubled over, heaving my guts up.

Back in my bedroom at the hostel, I cleaned the blood off my hand and nursed my bruised stinging cheek. I peeled off my dirty dress, removed the makeup that had smeared my face. I couldn't stay there long - I knew that. Not now I'd fucked up. I'd injured him, riled him up and I'd not got a thing out of him, save for his blood. He'd come after me pretty quick. Even as I took my clothes off, my phone sounded, making me jump. I ignored it, and then it rang again. I checked it, hesitated, finally picked up.

- Katy! Where did you go?

I warmed to the sound of Donna's voice.

- Scotland, I said.

- I've been worried sick.

- I just had a fight with Mike. I hurt him and now he's after me. And he's got a knife.

The words tumbled out of me before I could stop them.

- Come back. You'll be safe here with us, she said.

- I don't want to drag you into it. You're pregnant, I said.

- Pete will look after us.

Pete was Donna's partner - the manager of the shitty pizza place where we first met.

- If I leave, how will I get Cara back? Right now, at least I'm in the right place. I just need to get some help.

- *I'll* help.

- I need to go, I told her.

- Where, Katy?

I thought wildly. There had to be a way out of this mess.

- I could try find Caitlin, I guess.
- Your old school friend?
- Yes.
- I thought she hated your guts.
- She does. I paused, looking around the room. I got to go, Donna. I need to pack.

I knew I had to get the next train out, even if it were only to the neighbouring town. If I stayed in Kolcan, he would find me, surely as day follows night. Quickly I packed my things and headed to the station through my hometown's glassy streets.

JAMIE

It was raining as I left the house. A slow, monotonous drizzle. People were crammed together at the bus stop on Highbury Corner. A few of them smoked - tips burning through the wet. Two buses drove past while I stood, too rammed to stop. Finally I made it onto the third - I even got a seat, only to give it up seconds later to a rosy-cheeked, heavily pregnant woman, who reminded me forcibly of Rachel, only because she was everything my wife was not.

I got off at Fleet Street and walked down towards Blackfriars. There I queued for several minutes at the cash machine, and a further five for my coffee and croissant. Then I took a left, just before Blackfriars Bridge, and walked through a courtyard lined with Queen Anne houses to my office, in a modern building tucked around its grander neighbours' backs. My heart sank as I pushed open its heavy glass doors.

Within seconds one of the partners had accosted me by the lifts. Colin, in his forties, emanated the kind of corpulent smugness a minor partnership in an insignificant firm such as mine might produce in a man such as him. "Good trip, Jamie?" he asked, as with one fat finger he pressed the button to call the lift.

"Great, thanks."

We got into the tiny lift together and my florid companion pressed the button to close the doors, the soft paunch of his belly rammed up against them.

"Catch any fish?"

"I only hiked, but it was fun just the same."

The lift commenced its slow ascent. "Everything okay with your caseload? Celia Hammond - her claim settle in the end?"

"Yes, she was happy."

"Hardly surprising, given what she got. What about Stewart?"

"No, he'll fight."

"Surprised he's got the stomach for it."

"He hasn't, not really. He just won't accept defeat."

"You got that defence in the Myron case I asked for?"

I flushed. I had meant to do that before I left. "You'll have it by the end of the week."

I could see Colin weighing up whether this was acceptable. Fortunately, the lift ground to a halt, and he moved away, waving one chubby hand in my direction. "See you around, then."

I walked down blue and gold carpet to my office. As a senior assistant I had been allocated my own office, for which I was grateful. I sat down, swivelled round to face the window. The blinds, of the featureless strip variety, were drawn; I pulled

them apart and faced the City scene in front of me
- futuristic and alien. I thought of the Highlands,
the bleak hills and glowing bracken, the air so fresh
and cold it made my lungs hurt. I turned back to
my computer. There was an urgent meeting that
afternoon to discuss fresh marketing strategies and
loyalty discounts. I had a number of mails to send,
the first to a particularly awkward client, to tell her
her claim was hopeless. I sighed and tried to immerse
myself in my work.

My PA walked in, a momentary distraction. I
shared Sandra with a fair few other assistants. She
was candid and rather charming, if over-made-up,
and her love life was more colourful than most
in the office (bar mine, as of a few days ago). I
scored significant brownie points with her now by
remembering to ask after her aged mother, who I
recalled had been unwell, and she regaled me with
several details of her recovery, before taking with her
some urgent pleading I'd given her for binding and
promising me it would go 'to the very top of the pile.'

The morning passed uneventfully, in a series of
bitter coffees, tedious meetings and interminable
phone calls. Around twelve, Ian, one of the other
assistants, popped his head round my door to see if I
wanted to grab a bite to eat.

I rather liked Ian, though we were polar opposites
(he was smooth and political, with an eye to early
partnership), and I was just about to leave my desk

when an email from an unknown address popped up in my folder. Junk, I thought, but I was curious. A warning flashed up on my screen. I ignored it and opened the mail. I read it, then closed it, then opened it and read it again.

"Jamie? Shall we go?"

I had forgotten Ian. I looked up.

"You okay, mate?" he asked.

"Sure. Why wouldn't I be?"

"You look a little pale."

"Sorry. Something's come up. Give me five minutes. I'll meet you there. Usual place."

After Ian had left, I sat back, passed one hand over my eyes. Had I, in some moment of madness, told her the name of my firm? My *surname*? Perhaps I had. I couldn't remember.

She had had to leave Scotland urgently. She was taking a train back into London today. Could we meet? Later on? *Please?* She *needed* to see me.

I stood up and removed my jacket from the chair. What did she want? Sex? Money? Both, probably.

I sat down again at my computer.

"I can't see you," I wrote. "I explained why not." I hesitated and then I added "I hope you found your daughter."

I stood up once again, and then pressed send.

Two hours later, I found myself in a smart room

in Harley Street, sitting on a chair so comfortable I could have slept in it. Rachel was sitting next to me, wearing her most serious suit and highest heels, her whole being keyed up, her nervous energy, drive, determination all brought to bear on this one appointment. She had clearly thought of little else all morning, whereas I, I was desperately trying to keep my attention fixed on the glossy brochure in front of me.

Soon it became apparent the consultant was running late, and Rachel started to fidget. She looked at her watch repeatedly, getting up several times, once to harangue the receptionist.

I'd grown used to the fact my wife was physically incapable of sitting still. I placed one hand on her arm now, feeling how tense she was, how wired. But I was powerless where my wife was concerned. In this case she needed me to come up with the goods of course, but even so, Rachel remained at all times mistress of her own orbit, unaffected by anything I could say or do.

The consultant, male, had an unusually good bedside manner, asking Rachel for her complete history, which she delivered in minute detail, with her usual professionalism. At last he cleared his throat and adjusted his glasses, still running through Rachel's medical notes, before turning his attention to me. Did I drink? A couple of glasses a day, no more? Well, best to cut down. These things could make an enormous difference to sperm motility.

"So I keep telling him," Rachel cut in.

And did I smoke?

I thought of the furtive cigarettes I'd smoked recently. How could a few stolen drags of nicotine make any difference? I shook my head.

"He's given up," Rachel said. "Over a year ago now. Right, Jamie?"

I nodded mutely.

The consultant sat back and took off his glasses.

"Rachel, from the previous test results, there's no clear sign why you can't move beyond a clinical pregnancy. But we'll repeat the tests, just to be sure… and then we'll be in a position to move forward, right?" Rachel nodded vigorously. "All right, let me explain how this all works."

Rachel knew already, of course, though she still asked a multitude of questions, pushing, pushing, as she'd done to get this appointment, as she'd done to get me to this appointment, as she didn't know how not to do. She sat forward in her chair as she spoke, her hands folded on her lap, because she even had to control her hands, though Christ knows how she managed that. Only a stray muscle beat its wayward rhythm in her temple. I watched that pulse, fascinated, wondering if it gave the game away, or if I and I alone could see the concentrated terror that lurked beneath her cool surface, as if she were crossing a tightrope over a ravine.

But no; Rachel was in control. *I* was the one who was lost, sitting there trying to take it all in, and wondering how in hell making a baby had got to be so damned difficult.

"How are you with needles, Mr Kinsella? Because you'll have to inject your wife regularly with the requisite hormones," the consultant went on. "I hope you'll be up to the job."

Rachel eyed me sceptically. "I'll manage," I said.

"I'm sure you will." The consultant's smile was broad as he went through the success rate; a live birth rate of roughly thirty percent, but he was very hopeful, we were still relatively young and certainly healthy, so we should stay focused and positive… And now he was standing up, and Rachel too, so I followed them out of the room, onto the street, complete with various forms for all the tests we would need to take.

Rachel seemed to deflate the moment she left the room: now, standing on the street, she was small and pale and vulnerable. I put my arms around her.

"Coffee?" I muttered into her hair. It smelled of the same shampoo she'd used since I'd met her - the smell made me sorry and sad.

She yielded for a few seconds to my embrace, before drawing away.

"I have to rush back for a meeting. You have one - you look like you need it." She brushed my cheek with her lips and hailed a black cab. As she got in, I called out, "Rachel!"

She turned round. She'd put her glasses on, no doubt to read over documents in the cab; their dark frames made her face look even paler. "What?"

She was impatient. She wanted to get back to a world where everything and everyone made sense.

"I want things to work out, you know..."

"For me, or for you? Or for both of us?"

She closed the door before I could say anything else, and I stood, watching the cab pull away towards the City.

I picked up a coffee and ordered my own cab to take me towards Blackfriars as I did so. Just as I was walking into my office I got a call from Sandra. I recognised the tone in her voice, one of curiosity and apology.

"What's up?"

"You had a visitor while you were out."

"Who?"

"She wouldn't say."

A pulse started to throb in my temples.

"Presumably you told her I wasn't in?"

"I did. She said she'd wait, but..."

"But what?"

"She waited an age...and then she left."

"Oh," I said, hoping Sandra wouldn't notice my disappointment, and hating myself for it. I'd reached the office by now, and maybe I imagined it, but I saw a look exchanged between the receptionists as I walked in.

Sandra was still talking. I could barely concentrate on what she was telling me.

"Jamie, I'm sorry…I gave her your number."

I stopped short. "You did *what*?" I hissed.

The receptionists stared at me and then at each other, tittering.

"She said she was a friend. She…she was insistent."

She sounded less apologetic now, more intrigued.

It was my fault, I thought, as I entered the lift, for having a PA who consumed Romance as if it were chocolate.

Sure enough, the minute I sat down at my desk, my mobile rang. An unfamiliar number lit the screen. I ignored the call, but another came, and then another.

Finally, I picked up.

"You can't call me like this."

"I want to see you."

Her voice was low and lilting. My head lifted on hearing it.

"I've nothing to say to you."

"I've got your coat."

"Why didn't you give it to Sandra then?"

"I…I forgot."

I sighed. "Keep it. You'll need it."

"It didn't work out in Kolcan," she said.

I hesitated. "Why not?" I said, curious, in spite of

myself.

"I saw my mother. We had a fight. She never could stop herself, not after a few drinks. I wanted to stay there, so I called a friend, tried to get her to put me up, but-"

"Katy, I have to work."

"Have coffee with me."

"I can't."

She lowered her voice. "*Please*, Jamie."

"I *can't*. What do you want me to do? Ride in and make it all better, like a knight in shining armour? Well, this knight's already spoken for - he's too busy fucking up someone else's life, in fact, so he'll have to pass on yours."

"I don't need rescuing."

Sudden anger rose through me, like steam. "Then what do you need? Or do you just like to play with people - is that it?" I balled my hand into a fist. My fingers were pulsing.

"You're being cruel now."

I relaxed my fingers, my throat aching. "I'm not. I just can't get involved."

"You're already involved."

I held my breath, my mind racing. "What do you want, Katy? Money?"

"Don't insult me."

"What, then?"

"I need your help."

"How?"

"You lost your sister, didn't you? So you understand."

"I don't. And I've got a wife. I can't help."

"I know," she said. "About the wife."

"We're trying for a baby. Did you know that? We're trying really, really hard."

"Do you want a baby?"

"You're insulting me now."

"Haven't you thought about what happened, Jamie? In Glasgow?"

"Of course I have. I haven't *stopped* thinking about it. But it was a mistake, right? It was a shitty thing, the sort of shitty thing I never do."

"It didn't feel like a mistake."

"But it *was*."

"So you won't help me find my daughter?"

"I *can't*."

She was silent, and I thought she'd gone away. Then she said, so softly I could barely hear it "I'm back in London for a while. You've my number, Jamie. So, if you change your mind, use it."

"Katy - listen to me. I won't change my mind."

I heard her steady breathing down the other end of the phone, then silence, and this time I knew she'd gone.

KATY

Marcus was the first person I caught sight of, just as I'd stepped off the busy streets of Soho, and was helping myself to coffee, trying not to be blinded by the neon signs, the countless headache-inducing logos that marked out my place of work. He came up close to me, so close I could see the sheen on his pallid face, could smell his breath that was sour and stale, because he'd had too much to drink the night before and now he needed something to eat.

- Katy! Good of you to join us, if a little late.

- Sorry, I mumbled. Train was delayed.

- How was the trip? The very distant relative?

He stopped, peered at my cheek, while I put up one hand to cover it.

- What happened, sweetheart? I can make it better, if you'll let me, he said.

Then he looked at me like he always did, like he wanted to put his hand up my skirt (as he did when we first met), except then he saw my face, and he had the sense to leave me alone and let me work.

I was grateful to him for giving me the job, and I quite liked him because he could be funny and generous, though I wouldn't have wanted to get

too close, God no, with his thinning hair and
his just-developing paunch, made worse by not
enough hours at the gym and copious lines of
coke. Anyway, he had a stunning wife, Georgie
her name was, with long blonde locks, who I
knew hated my guts, and two blue-eyed kids and
a dog with a fancy collar and a coat, and a roving
eye that had got him into trouble before, but not
now he'd sworn blind to turn over a new leaf.
And right now he gave me calls to make and mails
to send and I was glad, so grateful to be fully
occupied.

I'd been working a while when one of the older
girls I was friendly with, Elsa, all bangles and
bling and big gaudy lips, came up to me and
asked if I was all right. I caught sight of my pasty
face in one of those big shining mirrors that lined
the place, and Elsa told me to go home and go to
bed, that she'd tell Marcus to go take a leap if he
tried to keep me late at work that night.
It was half seven, or near enough (though I was
used to working late - I shadowed Marcus, and
he never could get out of bed, but once he got to
work he never left), by the time I got on a second
bus and walked the crowded streets back to my
flat.
I'd moved to the flat after I'd worked for
Marcus for a bit (a friend of his had rented it to

me, on the cheap). It was tiny, but at least it was my own space, and much better than any of the other places where I'd lived. It was on the ground floor of an old and rather shabby house, nearer Euston than King's Cross. Now when I came in, the place was just as I had left it in a rush, with the remains of supper in the sink and the stink of Steve still on the sheets.

Quickly I turned on the light - the flat was always dark, with sombre paint colours that didn't help - and then I went through the kitchen cupboards, finding nothing but half a pack of stale biscuits to eat. As I ate, I texted Donna to tell her I was back safe, while I listened to the familiar noises of the flat, the dripping of the kitchen tap, the hiss of the water pipes, the constant scampering of unseen mice. I could almost hear the spiders spinning cobwebs, high up inside the kitchen window sash. Then those noises faded and there was nothing save for a slow seething inside my head, and I lay down on the sofa, and I slept.

I dreamed I was holding my baby again. She was gurgling as she reached to pull my hair and smiling at me, and I was smiling back, kissing her head, and smelling that sweet milky baby-smell that she had. Except now I was smelling booze, doctors, stale, rotting breath, and from the baby's swaddling there peered my mother's wrinkled face, and she was calling my name, her voice bringing smiling terror to my head.

I dropped the bundle, screaming, but now it was only the baby's face I could see shining like a moon amongst the dark cloth. And the baby was crying now; red-faced, screaming, little fists working free of the swaddling and reaching out to me. But before I could pick her up, my mother came and snatched her away.

- Give her back! I cried, but my mother ran out of the house, banging the door behind her, and all I could hear was the bang, bang of the door.

I woke in terror, clutching my hands to my clammy neck.

Bang! Bang! Bang! The noise of the door was real and didn't stop. Still shaking, I stumbled towards it.

- Who is it?
- Katy! Open up!

I let in Donna, who gathered me in her large, capable arms, and led me back inside.

- You gave me a fright, I told her.
- Why? she said, her large blue eyes glittering with shadow, shining through the gloom of the flat. Who did you think it was? And why are you sitting here in the dark? It's only nine o'clock!

She was holding a bottle of wine, and a bag of chips, which she waved in my face; as she did, silver bracelets shivered and chased each other up her wrists.

- These will sort you out, she said. Then you can tell me all about the trip.

She'd got even bigger since I'd seen her last; now her belly was pressing tight against the material of her dress. Sometimes I'd see that, and I'd feel pain so pure it was almost like pleasure. But I couldn't hate her too much for having a kid - she had a heart of gold, Donna did. Unlike me, she'd never had any trouble with drugs, she didn't have an addictive nature, she said - it was one of her three sisters who'd got herself into a mess, which is why she knew about that rehab place where I went. She acted kind of crazy, but she didn't put up with any shit. I wondered what made her so sane - I'd asked once, and she'd told me her older sister looked out for her (I envied her that because I was an only kid). She treated me like one of her younger sisters. When I was low she picked me up, when I was high she brought me down to earth, when my head came undone she screwed it back on tight. She knew some of the details of my life, more than any other person did - and though it hurt to trust, I trusted her, I really did.

Now she turned on the single overhead light, humming a tune I thought I recognised, while she unscrewed the bottle of booze that she'd brought.

- Jeez, you look sicker than I feel, Kay-tee, she said, sitting down and pouring the wine out. She stroked her belly with one hand. And I'm feeling sick as a dog, she said.

- How's Pete? I asked her.

- Pissing me right off!

- You haven't even had the baby yet.

- How was your trip? Did that bring you luck? she said, touching the necklace she'd given me - and then she looked more closely at the bruise on my cheek. Fuck, Katy, was that Mike?

She shook her head, and as she did so her long earrings trembled in the light.

- Didn't I tell you? she said. To leave well enough alone.

- And leave him with my kid?

- Does he even have her?

- You think I'm making her up? That I gave birth to some phantom kid? I shifted on my seat, made as if to get up, but Donna held out her hand and held me back.

- I never thought that. She paused, testing my mood. What's her name, anyhow? she asked me. You never said.

I swallowed. It hurt to say it, like a stone wedged in my throat.

- Cara, I told her.

- And what about Steve?

- What about him? I've no need for him

anymore, I said.

And then the last few days all came and crammed my head and I put my hands to my face, and I wept.

- Come on, Donna said, and put her warm arms around me, and even though she was not much older than me, there she was, pulling me towards her, like the mother I never had.

- Come on…didn't I tell you it was a crazy plan? You want her back; you go through the official channels. That's what I said. You know, Katy, you've got to get some proper help. I wish you'd let me help you. Look how I helped before, getting you to that rehab place. But you're still not right, and it's not your fault, but it doesn't have to be that way. People can change if they get the right help, and if they want to, she said.

She took my hand.

- Didn't I make that appointment with the GP a thousand times? And each time you said you'd go - and each time you lied?

I shook my head, suddenly feeling smothered, glad when at last Donna let go.

- The doctors, they could help. Marcus, he might even understand. Let you take the time off work. Miracles do happen, she said.

I shook my head.

- I don't need doctors, I said. I've found someone who can help.

- And who's that? Another shitty bloke, who'll just fuck you up, you and your life? Jesus, Katy, you make me crave a fag, and God knows, with the baby, I'm trying to give up!

She went and stood by the kitchen window, the light from the streetlamp sending her into big-bellied silhouette.

- Who is he then? And how is he going to help?
- I haven't figured that one out.

I told her a little about Jamie, how we met and how it was between us. I hesitated, and then I told her about his wife.

- Tch, Katy, be careful. The married ones, they mess with your head. He might turn out to be more dangerous than Mike.
- Donna, that makes no sense at all, I said.

As the night sky darkened outside the windows our chat became less focused with the drink (though I drank most of it) and in the end Donna's boyfriend came and picked her up because I was worried about her going back alone, even though she lived only a few streets away from my home.

After she left, I went to sleep pretty quick. One time I woke, it must have been the middle of the night, and as I sat up, I thought I heard knocking at the door again and then a scratching at the window, and the sound of footsteps moving away. I imagined Mike outside, one hand clutching his bleeding neck, while the other wielded my bloodied knife.

Thankfully I went back to sleep again, and this time when I woke I saw the dust motes dancing in the morning sunshine slanting through the shutters, and there came to me another plan, a plan so beautiful I couldn't believe it was only me had made it up.

JAMIE

That night I was holding Katy again in my arms. We were outside and it was dark and freezing, but her kisses sent fire through me. With each kiss, the urge to rip up my life's straight seams welled up inside me like tears. I felt as if I were being dragged through the stars towards the edge of a black hole. I kept on kissing her, until the black hole began to swallow me whole and I could no longer think.

Suddenly she turned and began walking away from me. I ran after her and pulled her to me. But when I turned her around, I was staring at my younger sister's flawless face, as it once was, before the accident and the drugs ravaged it.

"Sarah!" I went to put my arms around her, but she melted into them, disappearing altogether. "Sarah!" I called again, sitting bolt upright in bed, wiping the sweat from my forehead.

"Jamie?"

I fell back into the yellow circle of my wife's bedside light. "Rachel - I'm sorry."

"No need to apologise." She rearranged her features, smiling sympathetically. "Shouldn't you take some diazepam? You haven't taken it for a while."

"You know I don't like to."

"Or book an appointment - to see that therapist?"

"Dr Bowen? He was useless."

Had he been? I couldn't remember. I only remembered his sad, colourless eyes, the loose skin in folds around his cheeks, his soft, almost pleading voice, as he tried and failed to deal with the fallout over Sarah.

But who could have helped with that? Certainly not Rachel, who could barely cope with despair or desperation, least of all my own. I'd wondered often, as I did now, what had made her that way. Her background was solid, her childhood uneventful and happy, if rather structured, all of her leisure time accounted for with extracurricular activity from an early age. She and her mother were similar. Both of them had unusually phlegmatic genes and a singular lack of imagination.

Which was in no sense their fault. *I* was the one who was rather foolish, always running after the moon, the stars; never satisfied until I could hold them in my hands.

I turned to my wife now, put out a conciliatory hand.

"I'll be okay. It'll pass."

But nothing I did excised the memory of Katy's kisses. I tried. I worked harder, drank harder, even made love to Rachel with a tenderness that had eluded me for years (hoping that she was too wrapped up in work and our joint social life, full of childless couples like ourselves, to notice or to care that I was elsewhere). And when, on my way home, I passed pubs, lit and swarming, the people who stood outside, smoking and laughing, full of hilarity and freedom - they broke my heart. In quiet moments, when I thought I was safe, the memories crept in and crushed me entirely.

I was well practised at hiding feelings from my wife. But the turmoil in my head was so great that after a few weeks of this, even Rachel was driven to turn on me one day and say:

"Jamie, what in hell's name is the *matter* with you?"

Guilt. Desire. Guilt. Desire came in waves; fleeting, intangible as moonshine, and easily quelled, for it was as fragile as butterfly wings, but the guilt that followed was heavy as a tombstone, a tonne weight. And that crushed me completely. Alcohol was my only anaesthetic, and I drank a great deal of it, much to my wife's despair.

One night I called Peter from my cab home. I'd had a few drinks - so many, in fact, that calling my brother, in a conciliatory vein, seemed a sensible thing to do.

"All ok, Jamie?" Peter asked in a steely voice.

"Rachel's *furious* with me," I told him. "She knows, Peter. She just *knows*."

"How can she? Have you told her?"

"No."

"And nor will you. Pull yourself together."

"You make me feel like a child."

"You're behaving like one."

"Do you remember that hollow tree, Peter?" I blurted out suddenly.

"What tree? What are you on about?"

"In the grounds of Felbrigg? I used to run and hide in it. It had very shiny sides..."

"Well, you can't go hide now. Just *enjoy* the moment, revel in an unbridled fuck, then put this girl out of your mind. Didn't I give you the key to my flat? *Use* it, for Christ's sake."

I looked out of the cab, as the clubs and restaurants of Shoreditch bloomed into sight, then faded.

"You don't get it."

"No, I don't. Go home, drink two pints of water, go to sleep. Get up and resume your duties as husband. And possible father."

"I'm not going into battle, Peter."

"Ah, Jamie - there, you're mistaken - that is precisely what you are going to do. Give her a kid, she'll be happy as Larry. What do you have to do that's so very hard? Wank into a test tube?"

I lay back against the smooth leather seat of the cab, eyes closed. The taxi rocked slightly. "I never told you something about Sarah..."

Peter's voice was suddenly tight, wary.

"What's that?"

"That last night she came to see me-"

"You sent her packing with some cash. You told me."

"I didn't tell you something else. She...she was pregnant."

A stunned silence. "What the *fuck*?"

I closed my eyes. Thoughts of my younger sister blossomed in my brain: a headstrong five-year-old, working our garden swing too hard and too fast, while I, pasty and pock-marked, stood beneath it, pleading with her to stop. Aged seven, running out into the sea, out of her depth, and being rescued, screaming outrage, by our terrified father. A louche teen, recklessly promiscuous, raucous, bawdy, lolling on a sofa in a fog of cigarette smoke, eyes ringed with kohl, hair in the dark, hard bob she favoured, listening to *Vision Thing* and *LA Woman* and *The Dark Side of the Moon,* and wearing those high-heeled croc-skin boots she lived in. She had loved those boots...

"How pregnant?"

"I don't know. She wasn't....she wasn't showing."

"Why didn't you tell me this before?"

"I...I don't know."

"*For fuck's sake*, Jamie."

"She said she was going to have a termination." I struggled to get the words out.

"But what if she didn't? What if she lied about that, as well as everything else?"

He was right, I thought. What if there was a child around, a little kid, motherless, who needed help from us and wasn't getting it?

"I should have tried harder," I admitted now. "I should have looked after her harder. Made her stay at mine."

"Is that why?" Peter asked suddenly.

"Why what?"

"Why don't you want a kid? Because you failed Sarah's before you'd even got going?"

"Peter..."

It was too late. I heard the phone click and he was gone.

I sat back once again in the cab.

Peter was right.

I had failed Sarah.

And it was too late to make amends now.

Now I remembered that last time I'd seen her, how Rachel and I had heard a frantic knocking on the door late one night and had opened it to find Sarah standing on the doorstep of our new flat in Canonbury, looking dishevelled and broken. I could see the consternation in Rachel's face at the sight of her dirty face and broken fingernails. We'd just bought the flat, Rachel and I, we'd only been in there for five minutes, hadn't had a single guest over. The place was immaculate. I could tell Rachel didn't want

Sarah anywhere near it.

"Come in," I'd told her, but she'd shrunk back, shivering.

"Why are you in London?" Rachel had asked her.

She'd flared up at that, as she'd done on many occasions since the accident. Her mood swings were wayward and occasionally took a violent turn. She was paranoid too. Now she hissed "For fuck's sake. What kind of greeting's that?"

I'd turned to Rachel.

"I can handle this," I'd whispered.

"If you're sure," she'd told me doubtfully, retreating into the flat.

"That's right! Talk about me as if I don't exist," Sarah had shouted after her.

I took in her androgynous black clothes, the heavy make-up, the multiple piercings. She was wearing winkle-picker boots, and a Rivett's biker jacket. A line of silver studs climbed each ear, and there was a pin in her lips - I saw how swollen and bruised and bloody the mouth around it was. She barely seemed to recognise me; her eyes were lost and pleading, the pupils erratic, unfocused. Her skin was haggard and pale as a cadaver's, stretched tight over her cheekbones.

It was that face that haunted me in my dreams.

"How did you get that?" I'd asked her, pointing to a

dark bruise on one cheek.

"Walked into a door. It was shut, obviously."

"Stop lying, Sarah."

"As if you care."

"Of course I care!"

"Could have fooled me. You and your stuck-up wife, in your fancy flat."

"What do you want?"

"What do you think?"

"How much? And what for?"

I knew I could only ask before I gave her the cash. She'd disappear, the moment she got hold of it.

She'd grinned at me, a trace of her old charm still clinging to her like an elusive scent. "Rent."

"Peter tells me you're using."

She'd thrown her head back and laughed, as though the suggestion was hilarious.

"Actually…" She was suddenly serious and gave me a sideways look.

And that's when she told me.

"Are you sure?" I'd asked, shocked.

"Am I sure I'm pregnant or am I sure I'm going to get an abortion? You going to tell me what's what about my own body now?"

I'd backed away then. I'd actually said those words that had come back to haunt me in the countless nights since her disappearance.

"Fine. I don't give a shit what you do with the money. Just keep me out of it, OK?"

Then I'd left her there and gone in, to fetch the cash. I'd had a fair bit in my wallet as it happened, and I'd given it all to her.

"And here - take this." I'd handed her a wool coat of Rachel's, one she seldom wore. Sarah had wrapped it about her, still shivering.

"Come in, Sarah, please," I'd begged, as she'd backed away into the street, not even bothering to count the wad of notes.

"Doubt your wife will be very happy about that. I'm off to see a friend."

"What does he do, this friend? Is he the dad? Does he deal?"

"What would you care?"

"Where does he live?"

"Newcastle."

"Would I like him?"

"Yeah, I think so. What's with the third degree, anyhow? You're always on my case, hassling me. You don't give a shit really."

"Sarah, *please…*"

But she wouldn't tell me anything else. And then she'd disappeared into the darkness, as I'd always known she would.

Except, this time, she disappeared for good.

Her Satanist mate proved a red herring. He was prosecuted for ABH against another girl - not Sarah -

but they couldn't pin Sarah on him, or on any of his freaky friends.

Her body had never been found. Which wasn't surprising.

The surprising thing was that any body in any murder investigation was ever found.

Can you grieve properly for someone when you don't know for sure what's happened to her? Loss was different from grief, I thought suddenly.

Loss was infinite.

I shut my eyes. The cab's rocking motion was making me feel ill.

Suddenly my phone rang again, startling me into the present.

"I don't want any more lectures, Peter. Not in the mood for it."

"Jamie?"

"*Katy?*"

I could hear her breathing, ragged and heavy, down the phone. "I'm in trouble," she said at last.

"What sort of trouble? Where are you?"

"I'm..." There was a pause. "I'm at the station." Another pause. "Canonbury."

"What the hell are you doing there?"

"Will you come? *Please?* I'll tell you everything when you get here."

I didn't hesitate. "Give me five minutes," I said.

I leaned forward to redirect the cab. Alcohol made my brain foggy and slow, as if I were lost in some interminable maze.

As the cab arrived at the station, I checked the time. It was 11.40 pm. The station was still open, the ticket barriers unmanned. I walked straight in and down the steps to the platform.

It was empty. I moved swiftly along it, calling Katy's name. Where was she? *And what the fuck was I doing?*

There - there - a figure right at the other end, sitting on a bench. As I drew closer, I recognised her, and I felt drunk; gloriously, happily drunk, bursts of joy coursing through my veins like jolts of electricity.

"Katy!" I called out.

I stopped short when I saw the face she turned towards me - just visible on the dimly lit platform - pale and tear-sodden, a dark spreading bruise beneath the right eye.

"How did you get that?" I asked softly, reaching out involuntarily.

She flinched. "Never mind."

"Why are you here?"

"You have to help me."

Behind us, I could hear the distant rumble of an approaching train. A cold wind blew along the platform, a few bits of dirty paper flapped in the breeze. There was another couple, waiting some way away from us. The station lights shone eerily on the tracks.

I looked again at Katy, and pity shot through me, like the clean cut of a knife. I knelt next to her, so my face was level with hers. "Tell me what's wrong," I said.

She breathed out, hard, her breath making mist in the freezing air. "He's after me," she whispered.

"Who?"

"Somebody I used to know." She looked around the platform. "He could be here."

Unable to help myself, I looked round too.

"There isn't anyone here."

"He's following me, I tell you!"

"*Who* is?"

I could hear wheels on the tracks, see the steady beam of a train's headlights coming towards us.

The train seemed to scream as Katy made a sudden run for the edge of the platform. I lunged, and in a single motion caught and held her as the train hurtled towards and then past us. Relief flooded through me, as I felt the wild rhythm of her heart, and then I was kissing her, and she was drawing me back into the quiet dark space at the back of the platform where we both stood, reeling with the shock of what had happened.

I held her close. "Nothing's worth that. You hear

me?" I pressed my arms around her. "Do you think I wanted to find you, only to lose you again?"

"So you wanted to find me?"

"Of course," I breathed. As the adrenaline ebbed, I pulled her closer. I was startlingly aroused, my erection almost painful. I started kissing her, slower this time, holding her tighter than I'd done in my dream, in case she dissolved in my arms.

"Don't do that again," I whispered.

Kissing her induced a kind of feeding frenzy: once I'd started, it was almost impossible to stop. Finally, with an effort, I drew away, and she straightened her hair and smoothed down her skirt. I came up close to her again, feeling her warmth.

"Can we go somewhere else?" she whispered.

With no thought at all, I nodded. "Peter's place."

KATY

There wasn't much to the place once we'd collapsed into it: a living room with a galley kitchen along one side, a shower room, a bedroom with nothing in it but a big white bed. A pale moon shone through the sash windows onto the sheets.

Jamie made to kiss me again, but I played for time, had him make me up a drink instead. I listened to the sound of the ice hitting glass, the fridge door opening and closing, the hum of City traffic. Finally, he sank down beside me on the sofa, handed me my drink.

After the drama on that platform, I savoured the taste of the gin in my mouth. Finally, I put down my glass and pressed my fingers to my temples, where voices, like a rattle of static, were just starting up. My arms were shaking but Jamie stroked them gently, and eventually the voices calmed, and the shaking stopped.

- You've magic fingers, I said.

- Who is the man you were talking about? Your ex?

I nodded.

- He's coming after me. And he'll find me and hurt me again, I told him. It's only a matter of time.

- He can't. Not when you're with me, he said.

I thought he'd try and kiss me again after that, but he didn't - he watched me carefully while I finished my drink.

- Promise you'll never do anything as stupid as long as you live, he said.

I flashed him my best smile.

- You may not be around to stop me, I said.

I sat back against the sofa.

- I remember when I…I told him I was pregnant, he…he balled his fingers into a fist… and I was so scared, I ran, right out of his place. There was a busy road just outside and I…I didn't look where I was going… I just carried on running, I said.

I was shaking again. He pulled me to him, put his arms around me and rested my head against his shoulder, stroking my hair with one hand.

- Like I once told you. A death wish, he said.

- There was a truck. But I missed it by an inch…

I shivered, lit a cigarette. I offered him one, but he shook his head.

- So he was violent?

- Yes.

- You never told anyone, tried to get help?

- My mother, I think she knew, but she left me to it, I said.

- And the baby?

I didn't answer, only looked away from him.

- You said you lost her. How?

I shook my head.

- We had a fight after she went. And then I left.

- But how did she go missing? Didn't you try and find her? Ask the police to help?

His questions were making my head ache.

- What about your sister? I asked instead. Did you try to find her?

- I don't want to talk about her.

- How did she get lost?

- I don't want to talk about her, I said!

He put his hands over his face. He was quiet for a few minutes and then he took his hands away.

- I was drunk. I crashed the car. She...she was in the passenger seat. After the accident, she changed. When she needed me, I didn't help. And then she...she disappeared, he said.

I moved into him.

- The guilt - I can make it better. The pain - I can make it go away, I said.

It wasn't how I intended it. I hadn't wanted to tell him so much. I'd wanted him drunk and myself detached, as if I were watching me in this, some sort of film of my life. But somehow I'd given information up. And that was dangerous - the thought of that made me upset, until I let go, let my fingers play over his chest and down his back while I helped him to undress.

- Come with me, I said, and I led him to the bed.

As he moved inside me, I whispered

- Jamie, can I ask you something?

- Shall I stop? he said.

- No, no, I told him.

- What is it then?

He tried to pull away, but I held him to me.

- This isn't about sex, I murmured.

He kissed me, whispered in my ear

- What is it then?

I felt my body soften and sweeten, felt it curve towards him, like a question mark.

- You know I know a whole lot about you, Jamie. I know about your wife, where you work, where you live.

I felt him stiffen.

- Sandra. I'll kill her, he muttered.

- I won't do anything with that, I promise. Only…

And I asked the question now that I'd been wanting to for a while, waiting for the right moment, scared to open my mouth.

- Will you help me, Jamie? Help me get my baby back?

And I knew that he would say yes, that he would whisper it so soft I'd barely hear it, but that we both would know what he'd said. And a whisper can be murmur or a roar, of course, or a promise, a promise made that will be kept. And I knew that Jamie was the type to keep his promises, and that with him I could at last face what I had left.

JAMIE

I woke with a start next to a sleeping Katy. It was after three.

I could feel her breath against my cheek, the weight of her arm flung over one of my legs. For once she was quite still. I laid one hand upon her sleeping head, trailed my fingers gently down her hair to the side of her neck. There was a faint pulse beating beneath her ear where her skin was most delicate; almost translucent. I pressed that pulse very gently. It seemed to slow under my fingers.

Then I remembered my promise, and what she had said to extract it. I took my hand away. My phone sounded where I'd left it, in the pocket of my trousers. I got up, checked it, and ordered a cab.

As I was fumbling with my belt, I heard Katy stir again. I looked up to see her gazing at me in the semi-darkness.

"I have to get back," I told her.

"I thought you were going to help me. You promised…"

"You know I keep my promises, Katy."

"No - I don't. I don't trust you."

I don't trust you either, I thought. "I'll call you," I said. "Try to sleep now, and then let yourself out. I'll come back later and lock up."

"But you promised…"

I bent down and kissed her mouth.

"I've got to talk to Rachel. Then I'll call you."

"When?"

"As soon as I can."

Katy leaned back against the rumpled pillow. "What happens now?"

"Wait, just for a bit." I said.

I didn't kiss her again. I waited in the living room, listening to her toss and turn in the bed, and before too long I heard the rumble of the approaching cab.

The cab sped along Upper Street towards Highbury. Above the Fields I caught a glimpse of a fading purple sky, studded with silver points of light, stars like the tiny heads of pins. A few minutes later I'd paid my fare, and was walking, somewhat unsteadily, up my front steps.

The house was in darkness. I put my key in the lock and opened the door.

I didn't switch on the living room lights. I drank two glasses of water in quick succession, and then sat down. I'd go upstairs shortly, I reasoned, I just needed a drink first. I got up and poured myself a cognac, a large one. Desire for a cigarette made my knees go weak. As I drank, I thought about Rachel and me. Early memories of our first days together, still as fairly junior assistants, came flooding back: the first time Rachel had permitted me to visit her very white, very cold flat in Maida Vale, where we'd made love, and neither of us could get warm afterwards; or the very first flat we'd bought together, on Barnsbury Street: we'd sat on the floor shortly after moving in and eaten take-out pizzas from boxes. It was hard to believe the Rachel I knew now had operated that far outside of her comfort zone; I hadn't seen her sit anywhere but a bed or a chair for eight years, but back then we were still in our honeymoon period.

Now I remembered our actual honeymoon, at some very smart adults-only hotel in the Maldives - Rachel complaining about the mosquitoes non-stop, and the heat and the wine, which she said upset her stomach. The smell of the sun cream she'd used constantly on that trip hit me now. My stomach shifted queasily in response.

I went on sitting there, in a zone suspended in time and space, and my mind moved further back again; before Katy, before Rachel, until all I could see was Sarah, this time as a small child, scrambling up a tall tree in our garden, never looking back, knowing I was beneath her, arms out, trusting me one hundred percent...

Just at that moment, I heard a soft tread on the stairs. I turned, still holding my glass.

My wife was wearing a pale, almost translucent silk dressing gown. She looked like a ghost.

"Where the hell have you been?" she said. "It's a quarter to four in the morning."

"You've been back this late before."

"When I've been *working*, Jamie. Don't say you've been in the office."

I hesitated. "No, I haven't."

"Drinking?"

"Yes."

"Who with?"

"Ian."

That was true - if not the whole truth. I'd started the evening in Ye Old Cheshire Cheese with Ian in Fleet Street, as I told my wife now, and Rachel softened a little, on hearing it. She held out her hand and I took it. I hesitated, opened up my mouth to speak. I felt as if I were about to jump off a high board - that moment when you tip forward a little too much, and you know then that you're committed to the dive, even if the impact knocks your breath out, even if it kills you, in fact.

"I…have to go away for a few days, Rachel."

"I don't understand."

"I have to go to Scotland."

"What? *Why?*" She frowned, rubbed her forehead. "You just got back."

"It…it's Peter."

"*Again?* What's wrong this time? Just leave him alone, Jamie. He'll never…"

"He…he's got himself in trouble…"

"What sort of trouble? Don't tell me one of his girlfriends has blabbed. I told you. It was only a matter of time…"

She flicked the switch next to her and suddenly our faces were flooded with the overhead light. I winced when she saw my face.

"Oh fuck off, Jamie. It's not Peter, is it?"

I shook my head.

"What then? Or - *who*?"

She stood there, waiting for the answer, but I couldn't give it. Suddenly, she sank back, hand to her stomach, as if she'd been shot.

"You always were a hopeless liar, Jamie," she gasped.

"I…I have to…"

"*Who?*"

I jumped off that board. "A person, a girl, I promised I'd help."

I was pushed backwards with full force as Rachel came at me, raking me with her nails. I staggered, dropping the glass I was holding; it didn't break, only spilt its potent contents onto our plush carpet. The reek of fine cognac filled the air.

"You bastard!" she hissed. "What about the treatment? You promised me. You promised!"

I put one hand to my face. My fingers came away wet and red. "Is that all you care about, Rachel? All you want from me? A *baby*?"

"Don't make this about me when you're the one fucking someone else. You *promised*," she repeated, more softly this time. I could see the thin fabric of her gown stir with the swift rhythm of her heart. Her eyes shone.

There was a lump in my throat that was painful and throbbing. I felt as if soon it might explode and spread its noxious matter all over me.

"No. No, Rachel, I didn't."

Rachel turned away from me, suddenly quiet, almost calm. "Who is this person?"

"No one you know."

"How did you meet?"

I was silent.

"Where does she live? Scotland? What does she do?"

When I was still silent, she hissed "*Answer me, dammit.*" She came towards me, pushing into my chest with her fists. "How *dare* you, Jamie." She hesitated. "Does Peter know about her?"

I hesitated. "Yes."

Her fists were rammed up into my chest now and I was backed against the wall. "Rachel…"

"I didn't know you had the balls. Well, *fuck you,* Jamie. "

She turned and walked upstairs.

I followed her, taking the stairs three at a time.

She was already putting my clothes on the bed, placing them carefully in neat little piles to be packed. Her movements were pregnant with repressed fury, but on the surface at least, after that uncharacteristic rush of temper, she had gone back to being the Rachel we both knew and understood. She was eerily calm.

I reached out to her, but she moved away. "Don't touch me," she said. "Don't you dare touch me!" Suddenly she stopped packing and sank down on the bed. "I want the old Jamie back," she whispered.

"Come on, Rachel. I'm right here," I said to her. I sat down beside her.

"No, he isn't. He hasn't been since Sarah went. Before she went missing you were *present*. Every decision we took was a joint one. You were happy to participate. Now I feel I'm dragging you along on everything we do. I don't recognise this Jamie."

I blinked back tears. "It changes you, to lose someone, especially like that."

"But it's been so long, I'd hoped you'd have shed the guilt by now, started to get over it..."

"You don't get over something like that."

"Maybe not, but you've carried it for *years*. I've told you so many times - it wasn't your fault, Jamie."

My chest was hurting too much to answer her.

"You don't understand. You never..."

I didn't finish my sentence.

"What? My life hasn't been *tragic* enough - is that it? My childhood was too normal, almost boring, my parents too well-adjusted? Well, you're wrong - I understand you very well."

I stood up and moved away from her, taking up the packing where she had left off.

"You have to let go of her, Jamie. You're fucked up

enough as it is, and now you're wanting to fuck us up too."

"I have to let go. Willingly. Tell me how, Rachel."

I kept on piling clothes hastily into a suitcase, sweaty palms marking material with patches of wet. The thought of what I was about to lose made my head spin. Conflict raged inside me, my brain a seesaw of love and loss, my heart torn, bleeding as if it had been sent through a mangle.

But I knew I had to act. Staying still was impossible, like trying to withstand a mighty fall of water. I set my jaw determinedly as I worked my way through my bathroom cabinet, leaving spaces in the rows of pots and potions there.

"You're leaving now?" Rachel asked, as I came back into the room.

"I'll be away for a few days…"

"What do I care anyway? I don't want you here again."

I swallowed with difficulty, taking a last look around the room - the smart blinds Rachel had fussed over, the Descamps bed linen she was so fond of, the inbuilt cupboards she had designed with painstaking care.

There was nothing of myself in that room, nothing I was leaving behind.

"And I simply cannot understand why you and your brother are so obsessed with Scotland," my wife went on. "The food's foul, the houses are hideous, and the rain never fucking stops. And don't you think you can just call and come back as though you never left!"

"We'll talk about the treatment, I promise," I said tiredly.

"Oh, you can be sure we will, Jamie. I'll hold you to that."

Hot darkness swirled abruptly through my head, and I sat down again on the bed. We both fell silent, and the air was heavy with it.

After a while, I heard her ask "Are you all right, Jamie?" She looked genuinely concerned, which didn't surprise me. Rachel could never quite let go of her rational, civilised side. It was I who was letting go of that, probably forever.

I blinked hurriedly.

"You don't have to worry about me, not anymore."

"Don't go, Jamie."

"I have to."

I stood up wearily and made my way to the door, dragging my suitcase and carrying a further bag, which felt extraordinarily heavy, as though it contained every worry, every fear I'd ever had.

I turned back at the bedroom door. "I won't take the car," I said. "In case you need it."

She wasn't listening. She was sitting on the bed, her hand in the hollow where I'd sat. She seemed smaller than she'd done a while ago, almost child-like.

We could have had a child together, I thought, as

I moved down the stairs. We could have had a *child*. Someone to call me dad, to think the world of me, who wouldn't think I was some useless piece of shit, as Rachel did, as I myself did sometimes.

I thought of pouring everything I had into a child, trying to make that little person big and brave and strong, everything I wanted to be but wasn't, and my heart seized up, so loaded with pain, I could barely put one step in front of another.

And yet I did, somehow. I had no idea what I was walking towards; I only knew I was no longer running in circles, like some pathetic creature chasing its tail. I was moving forwards, with purpose, putting an end to the bitter constant of my marriage, stopping up the pot of misery that filled with each row Rachel and I had and emptied with each reconciliation, each hollow vow we made to work at it.

And so I made my way up Upper Street towards the Angel, my suitcase trailing behind me in the gathering dawn.

KATY

At first I was confident he'd come back - I'd
only have to wait a couple hours, I thought, and
then he'd come find me at Peter's flat. So I lay
awake, letting the minutes pass, and when at last
a blue dawn broke over the City and still he didn't
turn up, I started to regret what I'd told him, save
what I'd said to make him promise, save for that.
My brain was a blur, messy and confused, and
then my mind emptied out, and eventually I left
his brother's flat and made my way back to my
place.

When I stepped in I thought there was a strange
smell about the place, a trace of male sweat, or
maybe I imagined it, but I felt my own sweat
start up as I pictured Mike hiding in the shower
or beneath the bed. I moved into my bedroom,
looked around, fighting the temptation to call
out. The smell was still there. I knelt down and
checked under the bed.

As I came back up I heard a footstep behind me,
felt a hand cover my mouth. I froze, tried to turn,
heard a voice whisper

- It's only me, Katy.

I whipped back round, shaking. There was
Steve, looking the same as he always did, same

squashed up features and shiny head.

- How did you get in? I never gave you a key.

- No, because you never trusted me.

- Who let you in?

- Your neighbour. She recognised me, he said.

Play it gentle, play it nice, I told myself. No point in winding him up.

- What do you want, Steve? I asked him.

- I just was passing, he said.

- You don't live so near.

- I wanted to see your face. How was Scotland?

- I never got there, I said.

- You didn't find her?

- No. No thanks to you, I said.

I couldn't help it, and that was a mistake. He came up to me, holding the tops of my arms.

- Nor will you, he said.

- I will, I told him. If I try hard enough.

- No, because I heard you talking to yerself in the dead of night. And I heard what you said.

- And what was that?

- That baby's gone where no one can find it, even the most dedicated, he said. I should know; listening to the kind of things you came out with at nights. I could never sleep with you lying next to me, going on about shit.

I flushed.

- I'm going back to Scotland, I told him. And I'm getting help this time.

- Who is it who's helping you now? No doubt you're fucking him.
- Steve, *leave*. Please, leave, I said.

He hesitated, still holding me, a little bit too hard, and then to my relief, he backed away from me, started moving towards the door of the flat.

- I'm not sorry I kicked you out that car, he told me. You're lucky I haven't gone to the police with everything you said.
- So why didn't you? I said.

He came towards me and cupped my face in his hands, speaking in a softer tone.

- I loved you, in spite of it.
- You didn't know me, I told him.
- Doesn't make a difference, does it? he said.

I looked him over, almost feeling sorry for him, with his puggish eyes, his cheap aftershave and his creased and dirty shirt, sweat stains marking its sides.

- Where you staying now? At your brother's in Dagenham?
- As if you give a shit!

He backed away again.

- You know I feel sorry for 'im, whoever he is.

Then he was gone, slamming the door behind.

I showered quickly, washing his smell off, and afterwards I checked the place where I kept my extra cash and it was all there, all intact. I stuffed it into my purse and then lay down on the bed, all curled up, Steve's voice still ringing in my head.

Donna called just as I was making up my face to go to work.

- Steve's been in my flat, I said.

I looked around nervously. The walls of my small room seemed to have moved closer to me, as if they were listening. I shivered.

- What did he want? I hope you told him to get lost.

- I'm going away again, I told her.

- Katy - please.

- I'm going back to Scotland. This new man - Jamie - he'll help.

I told her we'd met up, but not how it had come about.

Donna sighed.

- I can't stop you, she said. Just promise you'll call if you get into trouble - any at all.

- I promise, I said.

She must have known my life was littered with promises I couldn't ever keep.

My phone sounded again just as I was leaving my flat. I could tell it was Jamie before I'd even picked up.

- I've left my house, he told me.

My heart took a leap.

- Why so quiet? Isn't that what you wanted?

- Yes, I said.

- Can I stay with you tonight?

I thought quickly.

- Not tonight, I said.

- Why? Don't you want me to see your flat?

I had come to a stop on the street.

- I want us to go to Scotland instead.

- What? This afternoon?

- Yes.

- Can't it wait?

- Jamie, she could be…she could be anywhere, I said.

He sensed the panic in my voice.

- OK, OK. I'll sort work out. Where…where will we stay?

- I know a place, I told him.

- And how will we get up? I…left the car with my wife.

- We can take the sleeper train. It'll be romantic, I said.

- We need to talk first.

- We can talk all the way up.

He sighed.

- OK. I'll see you at the ticket office, at Euston. I'll check the time, but I think the train leaves at five, so I'll see you just before, he said.

I was lucky: Marcus was in an expansive mood. He'd pitched for an account and won it and now he was like a man in love, though it was love that turned in on him rather than shining out. He asked me how much time I needed and didn't blink when I said a week, but he did ask me what I needed it for and I smiled and looked down, muttering something about a crisis and a bloke. I thought I might throw him off the scent: he was cynical, but he still had time for everyone else's love. And now he smiled, a great big greedy smile, with a shine to match the top of his head.

- I'm jealous, Katy, he said. Is it True Love? It'd have to be, to justify a whole week off. Then he gave me a peculiar look. I hope he's not married. I imagine you like 'em all complicated, he said.

Just before four, I rushed back to my flat and threw together what I needed for the trip. Soon I was standing amongst the roar of traffic, the seething mass of human life that characterised the Euston Road at that hour.

I imagined Euston station would look a little like King's Cross - high vaulting roof springing to the sky, iron beams scaling it like the rungs of ladders. But its neighbour was more like an underground bunker, with long lines of people and empty concrete walls.

Jamie came up to me at the ticket office and caught my hand, pressing his fingers and my ticket into my palm.

- It's good to see you, he said.

Trains were coming and going along the platforms, some fast, with a rush of sparks, and Jamie held onto my hand very tight as they passed.

We found our train and our carriage, and I sat down on one of the narrow beds and watched him store the cases overhead. Then he reached up and pulled the blind and I noticed the blur of graffiti and the rubbish littering the tracks as we began to leave London behind.

He sat close by me on the bed.

- Now, we've time at last. Tell me everything, he said.

I thought hard, winding a strand of hair around one of my fingers, round and round until I felt the tip of my finger tingle with the blood leaving it. Then I opened my mouth to speak.

Suddenly Jamie's phone rang, shattering the quiet. Reluctantly, he pulled it out to check it.

- Peter, he said.

- You didn't tell him, where you were going?

He shook his head.

- I know he was going to visit the flat today. Suddenly he flushed. Oh shit. I forgot to go back to lock up. And when he sees the state of it…

I knew he was thinking of that bed.

- He was calling to bitch.

- What will you tell him?

- That depends on what you tell me first.

He stood up and crossed the cramped space we were in, to look out of the window. There was now a blur of green on the other side.

- Tell me about your ex…he began.

- Mike, I whispered.

He turned to face me.

- Were you married to him?

- Yes.

- But you left? After your daughter went missing.

- Yes.

I hung my head as tears pricked my eyes. I thought about my baby, her smile like a flower unfurling, her tiny fingers clutching mine as if I alone could stop her drowning, and I remembered that pull we had one to the other, as if a rope of steel were hauling us together. I felt my heart expand again - and then yet again it broke, leaving only a pile of empty rags.

- I failed my baby, I said at last, wiping my eyes with my sleeve. I failed to make her safe.

He stood in front of me, then knelt down so that his eyes met mine.

- From whom?

- From everyone, I said.

- And you think Mike knows where your daughter is? That he took her?

- I'm sure of it.

- But he's dangerous?

- You can manage it.

I laid my hand on his, drew him to me.

- Can we stop talking for a bit?

He sat next to me, put his arm about me, pulled me close.

- Do you want something to eat?

I shook my head. I was too wired to eat.

- Do you have any friends in Scotland who might help?

I thought of Caitlin. I'd asked after her before I'd left Kolcan, at the scruffy inn and the caff opposite it. They remembered her at the caff - she was quite tricky to forget - but they said they hadn't seen her around in a while. I'd searched Google, but I couldn't find her. Perhaps Caitlin knew something, but I couldn't believe a word she said. So I didn't mention her to Jamie. What was the point?

Jamie was still holding me; his arms warm against mine. I leaned into him, closed my eyes.

- How do you know Mike took your daughter, Katy?

- Maybe my mother did it. She's a bitch. She did all sorts of crazy stuff.

- Like what?

- I don't want to go into it. Not now, I said.

- But...

- I don't want to go into it, I said!

- Will we talk to her?

- She won't bite.

- Where was the baby taken?

- I don't know. That's what we have to find out.

- I mean at the time - was she taken from outside your place, or inside it?

- I...I left her in her pram, outside the shop, while I went in for some cigarettes. I left her for two minutes, only two, and when I came back...

- Why didn't you call the police?

- Mike didn't want any fuss at first. He said he'd find her. He *promised*, and then we had a fight, like I said. And after that I ran off.

- Why didn't you call the police after you left?

- You don't understand. I was scared. I thought he'd kill me if I did.

- But your baby...

- I was a mess. All I could think of was to get away from all of them. I know; I know it doesn't make much sense.

- You weren't well.

I nodded.

- How not well? What was the matter, Katy?

I moved away from him and lay down on the narrow bed. I was so tired. His questions were like worms burrowing holes through the darkness in my head.

- I need to sleep, I told him.

I closed my eyes, but I could not rest.

Finally he lay down against me. I could feel his heart beat against my back. He turned me to him and very gently moved one hand over my forehead and the back of my head.

- I didn't mean to make you upset, he said.

I pulled him to me and kissed him, and as I kissed him, as our hot and tangled bodies met, I could feel my fear contract, and desire course through me instead. And it ran through me like a river, washing out the fear, and then I felt it pull me under and I relaxed into it and around it, until at last sweet oblivion came and claimed me in that tiny space.

JAMIE

I listened to her heart pounding in time to the rhythm of the train, until eventually I felt its beat subside.

"All right?" I whispered.

"I feel so safe, here, with you."

I circled her with my arms. "You're inside a circle of fire," I murmured.

"I might even go to sleep."

I tightened my hold on her. "You do that," I said.

Katy sighed, her breath hot against my neck, her luminous eyes resting on my face. "You know, Cara was a lovely baby. Her breath was sweet and soft and...and there was a curl on her forehead, just one, so fair, and...oh, she was just gorgeous," she said. "I almost died having her, though."

"You did? What happened?"

I felt her shiver against me. "I kept bleeding, just wouldn't stop. I was delirious with drugs and pain. I was calling and calling for her, but they'd taken her away - I had no idea where. I thought she was gone for good." She raised herself up to look at me. "I'll never forget how that felt. And then when I felt it a second time, that same pain, I took different drugs, and they helped, until they wore off and the pain came back..."

I didn't ask her what drugs she'd taken. Hadn't I felt

the same pain when Sarah went missing, the same disbelief and panic? I'd just dealt with it in a different way.

"But that first time at the hospital, when they brought her back…" She pressed her hands to her chest. "I was so happy - I felt it *here*, that finally everything in my life made sense. Everything that was wrong, I could put right. I felt so blessed. But then I left the nurses, and it was so hard. No one helped."

"With the baby, you mean?"

"Yes. They just told me I wasn't coping."

"Who told you that?"

"My mother…Mike… Even Caitlin, she said I was a mess."

"How not coping?"

She shook her head. "I still see them, you know. Even though I left. I see them *all the time…*"

"Where? When?"

"In the dead of night, their faces and voices…It's like they never left."

She fell away from me into the darkness.

"And now she's gone."

I tightened with confusion and frustration, before softening as she pressed her cheek against mine. *It will all become clear*, I thought. *I can help this girl. I just need to put one foot in front of the other. It'll be as simple as breathing.*

My forearm was starting to ache where Katy was lying on it. The whole room rocked with the motion of the train, as if we were in a giant cradle. My phone

rang again - once, no, twice - but I made no move
to answer it; I just carried on holding her, until
eventually I, too, fell asleep.

I woke to the alien wail of gulls. For so long it
seemed my whole world had become that tiny train
compartment, brimming over at times with the
sweetness between us. When at last I stumbled out
of the carriage into a grey dawn over Inverness, the
shock of the bitter cold was like immersing my head
in freezing water. In that sober moment, I turned to
my companion.

Katy had lit a cigarette. I watched the muscles
move in her neck as she smoked, the subtle, almost
brutal, flick of her wrist as she removed the ash. The
shadows under her eyes were cold and grey; her eyes
glimmered in the first light.

"This Mike," I asked her "What does he look like?"

"Why do you want to know?"

"A physical description might help if I'm going
to find him," I said, trying to keep my voice, level,
business like.

"Well, he's good looking for a start…" As she went
on, I wanted to slam my fist in his face. Instead, I
forced myself to stay calm, unflustered, as I pulled
out my phone.

"Where does he live?"

"Look at you - so dishevelled and unslept!" She
grinned. "I can't put you in front of Mike until we've
had something to eat."

She watched me work my phone.

"What you doing?"

"I'm calling a cab, to take us to a place where we can hire a car."

"Aren't you hungry?"

"We can eat when we get there," I said.

A couple of hours later, after a full Scottish breakfast and a fair few cups of coffee, we were drawing into Katy's hometown in our hired car. It was a soulless, desperate kind of a place, locked in by menacing mountains, by land that seemed to want to swallow it up. But Katy barely seemed to register her surroundings, showing me instead where I could park the car and then leading me through empty streets and air that smelled of burning peat in the direction of the only place that seemed reasonably smart, an inn, recently refurbished, by the look of it.

We were shown to a fairly large room, where Katy unpacked; or rather she strewed her things in a chaotic mess all over the place and I followed her with my eyes as she made the room her own.

Then she had a bath, leaving the bathroom door wide open. I watched her wash herself, curiously organised, her neck first, then her arms, then her stomach and legs, picking up my phone as I did so.

Peter was at his most surly.

"Where in fuck's name have you been?"

"Peter, I'm sorry about the flat. I can explain."

"You're a careless pig, Jamie. Lucky for you the

place wasn't burgled. And where the fuck are you now?"

"Did you speak to Rachel?"

"I did. She's upset, Jamie."

"I know."

"She told me you'd buggered off to Scotland again. *Why?*"

Katy had exited the bath, shivering, and was standing dripping, staring at me. I stood up, fetched a large towel, and wrapped it around her.

"Can I call you back later?"

"Are you alone, Jamie?"

"Peter…"

"Answer the question."

Before I could stop her, Katy had taken the phone from me. "He's with me," she said, in her most glowing voice, and then she cut the call.

When Peter called back, she held my arms to my sides.

"Ignore him," she whispered. She started to kiss my face, moving down to my chest. I shifted as I felt my cock stiffen, still conscious of my brother's incessant calling. "We don't need anyone interfering with us," she murmured. "You can deal with Mike yourself. You can. *We* can, Jamie."

Like a fool, I believed her.

KATY

It happened when I was least expecting it, just as Jamie and I were leaving the inn to get something to eat. My right arm was grabbed, Jamie grabbed my left and I felt a tugging, a tearing on both sides, as if I were being ripped apart. *Fuck, it's Mike!* I thought, and cool relief flooded through me when at last I was released into Jamie's arms.

I barely recognised the man in front of me. He had a cut down one bloodied cheek that needed stitching, his nose was bruised, broken-looking; there was another cut on the side of his head, where his red hair was all matted and unkempt.

- Mac, I whispered.

- Aye, so 'tis! he yelled. Look at me! You see? You see what you did?

- I didn't do it.

- You led him to me, like I was a piece of fuckin' bait! See what he did?

He lifted up his shirt, and I saw his skin covered in cuts and bruises and I turned from him and buried my face in Jamie's chest. As I turned I caught sight of his face - it was grey, the colour of ash. He moved me gently behind him.

- What you staring at? Mac yelled, squaring up

to him, and then, in a sudden rush, he punched Jamie in the stomach, and slammed one fat fist into his face, so that his head jerked, and he staggered back. I tried to grab onto Jamie then, to hold him back, but I could feel him straining away from me, towards Mac. There was a small crowd gathering; wary, and nervous. I thought I recognised some of the faces.

Mac pointed at me.

- That hoor, he yelled, his stubby finger stabbing the air, is cursed! You're better off deid than mixed up with her! You go run, you go hide, but no matter how fast you run, how far doon you hide, that devil will find you and he'll smoke you oot! And then, then you'll be sorry you was born, he said.

His words echoed around the square, into the whispers of bystanders. Suddenly he stopped and looked about him, furtively checking the streets with sideways glances, and I could feel the fury ebbing from him.

- I pity you, you puir sod, he said, jabbing that finger into Jamie's chest. You're not worth the fighting.

He took another quick, secretive look about him, spat once in Jamie's direction, a great globule of spit that just missed his feet, and then he was gone.

Jamie led me back up to the room in silence. Once inside, I went straight to the bathroom, locked the door, and threw up.

I stayed there a long while, breathing in the sour smell of vomit. Jamie kept banging on the door, but I wouldn't answer it. When eventually I came out, he was standing dead still in the middle of the room, holding his phone.

- Tell me who that man was.

- A friend of Mike's.

- A *friend*? Is that what that man does to his friends, Katy? The man you married?

A hot tear burned my cheek.

- I was young, I whispered. I thought I was in love. Sex makes us stupid sometimes.

- Doesn't it just?

He came up close now, leaning against me, every part of us touching.

- And this man wasn't dangerous, you said. Not dangerous!

- I never said that. I said you could manage it.

- Like *fuck*.

Then his phone sounded, and he moved away from me. He left the room and I heard him talking on the landing outside. After he'd stopped, he came back in, and he placed both hands upon my arms. I winced.

- I wouldn't ever hurt you, Katy.

- Who were you talking to? I asked him.

- Peter, he said.

- I don't need your brother poking about in my life!

- It's too late.

- He'll tell you stuff about me. He'll tell you I'm crazy.

- You're being paranoid, he said.

- He will! He'll be like the others!

- What others?

- Mike, my mother, all the rest of them. They said I was sick. After I'd had the baby... But at times I felt so good, like a god. I never felt better. I'd take her everywhere; we'd walk for hours in the park. I'd hold her and we'd try the swings or the rides. And there was no one else. I didn't need anyone. But then they said I wasn't fit. They twisted everything, I said.

I held onto him, leaning into him.

- Promise you'll tell your brother not to come. Promise! I said.

He sighed.

- Jamie, promise!

- Ok, he said.

And finally I felt his anger dissipate, like steam from a kettle, and I knew then that I could relax. And after that sex was easy, because anything was easier than having to talk. I didn't even have to think; I only had to let myself feel and my head would quieten with it. But then too quickly time passed, and afterwards, no matter what Jamie said or did, the voices and all the reasons I had to feel afraid came back.

JAMIE

"I've changed my mind," I told Peter. "Don't come after all. I can sort this mess out on my own."

"So you admit that you're in a mess?"

"No - damn, yes."

"Don't tell me - she's lured you in, the Siren, and only now do you realise there's something not quite right about Miss Fuck-Me-Eyes you've shacked up with."

"Fuck off."

"I'm heading in your direction right this minute."

"Don't - I promised you wouldn't."

"I'm already driving," he said.

Now I was waiting for him outside the café in Kolcan's main square, as he'd told me to do in a recent text, and he was late, as usual. Above me the sky was a lustrous shade of blue. In a couple hours, the streetlights would wreath everything at eye level in a fiery neon glare.

I was still wired after the morning's attack. I stubbed out the cigarette I'd been smoking and went inside the café to await my brother's arrival, and the inevitable barrage of questioning that would accompany it.

I didn't have to wait long. Peter's arrival at the café

was like that of a storm. He came in, stamping his boots and calling at once for hot, fresh, tea.

One look at my bruised face was enough for him. "Jamie...what the *fuck*? Where is she?"

Of course, I thought. He wasn't here to help me out. Curiosity would take him far, even as far as this dump.

"We're staying at the inn," I said. "The smart one."

"*Smart*? In this hole?"

"It's all relative, I suppose."

"What the hell happened to your face?"

"I got punched by some shady character from her past."

"Jesus, Jamie, you absolute idiot! You priceless A-grade moron!"

"If you've just come to call me names, you can get lost, Peter."

My brother gulped tea and swore again. "What's the fucking point?"

He sighed, signalled the waitress and paid her, with one of his most charming smiles. Then he stood up suddenly, the cramped, softly lit room seeming too small for his height and bulk. "Let's get out of here. I need to stretch my legs after that drive. Then we can get a proper drink."

We left the café and crossed the main square.

"Rachel called again," he told me, striding through the streets towards the canal, its ferrous reek assaulting our nostrils long before we saw it sliding through the early evening light. "She thought you might be staying with me. She's got something to tell you, she said."

"What is it?"

"How would I know? She's hardly going to confide in me now, is she?"

"What did you tell her?"

"Nothing, of course."

"She knows, anyway. I told her."

"What exactly did you tell her?"

"Enough." I stopped walking, and turned to face him, my chest tightening. "I have to move out the rest of my stuff."

"No change of heart then? Why don't you give it a while, see how this all pans out?"

I shook my head. "Shall we walk by the canal?"

I started down decrepit steps that led from the side of a graffitied bridge towards the towpath that bordered it.

"When am I meeting this insane girl?"

"You're not, not yet. You can meet her tomorrow."

"I want to meet her tonight."

"I haven't told her you're here yet."

"What the hell's going on, anyway?"

"Nothing."

"Bollocks."

I sighed. The water of the canal gleamed a rich chocolate brown where the lights by the canal hit it. "I have to find a man called Mike. Katy used to be married to him."

"Why does he have to be found? What's his

surname?"

"I don't know."

"That would be a start, Jamie. Where does he live?"

"Katy knows."

"Why him?"

"He knows where Katy's kid is."

"What kid?"

"The one she lost."

"How can you lose a kid? How *irresponsible*." Abruptly, Peter stopped walking to light a cigarette. He succeeded finally after a fair few attempts, cursing under his breath. "*Why* are you helping her, Jamie? What's wrong with you? And what's wrong with Rachel as a life partner? Calm, practical, sensible…"

I said nothing in response. All I could think about was the constant *pressure* of being married to Rachel, its continual squeeze a slow death.

"Peter, I know things are a bit…messy at the minute-"

"Wild understatement. You've lost the plot. You've been slowly unravelling since that fatal accident, in fact."

"Nobody died, Peter."

"Correction. Somebody did."

I winced. In the murky waters of the canal to my side, I seemed to see a face, circled by raven-coloured hair, its eyes steady and unblinking. I blinked, passed one hand over my own eyes, glad in spite of myself that my brother was walking beside me.

Peter punched my arm, only just not hurting. "You

messed up, Jamie. But how the fuck does *this* make it right?"

I sighed. I couldn't turn my back on Katy now - it was as if some giant fist were rammed into my solar plexus, pushing me towards her, the whole time. It *hurt* too much to go the other way. Peter could never get that.

"I want her," was all I said. "I want to be with her, to make her happy."

"Not possible."

"I want to *try*. And right now, to do that, I need to help her get her kid back."

Peter turned and scanned my face for a moment in the semi-darkness. "You poor, stupid sod," he said at last. "You'll miss Rachel, you know."

The water of the canal was so black by now it could reflect nothing; only suck all life and light into its murky, impenetrable depths. At the next bridge we turned to exit the towpath and started walking towards the centre of town.

By now, Peter had finished his cigarette, while around us the shadows had lengthened and darkened. Suddenly he stopped and smiled at me, one of his glorious, rare, beatific smiles, bathing me in a sudden burst of dying sunshine. "Let's do it then."

Overjoyed, I grasped his arm. "Thank you."

My brother smiled again. "This Mike chancer will be no match for me. Now, let's get back to this inn of yours. I need a proper drink."

KATY

I tossed fitfully in the hotel bed. This time in my
dream, I was carrying only a blanket, and it was
wet with tears, and it was sometimes light and
sometimes so heavy I could barely lift it to my
breast. As I carried it, I felt my chest tighten, felt
it squeeze.

I had reached a corridor, so narrow and dark,
the floor uneven and crooked. As I walked along
it, the walls of the space kept moving slowly
towards me, until I was forced to drop the blanket
and to hold my hands out to stop myself getting
crushed. But instead of solid brick, my fingers
met the soft pliancy of human flesh, and arms and
legs came out from the walls of the space, twisting
like a mass of snakes. I picked up the blanket
and ran, until I thought I could see the end of
the corridor. But there, right at the end, was my
mother's face - full, bloated, a massive leer all over
it, blocking the exit of the place.

I screamed. Panic rode through me. The scene
faded and my mother's face vanished with it,
and there was only Jamie holding me while I
caught my breath. But even with my head pressed
into his chest, I could still hear the voices of
my dream. If I let myself listen to them I might

even hear what they said. I didn't want that, so I carried on pressing into Jamie's chest and eventually the voices subsided, and I slept.

The following morning, as Jamie ushered me out of the room, I asked him where he was so keen to get to so early.

- Breakfast, he said.

As we came up to the caff opposite, a man stepped forward, a man so tall he towered over both of us. Instinctively I took a step back.

- This is Peter, Jamie told me.

- You promised he wouldn't be here. You lied, I said.

- A simple 'hello' would have been more charming, his brother told me, as he offered me a cigarette.

I could feel the burn of his eyes on me as I shook my head.

- I can see now why he left his wife, he said.

I wondered at how different he looked to Jamie, how confident.

- What do you want for breakfast? Jamie asked.

- The full works, Peter told him.

Jamie hesitated.

- Do you think I'm going to kidnap her or something? Go on in and order. And don't forget the black pudding! he called after him.

He continued smoking, looking at me steadily.

- You look like an animal in a trap, he said.

He put a hand out to me.

- I promise I won't bite.

I winced, shook my head.

- So, you're smitten with my brother, are you? Can't think what you see in him. You could have had your pick.

- But what if he's the one I fell for? What if he's the one for me?

- *Really*? So you're a one-man woman? How *interesting*, he said.

His eyes were like lasers, scoring lines in my flesh.

- I've loved him since we first met.

- Love at first sight? How *refreshing*, he said.

I knew then he'd never really trust me, and not in the same way I couldn't trust, it was way more personal than that.

- Where you from?

- From here. Kolcan.

- What, this dump? What about your mum and dad?

- My dad's dead.

- Your mother?

- My mother's an evil bitch.

- Has Jamie met her?

- Not yet, I said.

I closed my eyes, wishing he would stop, that I

could control his desire to know me, to *consume* me, knowing he would manage it before his brother did.

- I need to find Jamie, I told him.

I made to go into the breakfast place, but he put out one arm, held me back.

- Not now you don't, he said. Now you need a cigarette.

So I waited while he handed me a cigarette. And as he held out his lighter I noticed he was clean-shaven and smart, his hair thick and nicely cut.

- What about your ex?

- What about him? I said.

- I hear he's a complete shit. So, why are you throwing Jamie to him? Like you would a lion a piece of meat?

I was silent.

- Tell me exactly where he lives.

- We don't need your help.

He took a step closer to me, so close I could smell the sweetness of expensive cologne mixed with stale cigarettes.

- *Don't fuck about.*

Reluctantly I told him Mike's address. He assessed me as he did so, his eyes full of it.

Then he took hold of my arm again, his fingers holding on just a bit too tight.

- I'm a sucker for sex. Just like the rest of them. But I see it for what it is. And I see that you're a lunatic. You could ruin Jamie with a single step. But if you do, you'll have me to answer to, understand? I've quite a temper, he told me. And I lack his…what is it? His ability to *empathise*, he said.

I felt his shadow move cold over me and I saw his other hand make a fist, and all I could think of was that fist in my face.

- Oh, I'd love to… he breathed at last. His fingers relaxed on my arm, caressing it instead.

He dropped my arm, unfurling his fingers and holding his hand out.

- But for now let's try to be friends. I think that would be best.

When at last we went inside, I was shaking, the skin on my arm tingling where his fingers had had the chance to touch.

JAMIE

On the drive over to Mike's place, Peter grilled me again about Katy.

"What I don't understand is, why no police investigation after the baby went? Sounds like a cover up to me," he grumbled at last.

"I guess we'll find out."

"If she's a baby-boiler as well as a nutcase? I guess we will."

It took all my self-control not to make him stop the car then and get out, but the truth was I needed him. I had to accept that. I remembered vividly playground fights where older tougher boys or simply those with harder stomachs had got the better of me - Peter had pulled them off me with ease. His intellectual capabilities might be flawed, his softer side non-existent, but he was fearless, ferocious. Yes I was mad at him, but I was glad he was with me now.

At Peter's insistence, I stopped to withdraw a wad of notes from the only cash point in that desolate town, before we drove over to the address Katy had given to us.

The house was in darkness. We sat in Peter's car, waiting. The cold was penetrating, even in the car. I thought of Katy's parting words to me as she waited for Peter to start the car, the sun making her hair shine like it was on fire.

"Try to stay safe," she'd whispered, and though she'd spoken quietly, Peter had heard, and he'd quipped "That's something he'll never be as long as you live."

My heart beat faster whenever I heard footsteps. But no one matching Katy's description passed us; and certainly no one walked up the steps of the dark, empty house.

"Fuck him. He's not coming back," I swore.

"Let's go."

"Where?"

"To make some enquiries."

We walked to the end of the street, to the inn we'd seen at one corner. Small freezing snowflakes bit into my cheeks, the cold burning where they landed.

The nearest inn was crowded, filled with red, shining faces, the air smelling sour, of beer and sweat. I saw Peter talking to the barman, passing him a large note for his drinks, without picking up any change. The man kept shaking his head, then took Peter over to one end of the bar. There, they spoke again, their backs to the crowd, until eventually my brother returned, carrying our drinks.

"That was hard work," he said, as he came back, putting a glass down in front of me. "The man was petrified. But also broke, fortunately. Mike's left that house. He's in a travellers' site now, on the eastern edge of town. Police were after him because of that mate of Katy's he beat up, so he had to hide."

The whisky was burning a small hole through the ice inside of me. My thirst remained though - the drink did nothing to slake it. I thought of Katy's friend - the cut to the side of his head, his red hair matted with blood.

"Drink up," Peter told me. Grimly, he pulled his hat down on his head. "Let's go find this bastard."

As we drove east, my tongue felt dry against my mouth, my insides shifted uneasily. Finally Peter turned left from a smaller road down an unmarked black track. Fronds of bracken lurched out at us through the blackness, bleached by the white beams of the headlights. Around these, hundreds of snowflakes whirled.

Once the first caravans came into view, like white birds nesting in the shadows, we parked up. Peter delved into the glove compartment.

"Here, take this," he said to me.

The brush of cold metal on my hands was like an electric shock. I remembered Katy's knife, the flash of its blade like the beam of a torch. I remembered the blood, warm and wet, on my hand...

"We don't need this," I protested.

"Yes, we do."

"Don't you want to carry it?"

"I'll take the cash," he said, as he stuffed the wad of notes in his pocket, then delved into the compartment once more to find a torch.

A rank river smell hit me as we left the car. Soon I could hear the sound of water rushing to our right. Wasn't the river to the west of the square, I thought? I felt disorientated, confused.

We walked side by side through the failing light towards the caravans. The snow was fast covering ground littered with broken glass. A mangy dog passed us, its eyes glinting in the light from a meagre fire. We stopped to give a pale, scrawny child some money, and were directed towards a lone caravan at the far end of the field. As we walked, Peter muttered, "Christ, you owe me one, Jamie: I should be tucked up in bed with a girlfriend right now, not stalking some bloody maniac across a stinking field."

I breathed in a mouthful of snow and dug my hands deeper into my pockets, suppressing a nervous, mad desire to laugh.

We stopped a hundred yards from the caravan, on Peter's suggestion - we'd try and get Mike out of his bolthole, hopefully away from any stash of weapons inside it. It was so quiet; I could hear the rush of snow falling to the frozen ground.

"What a godforsaken place," my brother said, stamping his feet.

I called out Mike's name. Behind the caravan, the wall of trees gave back a faint echo. I called again. Nothing.

"Bugger it. We'll have to go to him."

We came to a stop right outside the caravan. There was nothing to distinguish it from the others. A fire was burning outside it, a discarded pan by its side, holding the remnants of some meal.

Inside the caravan I could now make out the sound of footsteps, and I called out a third time.

At last the door of the caravan opened, and a man stood at the threshold, staring at us. I knew at once that this was Katy's Mike. He was just as I'd imagined him - tall, striking, well-built, his hair thick and dark. The light from the caravan illuminated his bullish neck - bunches of veins protruding from it like ropes - and the large grimy hands at his sides. The thought of those hands touching Katy sickened me.

I stepped forward. "We've come to talk," I said.

Mike came towards us, his dark bulk hovering near his fire, its flickering light making him look bigger. He was so close now, I could feel the menace that emanated from him, and I could smell him - tobacco, and something else, something sweet and sickly, like pollen.

Mike turned to Peter, who stood his ground.

"Who are you?"

"Friends of Katy's," I said.

"She doesn't have any friends."

"We want to talk to you," Peter told him.

"What aboot?"

"Her baby," I said.

Mike took a step towards me, and as he did so I saw

a long thin cut on his neck, fresh bruising around his left eye. I moved back, until I could feel the heat of his fire on my legs.

"Fuck oaf, the pair of you!" Mike hissed. "I want nothing to do with that lying hoor. If I find her, I'll kill her." He pointed at the bloody cut on his neck. "See this? Aye, she did that, and more! You're welcome to her. She's a waste of space, the fuckin' slut, and she knows it."

Instinctively my fingers curled into a fist. I took a step closer to Mike, before I felt Peter's hand grip my upper arm.

Mike laughed. "Aye," he said. "You just try it, mate. You won't ken what's hit you, I promise. Thirty seconds, it'd take, to make a sorry mess of both of you." He spat at us as he stepped back, the globule just missing us, pooling on the ground at our feet. "Now clear oot of my space, go on - get back to that lying cunt you've hooked up with."

Before Peter could stop me, I flung myself at Mike - with a lucky, flailing punch I sent him stumbling, almost falling. He was up in an instant, his face drawn into a snarl. "I thought you only wanted to talk," he said. The menace rolled off him, strong as the smoke from his fire.

Quickly Peter stepped forward. "Forgive my brother. We just want information - and if we get it we'll make it worth your while." Casually, he pulled out that massive wad of notes.

Mike grinned. "Now you're *talking*. Come along in, then."

"We'll stay out here, thanks," I said.

"Suit yourselves."

Mike sat down by the fire on a broken camp chair and pulled out a tobacco pouch. His mood had changed - he was relaxed now, as if he had all the time in the world. He rolled himself a cigarette, lit up and began to smoke slowly, savouring each lungful. Then he looked up at us and smiled again, showing a line of eerily perfect teeth. "What do you want to know?" he asked at last.

"We're looking for the baby," I said, forcing myself to speak calmly. "Katy told me she went missing a while back."

Mike threw out a cloud of blue smoke as he laughed. "*Went missing*? Is that what she told you? Jesus..." He shook his head, his eyes shiny and wet; then he looked up at us. "So, which one of you is fucking her? Aye, one of you is, why else would you bother?" His eyes rested on me. "That lassie's no good, man. She's like the apple in the fuckin' fairy story - looks the business, but one bite and you're deid. She isnae right up here." He tapped his head with one finger and leaned towards us, his face pasty, ghoulish in the firelight. "Gets you by the balls, though, don't she? Fuck, she gives it good..."

He broke off in a violent fit of coughing and Peter

put out his hand to me in warning as we waited for it to pass. In spite of the fire, my feet were slowly starting to freeze. I was edgy and anxious - Mike's words had trampled all over my nerve endings. A part of me believed him, of course, a deep-down distrusting part of me I tried to suppress. "She's fuckin' crazy," Mike went on, throwing his words out to me, as if he knew this. "Aye, just like her ma - though the drink doesnae really do it for her. She didnae tell you aboot her wee brother? Found dead in his cot, poor wee bairn. The people in the know said it was cot death, but most people think in these parts think differently…"

I couldn't help myself. "What do they think?"

"They reckon the da smothered him. *But some say it was the ma,*" he whispered. "She was half-mental even before the da left - and ratarsed half the time, which didnae help. And after the bairn was born, I hear she became a total loon." Mike ground his cigarette butt under one heel. "But we'll never ken exactly what happened."

I could see Peter shifting impatiently as Mike bent again over his tobacco pouch, speaking slowly, reluctantly.

"I knew aboot her brother before she got pregnant, see. So, after she had the bairn, I watched her day and night. She was melted, fuckin' all over the place - tears, tantrums, the works. Her head was fucked already, well and good - no surprise, with a ma and da like she had herself, and the wean fucked with it further. I didnae like to leave her alone with the bairn in case she did something stupid. She was seeing and hearing all sorts of shit. One night she said the bairn was burning up, said she could see the flames. Stripped her down, doused her with water. Almost drowned the wee thing. Another time, I caught her leaning out the house, the bairn in her arms. Claimed she was being followed, they were going to take the baby, she was going to jump oot... Well, after that, whenever I went oot, if I could I'd take the bairn with me. One night, though, I had some urgent business to attend to. I was only gone about ten minutes but that was enough. When I got back, she was stood there, tears streaming, eyes white all round - fuck knows what she'd taken that time. She was on all sorts of shit whenever my back was turned.

"Where is she?" I said to her. "Where's the bairn, you cunt?"

"You wanted rid of her," she told me. "She made too much noise, you said. So I got you some peace and quiet, like you wanted."

"What did you do with her?" I yelled.

But she wouldn't tell me, and I couldnae find the wee thing in the house, so I left again, went oot to look..."

Mike's massive hands were trembling.

"And...?" I whispered.

Mike sighed. "Ach, nothing. I couldn't find the

bairn. After that I gave her hell, but she wouldn't tell me owt - where she'd left her, if she'd left her alive or dead." He rubbed absently at his eyes with one hand. "She could have tossed her in a burn, left her at a bus stop; I wasn't ever going to find her, just like she said."

Peter and I were silent. "Why didn't the police help?" my brother asked at last.

Mike contemplated his tobacco pouch, turning it over and over in his hands. "I didn't tell the polis or anyone, bar her mother," he said. "I couldn't watch Katy go doon. I'd loved her once. You ken what that's like." He looked at me.

"But didn't friends, neighbours realise she had gone?" I said.

"Ach, we kept ourselves apart from anyone. And the bairn, she hadn't even started school. Anyways, the polis wouldnae have found her. Katy was too canny for any of them."

"What about the social services?" Peter butted in.

"Aye, they were aboot at first when the bairn was around, and then she pretended all was fine and they fucked oaf before the bairn went. Fucking useless anyway."

"What happened then?"

Mike looked up warily. The firelight flickered on his face, softening its jagged edges. "She went totally la la, is what happened. Couldn't take the rumours in town. I tried to help her, but in the end she just wore me doon…"

He looked up at my stricken face and laughed. "Looks good enough to eat though, doesn't she?" He stood up and came up close. I stepped back, reeling from the rot in his breath. "And don't she taste good, too? Don't she taste fuckin' fabulous for a murderess? Enjoy it, man, while it lasts…!"

Before Peter could stop me, I lunged at him again then staggered back as he sank his fist into my guts, doubling me over.

Mike turned to my brother. "Give us the cash quick, and leave before I make you sorry," he said.

For a second Peter hesitated, then he put his hand in his pocket. "Fucking bastard," he muttered under his breath.

Mike took a step towards him, into the circle of darkness that edged out from the fire, where its heat had melted the fallen snow. "What did you call me?"

"I called you a fucking bastard," my brother said calmly. He walked towards Mike, his hands in his pockets.

"Peter!" I yelled.

I saw my brother's fist slam into Mike's face, and then the two men were grappling by the fire, their shadows dark against its dying light.

I gasped, still winded, trying to catch my breath. In my pocket, my fingers found Peter's knife. A swirl of snow blinded me, as I staggered to my feet. I heard a cry of pain, then the thud of a body hitting the stony ground.

Stop!" I cried, I took in a painful lungful of the freezing air and moved forward.

Peter was down, Mike standing over him. I saw him land a kick to Peter's head. He was holding something in one hand that flashed in the flickering light.

I cried again and lunged towards him. Just briefly, Mike looked in my direction, and grinned. For a few seconds he paused, his black shape silhouetted against the fire, and then he raised his hand and brought down his knife.

KATY

- I'm in hospital, Jamie told me.
- *Hospital?*
- There's been an accident, he said.

I stood there, holding the phone to my chest.
Now I was eight years old again - my small
fingers shaking as I dialled 999, leaving smudges
of blood on the buttons of the telephone.
- There's been an accident, I told them.
Then the scream of the ambulance through
the streets, and people bending over my mother,
winding bandages around her wrists. One kind
lady sitting by me, asking questions.
- Where's your dad? she asked at last.
- He doesn't live here anymore, I told her.
- You're a brave girl, she said.
- How are they going to stop up all the blood? I
asked her.
- Watch - they're bandaging up her wrists.
- Will she die?
- Not now, she said.
- Was it my fault? What she did?
- What? No! You saved her life.
And now I thought *Why did I bother, for such a
bitch?*

I was shaking now, the voice of that lady still buzzing in my head.

- Who's hurt? I asked Jamie.
- Peter, he said.
- How bad is it?
- He's in a coma.
- I'll come, I told him.
- Don't, he said.

There was only one hospital on the outskirts of Kolcan, easily reached by bus, and now there it was in front of me, a concrete block of a building, like a prison, snow falling all around it.

I'd been there twice before - once with my mother, that time she almost died, and the other time when I had Cara, when I almost did.

I ran up the path towards the hospital, then I crept through to the A&E section, where the corridors were silent, and dimly lit, and familiar, because I remembered walking through them last with Mike, when I heavily pregnant with Cara, and the long night after she was born when the bleeding wouldn't stop, and how foul he was after that.

Jamie had his back to me, but I recognised him by the firm set of his shoulders. I called out to him, and he turned, and I caught my breath, seeing the vicious purple bruise on his face, his left lid all swollen and puffy, the eye itself a tiny slit.

He flinched when I tried to touch.

- That's nothing. Compared to Peter, he said. I was too late.

- What happened?

- He scarpered before I could reach him. But before he did, he got busy with the knife.

- And now?

- Why do you give a fuck?

- Jamie, what now?

- Now the police are looking for him, he said. He scanned my face.

- Where do you suppose he is?

- You could try my mother's place.

- I'll tell them that. Give me the address, he said, and so I did. Then I moved towards him, putting one hand on his arm.

- I'm waiting for Peter's wife to come, he told me, and I've no idea what to say to her when she gets here. He paused. What do you suggest?

- What did Mike tell you? I asked him.

- What do you think?

- He's lying, I swear on my life.

- Why would I believe you? And what does it matter, with Peter like this?

He sank down onto one of the plastic chairs near the coffee machine, putting his hands to his face.

- This is all my fault, he said.

I sat down next to him, took his hand.

- It's mine too, I told him.

He took his hand away.

- Maybe you don't have a death wish. Maybe you wish death on others instead.

- I never…

- You know, Katy, I don't care what you did.

- Whatever he said, he *lied*, I said.

- He told me you left your baby out to die, he said. Or worse still, you…you…

- I did not! My mum…

- What's she got to do with it? For all I know all this could be a stupid game to you, spending your whole life looking for something you'll never find. And dragging others in and ruining their lives.

I covered my face with my hands.

- You have no idea, Jamie. No idea what he was like.

I watched the struggle in his face.

- I don't know you, he said.

- Do you have to know me to love me? I said, and he was silent, and I thought *Yes*.

- Do you want me to stay here with you? Until they tell us Peter is all right?

- I'm not sure they're ever going to tell us that.

Then his phone rang, and he turned his back on me while he picked up.

- That was his wife, he told me afterwards.

He stood up.

- I'm going to go meet her. You go home, Katy, he said.

- I haven't got a home, I told him.

My breath came out in a sob. I saw a few people staring at us then. My hand flew to my throat.

- Jamie…

- Katy, just go. I need to work out a way through all of this.

- But I can help you.

- Haven't you done enough already? Go home, he said.

I backed away from him, towards the exit of the hospital, then through the wall of snow that hit me, not turning, never turning, only moving down one street and the next, until eventually I had to stop to catch my breath, watch it tear through the air in blasts of smoke.

I sat down in a doorway, where the fresh snow hadn't yet collected, and breathed in the silence and the space. The freezing air made my head spin with a single thought:

Now he's not with me, where will I be safe?

And as I thought that, I felt sweat soak my arms and my back and there was no calm, no quiet in my head, only a scream, a constant clamour of voices, and my own voice trying to answer, but in my head, only in my head; because when my mouth was open, no sound came out.

JAMIE

When I woke it was after midnight, but time has no meaning in hospital. I had fallen asleep in a chair by my brother's bedside. I shifted now, sharp cramps flooding my thigh, and stared at Peter, lying waxen and still, his head swathed in bloody bandages.

I understood that the scope of his head injuries remained uncertain. There was possible trauma to the brain, damage to the cerebral cortex. A coma had been induced, to stop the swelling while they investigated. One leg was in plaster, and there were numerous tubes running out of his body. As well as his head wound, he had multiple cuts in his arms and a deep slash in one thigh, a broken bone in his right leg, a broken nose and a couple of cracked ribs.

I continued staring at my brother, unmoving, for once eerily silent. *I'm the murderer,* I thought. *And not Katy or Mike. I might as well have been the one with the knife...*

I remembered another hospital room, a different bed, and my sister lying in front of me, deathly pale, like a corpse. I'd wanted to rip the tubes out of her body, tear the bandages off, shape her by force back to being the Sarah I knew, so that I could pretend the past had never happened. Instead I was forced to wait, as now, silent hysteria mounting inside me, until I couldn't bear it another minute, another second. I could only hope she'd open her eyes at last, that she'd know who it was who had been watching over her all that time.

When she did finally wake, it was like there was a piece of her missing, a key piece of the puzzle that was my sister, that had slipped from her, like steam from a kettle, to evaporate into the air.

I still loved her, regardless. Except that now guilt was mixed in with it, a form of contamination, like spots of oil amongst the water.

My mobile rang, cutting into my thoughts.

It was only Emmeline, to tell me she was on her way up.

A nurse came by to check Peter's pulse, check his fluids.

"When are they going to wake him?" I demanded.

I must have asked that now one hundred times, always with that familiar sense of déjà-vu. Though with Sarah it had been Rachel who'd asked the questions, while I invisibly fell apart.

We never did get much of a response.

"When is his wife coming?" the nurse asked softly.

"Any minute now."

"Perhaps you should get some sleep," she said, not unkindly, her eyes scanning my face.

"I can't," I said.

I heard the click of Emmeline's heels before I saw her walk into the room - saw her flawless features finally collapse.

"Oh!" She scanned the form at the end of the bed. "Basal skull fracture…intracranial hypertension… possible cerebral contusion…" She turned to me, incredulous. "Knife wounds, Jamie? *Knife* wounds?" One hand flew to her mouth. "What happened? *What did you get him into?*"

I hung my head. "A fight," I whispered.

"*Who with*? Peter never loses a fight!"

I thought of the flash of Mike's knife in the firelight.

"He lost this one."

I stood up to let Emmeline sit down. She grasped one of her husband's hands, then let it drop.

"I called your wife," she said. The diamonds in her ears glimmered. "I thought you'd want her to know. She keeps calling our house. She wants you to call her." She turned back to Peter. The light above Peter's bed cast an unhealthy sheen on his skin. "You hot-headed fool," she whispered. "When are you going to wake up?" Her voice rose an octave. "Are you *ever* going to wake up?"

Her unanswered questions bounced around the room.

"He'll be OK," I whispered, resting one hand on her shoulder.

"I think we both know that's a lie." She put her head in her hands. "I need a coffee. Fetch me one, please?"

As I walked through glaring corridors towards the coffee machine, I saw two police officers walking towards me; instinctively, guiltily, I increased my pace. The officers, an older man and a woman, turned into Peter's room, but as I was pouring hot water into plastic cups, I felt a hand tap my shoulder.

"Mr Kinsella?"

"Yes?"

"Can you just answer a few questions? It won't take long."

Stay calm, I thought, as I followed the police into a small room filled with medical paraphernalia. You've done nothing wrong.

Inside me a voice chided derisively: *Who are you trying to kid? You took up with some deranged stranger, fucked your wife over and led your only brother into the jaws of a known psycho. More like you've done nothing right.*

I tried to silence that voice without success as I stood opposite the police, sipping my burning coffee.

It was Mike they were after, of course - a detailed

physical description, the exact location of the site, and his address before that - that kind of thing. But they also wanted to know what Peter and I were doing on the site in the first place, why we were tracking down a character like Mike, and lastly, why Peter had a heavy wad of blood-stained notes in his pocket.

Mike hadn't even had a chance to take the money before he'd scarpered off.

"The notes were by way of a bribe," I said.

The policeman raised one thick eyebrow. "Do tell."

So then I had no choice but to explain we were looking for a baby that we understood had gone missing three years ago, and we had reason to believe that Mike knew where she was. And then, of course, they asked "Whose child was that?"

I could feel the plastic cup I was holding burn the tips of my fingers. "Mike's," I said. "And a girl called Katy's."

"And who's Katy?"

I remained silent.

"Is she your girlfriend?"

I flushed. "Yes. Well…no. Actually, I have a wife. I'm still married."

More eyebrow-raising as I went on, hesitantly, "Katy was once…married to Mike."

"And where is this Katy now?"

I hesitated. "We're staying at The Wanderer's Inn," I said. "In the centre, dead opposite the statue of the man on the horse."

"Can you give us a phone number for her?"

A number of options raced through my mind. I could refuse - no, impossible. I could give a false number - I could fluff one digit. How tempting that one was! But I didn't do it. Reluctantly I gave them Katy's real number. Then I braced myself for more questions - but all they said was, "We'll leave it there for the time being. When we've found Mike, we'll talk to him - we'll talk to your...girlfriend, and then we may ask you to come in for further questioning later on. We'll also talk to your brother when he wakes up. *If* he's able to talk, that is."

They were pretty confident they would find Mike - they already had a few leads from witnesses who had seen the attack, or the end of it. Mike was wanted for several assaults already, they said. They would call me back when they needed me. I was to stick around until they did.

I thanked them and walked back along the corridor. Emmeline was still sitting, motionless, by Peter's bed. Streaks of paler grey marked the sky I could see from the small window of the room; snow was still falling. The scene had the eerie quality of a still life.

The air in the room was warm and stale, pressing on my chest. A sudden craving for the familiarity of London's chequered streets overwhelmed me. I felt a desperate urge to submit to its great grubby bosom and take comfort there.

"I'm going back to the inn to take a shower, catch some sleep," I told Emmeline gently, placing the now tepid coffee in her hand, watching her rings flame in the overhead light. "I'll be back in a bit."

She didn't appear to be listening. She just continued to sit, unmoving, seemingly unmoved, barely acknowledging my parting words, as I backed out of the ward, walking through hospital corridors that seemed to pulsate with the memories of pain they'd once witnessed, and now observed my every move as I walked away and out onto the frozen streets.

KATY

I had no proper plan in mind, only that I had to leave that place. I had to go as far from him, from all of them, as I could. Or soon there would be no way out. I would be trapped.

And so, once again, I packed hurriedly in the half-light, cramming my belongings into my small navy suitcase.

The voices were with me now, as clear as they were the night Cara was born. But this time I was alone with them - there were no nurses in white to tell me it was alright, or to offer me oblivion in the form of little white pills.

- *Run!* the voices kept saying. *Keep running! Or she'll find you.*

- *Who will?* I asked them.

- *She waits for you at the base of the cliff. She'll wait for you forever,* they said.

- *Who?*

- *Karma,* they hissed. *Her head is shaped like a dog's, her eyes red and luminous. Be careful. Run. Run! Or you'll fall towards her fast, too fast… She's waiting for you,* they said.

- *But what about my kid? If I run away, I'll leave her behind. I can't. Not again,* I said.

- *She's gone,* they told me. *You know it,* they

said.
- *Where has she gone?*
- *Where you won't find her*, they said.
- *How do you know that?*
- *We know everything*, they said.

And so I left the inn and started to run as fast
as I could through the snow. And as I ran I heard
the voices whisper
- *Faster, faster! She's in two places at once.
She's chasing you and she's waiting for you. You
can't see her clearly, but we know she's there;
she's always been there, lying in wait...*

I ran until my body was begging me to stop. I
ran until I could sense there was nothing ahead
of me, only a dark void, empty but for stars. And
still I ran, though at times I felt as if I was falling,
falling through darkness impenetrable as ink, and
through space I knew would have a stop...

Finally I came to the main road that fringed my
hometown, that led not to the South, to London,
but to the Northern Highlands, further up. There
I stopped, outside a truckers' caff, watching
gritters lumbering like ponderous beasts through
the snow, and cars moving at a slow crawl along
the white roads to the frozen hills.
I came to the side of the road, right to the edge

where my feet sank into the dirty snow. There, very tentatively, I put my thumb up.

I waited a long while with every car driving past, and then I remembered standing on the Holloway Road after that row with Steve, and seeing Jamie as he drew up outside that light and what I did to make him stop, so I grew bolder, and, tightening my coat about me, I stepped out further, smiling at each new car as it drove along.

It was then that I heard a horn sound behind me, and I turned and saw a truck outside the caff, though I couldn't see who was driving it, as I was blinded by its lights. I held my hand up, shielding my eyes, now catching a glimpse of the dark shape of the driver huddled at the wheel.

- Where you heading? I heard a rough voice shout.

- Up North. As far as you're going, I said.

There was a pause, and then

- Jump in, the voice told me.

I climbed the two steep steps into the cab and settled next to the driver, who I could tell was smiling at me, while I busied myself with my seatbelt.

I sat back, waiting for the questions, and was relieved when the driver merely handed me a packet of cigarettes.

- Have a smoke, was all he said.

It smelled of cigarettes in that cab and of the

sharp reek of stale breath. I closed my eyes. I wished I could fall asleep and wake up in my new place, finally safe. Instead I smoked and looked at my new companion - his shaved head, the untidy beard that hid his craggy face, the blue veins running along his arms and the calloused red fingers that stroked the wheel of the truck. I tried to stifle the fear I felt; that was nothing compared to the fear of what I'd left.

I pointed to a picture of a woman that was hanging by the mirror, with a little kid.

- Is that your boy?
- Aye, he said.
- How old is he?
- Six, he told me.

I swallowed, blinked back tears.

- You got any wee ones? he asked me.
- I did have a daughter, but I…I lost her.
- What happened?
- She…died.
- Ah'm sorry, he said.
- It's good. She…she's safe now. They can't come after her. I kept her safe…

I turned to him.

- They say I…harmed her.
- And did you?

I put my head in my hands.

- No, no. They were going to though. I know they were. If I hadn't done what I did. If I hadn't kept her safe.

I shook my head.

- It doesn't matter. They can't now. Now she's gone. She's really gone, I said.

My ears were ringing, and fog was moving through my brain. *I was a mother once, I thought. And now no longer. And only myself to blame for it.*

- If it's ok, I told him, I'm going to try and sleep. Will you wake me when it's time to get out?

He grinned, showing his jagged teeth.

- Ach, that'll be a wee while yet. I'm headed to Kinlochbervie, he said.

- At the top? With nothing beyond? Only sea?

- Aye. Ah'm on the road to nowhere, he told me.

I didn't hesitate.

- Take me with you, I said.

He smiled, starting the truck up, and it began to sway very gently on the icy road. I clutched my hands in my lap, willing it to go faster. Kinlochbervie would suit me just fine. It was as far North as I could get - there I could hide, where it was most remote and desolate, and there I would shake off Mike and anyone else who came after me, wanting what I couldn't give.

I would go underground, take on a new name, change my hair, my face.

I would stay up there a long time, maybe forever.

I wouldn't ever think of coming back.

I was too scared to sleep. For hours it seemed
I sat there, my hands folded, my eyes staring,
unblinking, straight ahead, while all around me
there was nothingness, only empty space, and the
truck moved onwards through the falling snow;
ever onwards, towards the dark heart of the
night.

JAMIE

I moved away from the hospital as fast as I could. The snow had silenced the world, sucked all life from the street, suffocating it under a pale blanket heavy as a shroud. I had to warn Katy about the police, I thought, as I waded through it. So that she could… what? Escape by falling underneath another train?

I called her number. There was no response. I called again, and again. Nothing.

I had to get through to her. I'd promised I'd keep her safe, hadn't I? I couldn't fail her now. No matter what she had or hadn't done.

I could only hope the police hadn't contacted her already.

Eventually, I reached the inn and hurried inside, stamping my feet.

The place was deserted. I rang the bell at the reception desk furiously. Eventually the landlord emerged from the back room, blinking sleepily.

"Is Katy upstairs?" I demanded. When he didn't respond, I went on "The girl I was with. Long fair hair, grey eyes…"

The man smiled at me, sleepy lechery evident in his grin.

"She left," he said.

"When?"

"About half an hour ago, I'd say."

"Did she tell you where she was going?"

"No. Seemed in a hurry, that's all I know. As if she was being chased by something or other. Ignored me when I called out to her."

Scarcely believing him, swearing under my breath, I took the stairs up to the room, three at a time.

The door was unlocked, the room empty, though a faint trace of Katy's scent seemed to permeate its walls, clinging to the crumpled pillows and tousled sheets.

I sank down on the bed and groaned, picking up my phone again.

The phone rang endlessly, as it had done before, didn't even connect to voicemail.

I stumbled into the bathroom, my bruises livid in the mirror's bright glare. I doused my head in cold water and went back to the room, turning my phone over and over in my hand, willing it to ring. It didn't. I drew back the curtains and looked out.

The square was carpeted in snow, glowing faintly with the blue light of dawn. Over it the skies were vast and empty, while around it the barren white land brooded in silence.

Somewhere out there, Katy was hiding. From Mike, from the police, even from me.

Especially from me.

The sudden ringing of my phone cut through the silence. I pounced on it.

"Hello?" The voice sounded familiar; strained as the taut string of a violin.

"*Rachel?*"

"Yes, Jamie."

I could hear travel noise in the background.

"Where are you?"

"I'm on a train. On my way up to Inverness."

"You - what? *Why?*"

"To see Peter. And you."

"You don't need to do that."

"Oh, but I do. It all sounds terrible. Peter getting beaten up. Badly, Emmeline said. And all the rest of it."

"It's nothing I can't handle."

"I doubt that."

I sighed. "Rachel-"

"Where are you staying?"

I told her. "But it really isn't necessary. With the snow, it'll take ages to get here. And seeing Peter - as he is - will upset you…"

There was a pause. "It's a bit late for this… sensitivity over my feelings, isn't it, Jamie? Besides, I have something to tell you."

"What?"

"Wait till I see you."

I cut the call, lay down on my bed and closed my eyes.

Please, God, let Peter be ok, I prayed. *Please make everything ok. If you do, I won't try and find Katy. I won't care if I never see her again... Just please let him be ok.*

So I lay there, making wild bargains with a god I wasn't sure I believed in, while the hours slid by, unnoticed, uncared for, and my blood beat an unhappy rhythm through my aching and unslept head.

And then I found myself standing on the threshold of the café opposite the inn, waiting for my wife in the early morning light, until at last I heard a voice calling my name and I saw Rachel approaching cautiously, stumbling and shuffling, almost comically, in her heels.

"You shouldn't be wearing those things in this weather," I scolded, stepping forward to give her my arm.

She brightened at my concern, and we stood a few steps apart, acutely aware of each other, until at last, by force of habit, I reached to kiss Rachel's cheek. Her face was closed to me, as if under lock and key.

I studied my wife. Her outfit was understated - cream cotton shirt buttoned up to her neck, smart black trousers without a single crease; only her hair seemed remotely expressive: as full and sleek as ever, flowing over her shoulders in a single, unbroken fall of silk. Seeing it now, that smooth fountain, I remembered it then, how it was when we first met. The memory made me catch my breath. I looked at my wife, as if seeing her for the first time.

"You look well," I told her.

Her eyes, warm and centred, met mine. "Thank you," she said.

I led her into the steaming café nearby, whose honey-coloured walls now dripped with condensation. She signalled to the waitress and ordered scones, with cream and jam, for both of us.

It was curiously comforting to sit, sipping scalding tea, cramming our mouths with strawberry jam, sour and sweet, and listening to the chatter around us; my world that had been wobbling on its axis seemed to straighten as I drank.

Rachel smiled, almost apologetically, through a mouthful of scone. "I gave you the run around over what I ate, didn't I?"

"You did."

She smiled at me. "I've relaxed a little," she told me.

The waitress came to ask us if we needed anything else. I shook my head as my wife stirred her tea, the colour in her cheeks heightened.

"How are you?" I asked, solicitously. "Are you ok? Have you been working?" I saw, with a pang, that there were still dark circles under her eyes.

Rachel's smile was tight. "Yes, I have. Very little puts me off that. How's Peter?"

"They're still doing tests."

"Oh, Jamie…" I caught a distinct whiff of reproach in these words and stiffened. Rachel must have sensed it, because she changed tack. "Have they caught the man who did it?"

"Not yet."

"Who was it?"

"No one you know."

"But someone your girlfriend knows, presumably?"

I was silent, while Rachel wiped her face with a napkin and sipped at her tea, her movements precise and ordered as ever. I wondered if I missed that precision, that order, and then, quite deliberately, I put the thought aside.

"So, how are you, really?" I asked her.

"What's it to you?"

"I *care*."

"Do you?"

"Of course I do."

She looked straight at me "Tell me about her," she said.

"Rachel, please…"

"I'm curious, Jamie," she went on, in a light, easy voice. "What was it about me that made you want to marry me in the first place? You weren't in love with me, that's for sure. I think, perhaps, if it hadn't been for the accident and then Sarah's disappearance you never would have married me at all. But all of that somehow…diminished you…"

I thought back to the harrowing aftermath of the

accident, my life spinning out of control, just like the car carrying my sister. How I'd craved some kind of order that would stop the chaos.

"Were you in love with me?" I asked suddenly.

It was a cheap answer. But I couldn't help myself. Besides, I was curious.

"I've told you before - there were several men I could have married. Kind, eligible, loving men, all of them. I'm not sure what made me choose you." Her eyes turned to me with a flicker of curiosity before returning to her tea. "I'm not really a betting person, so I guess you could say I picked the wrong horse. I was never romantic in that sense. Even as a teenager, the idea that there was only one man out there to make me happy filled me with a kind of horror." She turned to me. "I always thought you felt the same way. But I was wrong about that, too, it seems."

She rested her chin in her hands and looked at me again, weighing me up, my pleasing qualities and my less pleasant ones, as if she were the proud owner of a finely balanced set of invisible scales. And I looked back at her, this woman sitting opposite me, who at least was real, who wasn't a murderess or a drug addict, who had never wielded a knife or wept tears of undiluted grief or taken a drug to help her sleep or even smoked a cigarette, and pain rose from my gut, filling the cavity of my chest, stopping my breath.

"I'm sorry," I said, when at last I could trust myself to speak.

The words fell small and flat into the room, pitifully inadequate.

"So, are you finally able to tell me what she's like?" she asked again. "I imagine she's rather alluring, beautiful in an overwhelming sense, and brilliant in bed, of course. Or perhaps she's none of those things but she brings out the protective instinct in you. Maybe you think you can redeem yourself by looking after her, that you won't cock up so much this time. Maybe…"

"Her name's Katy," I sighed. "She's from these parts…"

Rachel was leaning in so close now I could breathe in the face cream she used, its clean, clear scent so familiar to me. "You don't get it, do you, Jamie? I'm asking you what she's *like*."

I shook my head, shaking memories out of it - the corners of Katy's eyes that turned up when she laughed, how they softened with her crooked smile, the flush that spread from her throat to her chest when she came... There were all these things, and others, that I couldn't begin to tell Rachel.

She continued softly. "Isn't it strange? I thought I knew you, what you were capable of. But I was wrong. And look at you now, such a mess - I'm guessing she's run off then? Why does every woman you truly care about do a disappearing act on you, Jamie?"

Rachel continued to concentrate on her scone,

eating as immaculately as she had sipped from her cup. I swallowed, to make the bile in my throat disappear along with the food I was eating.

She looked over at me. "Only the other day I was remembering that holiday we had in Crete in May that time, over six years ago now. Do you remember? We walked for miles along the coast. The wildflowers were out. And you swam in the sea."

"And you wouldn't go in."

"In May?" She shivered.

"At any time."

"No," she admitted. "Swimming in the sea - not my thing. But we had a nice time, didn't we, Jamie?"

I nodded. It had been a pleasant break from a particularly stressful time at work.

"And do you remember that trip we took to Bordeaux? The wine tasting? The siesta after lunch? We didn't sleep much, did we?"

I remembered it now: the sunshine shifting through the shutters, slow French music playing on the radio next door, and we, loose-limbed, slightly dishevelled after the tasting, making love in languid light of an empty summer afternoon.

I swallowed, meeting her eyes, my chest feeling light, almost hollow.

"You said you had something to tell me," I said.

She paused. "I'm pregnant." She hesitated. "Again."

"How many weeks?"

"Six."

"And…?"

"I saw a heartbeat."

"*You did?*"

"The doctor says the hormone levels are normal."

We looked at each other. There was a strange light shining in her eyes. I had never seen them shine like that before.

"I'm glad," I said.

"That's why I came up here, Jamie. To tell you to come home." The words came out in a rush. "Things will be better, Jamie. We'll pull together with a child. You'll see."

I felt her eyes pulling me, inexorably, towards her.

"*Please*, Jamie." She pressed her fingers into my hand.

A faint longing for her, for the organised civilised life we had once led, rose up in me. And to agree would be to assuage my guilt. How satisfying that would be, as satisfying as a deep tissue massage for an aching joint…

"Rachel-"

"You and I, at our best - we're *OK*," she whispered fiercely. "We've got a lovely house, good friends, and now we'll have a child. A joint enterprise." She laughed - Rachel, laughing! - and then looked me steadily in the eye, a slow spot of colour staining each cheek. "You can't back out now, Jamie. You can't pursue this feeble romantic fantasy any longer. Not when there's going to be something real between us.

You'll have to grow up, painful as that is."

I ran my hand over my eyes. Katy was gone - perhaps forever. God knows what sort of a person she was anyway. What if everything Mike had said was true? And here was Rachel, right in front of me, offering me a vision of the future that, though far from perfect, was at least possible. I just had to reach out and take it, take hold of her, press my lips to hers...

But with Katy I could make the difference that I'd failed to do with Sarah, that I could never do with Rachel. My wife was so complete, so self-contained, I felt powerless to effect any change, to give her more than she already had - with the exception, of course, of a child.

And that I'd done already.

"Rachel - our life together...we weren't happy."

Abruptly, she moved away from me. "*Happy?* You sit there with a list of fuckups as long as your arm and expect happiness presented to you on a plate? *I* can't wave a magic wand and make you happy. You were never that way anyway, and you were worse after Sarah. And are you any happier with this girl? She isn't even *here*, Jamie. She's more messed up than you are."

But I'd loved her, I thought. *I still love her.* Even though she wasn't the person I'd thought she was, the one I'd wanted her to be. I loved her in spite of that.

But now she was gone. My heart squeezed painfully.

If I could forget Katy, Rachel and I could have a chance, start over. I'd tell Rachel I'd think about it. No - I'd tell her I wanted to try.

I opened my mouth to speak.

Just at that moment my phone rang, filling the café with sound. People looked up, startled, irritated.

"Aren't you going to answer it?" my wife demanded.

I shook my head miserably.

"Go on, *answer* it," she said.

But the phone had stopped ringing, to be replaced with silence more deafening than its sound.

Rachel stood up, stony-faced. "Good luck, Jamie," she said.

"Don't go," I said.

"It seems you have business to attend to, apart from the bill, that is."

"Rachel, listen."

But she was already backing away.

I swore softly under my breath. "Look - I'll call you."

"Call her first."

Through the streaming window, I watched her make her way tentatively down the street. I stood up and left some money on the table. I walked out into the frozen air and called after her. She stumbled, but she righted herself, turned and with the briefest of gestures, waved me away. Then she continued walking away from me, steadily this time, her feet negotiating with considerable expertise the thin sheet of treacherous black ice that coated the shining streets.

My phone sounded again. This time I took it out of my pocket and answered straight away.

"Peter's awake," Emmeline said. "And he's asking for you. Come right away."

KATY

Now the wild mountains surrounding Ullapool were looming up ahead. I shivered as I felt An Teallach throw its vast shadow over the truck. It had stopped snowing, but the waters of the loch reflected an unbroken mass of grey cloud, and the air had the sharp pinch that signified more snow to come.

The driver stopped the truck near the choppy waters of the harbour and cut the engine.

- Aye, she's a bonnie sight, Loch Broom, he said to me. Now, oot with you, bonnie lassie. I need something to eat, and I ken you do too.

Mutely I obeyed, cramp sending shooting pains up my left leg as I stumbled from the truck. I waited while my companion went towards another truckers' caff, grateful to be on my own, if only for the length of a cigarette.

I watched as my driver queued up. There was something familiar about him. Perhaps I'd met him once, in the life I'd had before Mike. Or perhaps I'd just imagined him; I imagined all sorts of things. He could have been a spectre from some old and best-forgotten dream. He'd been silent for most of the journey, while I willed him to be harmless, simply doing a kindness to one in distress.

I walked along the harbour, listening to the scream of gulls, pulling Jamie's coat around me against a bitter wind that whipped the water, making white foam run. All around the dark sea and sky rose hills that were darker still, save for gleaming snow at their peaks. The voices in my head had dropped to whispers that welded to my blood.

Finally I stood still, looking out across the water. Should I take the boat to Stornoway, I wondered, or continue North? But I knew people who had moved to Stornoway; it felt too close to home. The Hebridean community was too small - people would talk. People had always talked about me. That was just the way it was.

The mountains seemed to beckon to me. I would follow them, I thought. I would follow the road to Kinlochbervie. Surely no one would chase after me as far as that; not all the way to Cape Wrath.

Suddenly, my phone sounded. I hesitated, then pulled it out to answer it.

- Where the fuck are you?
- Nice to hear from you too, Donna.
- Fuck that. I've been worried sick.
- I'm in Scotland, where I told you I was going.
- Did you find your daughter? With that bloke you spoke about?

- We…I couldn't find her. She's gone, I said.
I forced out the words against a violent gust of
wind that wanted to snatch them away.

- Where exactly are you now?

- Ullapool, I said.

- Where the fuck-? Should I come up?

- In your condition? In this weather? Don't be
daft!

- I…I think it's almost time. I've been having
pains. Need to go back into hospital today.

- Oh Donna… Even in my state I could feel for
her. I touched my own belly in sympathy.

- Don't worry about me. Pete's looking after me.

- Anyways, we found a nice place to stay, Jamie
and me. Let me know how you go, Donna. I'll call
when I'm back.

I couldn't help it - had to lie to get her off my
back.

- Hold on - before I forget. There's somebody
been in touch through Facebook, looking for you.
An old school friend, she says.

- What does she want?

- Wants to talk, she says.

- I'll bet it was Caitlin, I told her.

- Maybe you should talk to her. Maybe she
knows something, Donna said.

- She was a right manipulative piece, back in the
days.

- Ah, come on, Katy. You were close once.

260

- That was before I met Mike. She was so jealous of my kid - she didn't even send a gift.

- I gave her your number.

She spoke hesitantly, scared I was going to tear a strip off her, which I did not.

- You're not cross?

- No. What's the harm? I said.

She went on a bit after that, but I was barely listening, until at last I felt her relax enough to let me go, and I walked back towards the truck and waited there for its driver.

Eventually he returned with tea laced with sugar and a toasted teacake dripping with butter and handed them to me, and I was grateful for the food and the monotony of the motion of the truck on the open road.

We had been going only a while when the light began to fail, smothered by cloud, and after a bit I was conscious only of the snowflakes in the headlights, steadily accumulating on the road ahead.

Our progress slowed to a crawl.

- Ach, my driver muttered, I didnae want to have to stop.

He turned the car radio on, and I caught the faint whiff of plaintive melody over the crackle of static.

- What you taking up? I asked him, by way of conversation.

- Ah'm taking nothing there, he said, But ah'm taking a whole load of fish back. He coughed, a phlegmy rattling cough, and went on, You been as far up as Kinlochbervie?

I shook my head.

- Tis a lonely place, all right. He reached for a flask from the glove compartment and tipped it to his mouth. Aye, you'll see - if we ever get that far up.

He was quiet after that and I could feel my eyes closing, even after the strong tea that I'd drunk, even knowing that it wasn't quite safe to sleep. But I'd been awake for…how long now? I couldn't think - only that to sleep seemed sweetness beyond belief. Still I fought it, peering at the snow outside, but after a while of that the rocking of the truck defeated me, and my eyes closed, and I slept.

This time I dreamt I was being pushed forwards. I could hear feet behind me, could feel cold fingers on my back. I was being forced towards the edge of the cliff, and in front of me I could see a void, mist rising through it. I closed my eyes, expecting to fall, but then I felt something cold being thrust into my hands and a voice said Dig!

I opened my eyes. I was holding a spade. The metal handle froze my fingers. Then again I felt silent hands pushing me forwards and I shut my eyes again.

I felt one foot touch empty space and I screamed and backed away. But when I opened my eyes I was staring not over the edge of a cliff but into a hole, around five feet deep.

A very small child lay in the hole. Her face was heart-shaped, like mine, and she had dark curls, like Mike's. And she had my eyes, golden and luminous, save that they were blank and staring straight ahead.

Dig! the voice commanded. I couldn't recognise the voice at first, which scared me even more. I began to dig.

The earth was dry and frozen at first, and then it was dark and sticky, and the smell and colour of rust. Soon sticky clots of earth were all over the child's body - one covered her fingers, another clung to her hair, yet another stuck to her lips. And, as I stared, a single line of red began to move down her forehead.

I screamed again, trying to scramble back - but those hands pressed me forwards, so that I, too, fell deep into the hole, and then I felt cold earth rain upon my head.

Through the thick clods of falling earth, behind the spade's blade, I could see my mother's face.

Again I screamed - and then I woke.

I felt a hand on my arm, and my first thought
was *Thank God, Jamie's back.* But the skin of the
hand felt too rough, and when I opened my eyes
I was still in the truck, and there was only the
driver there - and he was near to me, too near, his
breath clinging like smog.

- What's wit the screaming? he said.
- Why did you stop the truck? I asked.
- I couldnae drive wit all the noise, he said.
We're close now, but there's so much snow on
the road - I thought maybe we'd stop here a wee
while and rest. Ah'm well shattered, he said.

I looked outside. We were in a lay-by, but I
could barely tell where the road ended, and
the white verges began. There was silence
outside and now in the truck only the sound of
my companion's breathing as he took another
swallow from his flask.

- Here, he said, passing me the flask. Have a
wee nip. It'll warm you up.

I took a sip. The liquor sent a small flame
through my insides.

My driver reached round to the back of the
truck and lifted out a heavy blanket.

- There. That'll keep us from freezing, he said.
He spread the blanket over us.

- If you've bad dreams, I ken just the thing, he

told me. You'll sleep good and proper by the time ah'm done….

I felt his fingers drift up one leg.

Suddenly my phone lit up, pealing through the cab, startling us both. I didn't answer it. Again it rang, and then it stopped.

I moved away from the driver, leaning against the door of the truck.

- I need to leave, I told him.

His eyes flew open in shock.

- You want to get oot? In this? Ach, lassie, I cannae let you do that. You'll freeze to death. Let me take you into Kinlochbervie. I'll not try anything on, I promise.

I shook my head.

- Let me out! I said. I tried the handle of the door, then again, more insistently. I was struggling to breathe now in the cab of the truck.

- OK, lassie, you win. Oot you go, my driver said. His voice was a low rasp, soft and guttural, as he leaned over me and opened the door of the cab.

I tumbled out quickly before he could change his mind.

The sulphurous light of the cab turned the snow in front of me a sickly yellow, as though someone had peed on it. All around me in the lay-by trucks lay like sleeping giants. I started walking past them towards the main road, which I could sense rather than see because dim halo of light from the streetlights over it. As I walked, snowflakes flew against my face.

It was hard to move through the snow; I had on an old pair of boots, but these were soon soaked through. The voices had started running through my brain again, like the rising wind, except they weren't speaking in unison now; they seemed angry, discordant, at war. I couldn't even make out what they were saying. When I'd left the trucks behind, I squatted down to empty my bladder, covered my ears, and stumbled on, until there was only snow around me, and a few silent houses by the roadside, glimmering faintly.

Across from me, on the other side of the road, there was a verge that rose sharply from the edge. Any traffic was moving so slowly that I was able to cross to that side without difficulty. From there, I kept walking up to the top of the verge. The discontented roar of the voices in my head seemed to be urging me further and further on. It was as if I were moving towards the edge of that cliff, as if, only by walking off the edge, could I at last silence them.

The truck had been as claustrophobic as fear itself. And now I was drunk on fresh freezing air. I kept moving until I reached the top of the verge.

But there was no sheer drop below it, only a gentle incline towards the outskirts of

Kinlochbervie. The nearest houses were mostly still in darkness. Far beyond these, I could sense the vast space of the sea.

Shaking, I took out my phone. The battery was running low, its feeble ghost light trembling as I turned it over. There were missed calls from an unknown number, but I didn't return them. Instead, with one of my hands, I steadied the fingers of the other, so that they could press the keys of my phone in a familiar pattern.

There was no response, just the answer machine. I breathed out in relief. Could I please leave a message, the familiar voice said? So I did. Just a few words, but I knew they would be all I needed.

And after that the phone went dead.

JAMIE

Peter was lying still, his eyelids closed, flickering very gently. When I approached him, one eye opened, and then closed again.

"When did they wake him up?" I asked Emmeline.

"Only an hour ago."

My brother's face was pale on even paler pillows. As I looked, both of his eyes opened, to blink in shock at the flare of neon over his head.

"Peter?" My voice brimmed with joy and relief. "It's Jamie!"

I saw my brother's head nod imperceptibly; then his eyes closed again.

I grasped his hand and pressed it. It felt cold and limp in mine. I pressed again and smiled. My brother didn't smile back.

I stepped back from the bed. "What are they saying?" I asked Emmeline.

"That he'll feel a little disorientated at first, but that there's been no serious damage. He's likely to make a full recovery," she told me.

Tears prickled hot behind my eyes. "A full recovery?" I whispered. "*Really?*"

Emmeline nodded, sucking in her lips, so that her mouth became a bloodless crack. "He'll be back to his old self before too long, they say." She paused and then continued in a low voice. "Back to that self I thought I couldn't stand."

"Emmy..." I murmured.

She turned to me. "Oh I know about his little frolics, Jamie. I always have done, from the start - there's been a fair few of them over the years."

Registering the shock on my face, she went on hurriedly: "He has no idea I know. It's that little fiction that keeps our marriage going." She paused. "It's strange, isn't it? How something like this makes you re-evaluate? When I thought I'd lost him, that love I once felt, that I thought I'd lost forever, came at me again. Like a tidal wave." Her blue eyes flicked to Peter and turned back to me. "Perhaps you should reconsider Rachel and your future."

I had never heard Emmeline make such a long or impassioned speech before. I stood up, came over to her, placed one hand on her shoulder. "I'll hang around outside the room for a bit," I said. I found it difficult to force the words out and over the lump wedged in my throat. "Until he feels a little brighter. Call if you need me."

Later, when I came back, Peter was sitting up, propped against the pillows.

"Peter?"

He returned my smile with a grimace. "I know it's you, you dolt."

Behind me, I heard a footstep and turned, to see

Rachel lingering in the shadows by the door. As she stepped forward, Peter inclined his head slightly in greeting.

"You," he murmured, not unkindly. "Tell me he didn't try and involve you in this mess as well?"

"I tried to stop her coming," I protested, hot with shame.

"Not hard enough, it seems. Fuck," he grumbled, "I hurt all over. Every bloody bone aches."

"At least you're awake. And there's nothing wrong with your brain, as far as they can tell."

"It certainly feels as though there is. That bastard broke me into bits, Jamie."

He gestured imperiously to the water by his bed, and I held the glass to his lips. "Emmy's gone in search of decent coffee. Can't speak to the police without it. And they want to speak to me, I'm told. Soon."

He shifted his torso slightly to face my wife. "So, Rachel, Jamie has a nasty habit of putting his siblings in hospital. And it seems nothing can cure him of that, even your sweet self."

Rachel's smile was tight. "No. He will go his own way."

"So I tell him."

"I think I should leave you two to it." She turned to me and lowered her voice. "I'll be heading back to London soon, Jamie. So if you want to talk again first, come and find me."

I nodded, watching her perfect posture, the straight

set of her back, as she left the room.

"What's all that about?" Peter asked me after she'd walked out. "And why the hell is she here? It's not on my account, that's for sure."

"She's pregnant again."

"How pregnant?"

"Six weeks. The hormone levels are where they should be this time, she says…"

"Is it yours?"

"Jesus, Peter!"

"Just checking. You've been a busy boy, Jamie." He tried to laugh and then choked instead. "And I suppose now she wants you back? She wants you, you wayward sinner. She's prepared to take you, warts and all…"

"I see your sense of humour hasn't suffered."

Another fit of coughing overcame him.

"Can I do anything?" I asked, solicitously.

"You've done enough, you idiot," he gasped, between coughs. "Get me some water!"

"I couldn't think why I was here at first," he told me, after he'd drunk. "I was confused - that's not like me, I know. But now I remember most of it, what that bastard said and did. Have they caught him yet?"

"No."

"Nor will they for a while. I'll bet that worm knows every secret hole on these godforsaken moors in which to bury himself." He coughed again. "And where's that girl with the fuck-me eyes you were so taken with? No doubt the police will want to know that too."

"Katy?" I turned my phone over in my hands. "She's disappeared too. I've tried calling her, but-"

"Where's she gone now? Not to be with *him* surely?"

"Jesus, Peter, you can be an insensitive shit."

"Well, if trouble's out there, she'll be sure to find it. Why did she run off anyway?"

I hung my head. "We had a fight," I admitted.

"So? The whole world fights. Where's your romantic enthusiasm gone? You were so full of it." He paused. "You didn't actually believe what that scumbag said about her, did you?"

"You think he was lying?"

"One of them is. Does it matter which?"

"Of course it does," I burst out. "If he's telling the truth, God knows what'll happen. She could end up in jail."

"I don't understand why the police didn't investigate at the time. Social Services were involved, weren't they? Why didn't they follow through then? Was she that good at fobbing them off?" He scanned my face, the ghost of his once magnificent smile playing at the corners of his lips. "You really love her, don't you?

I nodded.

A flicker of curiosity, bordering on concern, crossed my brother's face. "What are you going to say to Rachel?"

I stood up. My legs felt steadier, but a dense fog had settled in my brain that I couldn't shift.

"What would you advise?" I asked him.

"Really?"

"No. I can make my own mind up, thanks."

"Perfect."

"I'm going to go find her," I told him. "I'll come see you again later."

"Good for you." Peter raised one feeble hand, partly in dismissal, partly as if he were raising a toast. As I backed out of the room, I wondered what he wanted for me, if he really wanted me to go out and live an alternative life to his own - an exposed, confused, honest, dangerous life. One of us had to, I supposed.

On my way out, I passed the police in the corridor, on their way to see my brother. Behind them walked Emmeline, her make-up still immaculate, her high heels beating their own sleek, sophisticated tune on the dirty plastic linoleum that lined the hospital floors.

KATY

In the end I hadn't had to wait long, standing
in the slush by the side of the road, sticking my
thumb up. And the journey to Kolcan had seemed
shorter this time, taken in daylight with a young
couple in the car, the man driving as fast as
conditions would allow, the woman charging up
my phone for me, and asking a lot of questions
without caring too much about the answers,
fortunately for me.

I asked them to let me out once we'd reached a
stretch of the canal I recognised. And as I walked
through the frozen streets, it seemed as if there
was a face staring back at me from the ice, the
face of a young child, barely three years old, jet-
black curls all over her head. I followed this child,
followed her smell of shampoo and of soap, that
brought back the baby, the sweet baby I held in
the crook of my arm, who watched me from her
bath with that look of trust so total that to breach
it would have been unthinkable...or so I thought.
And in my head I heard her voice above all
others. *Why you taking so long?* she asked, as my
feet slipped on the black ice; and once I thought
she held her hand out and looked at me, blank but
curious, curious but detached. But most of the

time she was always just ahead of me, and always out of reach.

Then she disappeared for good, her voice faded from my head, and I felt sick with the realisation of what I'd lost, and the sickness soured still further as I drew closer to my mother's house.

The windows were in darkness, but I banged at the door loud enough to wake up the whole street.

It didn't take long for my mother to open up; this time I pushed at the door when she opened it, a push that sent her scuttling back.

As I entered that house its familiar smell hit me - the sour smell of booze and food, and other things not well kept, left to moulder and decay, to turn to dust or rust. I remembered the hall as it once was, stuffed full of muddy wellies, coats and hats, the busy belongings of a family, nothing like the empty corridor I now faced.

My mother backed away from me, retreating to the darkness at the back, and I went after her, into the kitchen. Here things were little changed. I remembered the old clock over the mantelpiece, with the moon's face on it, the brown enamel kettle on the ancient range, the table, covered in the scratches I'd once made, traces of felt tip pen all over it.

I turned the lights right up, then took hold of her, and turned her round, so that at last we looked at each other face-to-face.

I started to shake her, and she was as light as paper that crumples beneath the touch, and when I shook her, her hands trembled like leaves that turn the palest of bellies to the breeze.

- Where is she, mum? Where you hiding her?

But she just started grinning, a grin that showed every crease and line on her face.

I forced her to sit down at the table as I stood watching her, her hands still shaking while she turned the teacup in front of her, twisting and twisting it round, and she still smiling as I sat down.

- What's in the cup, mum?

- Nothing you need know about.

The menace of that smile was making the air around her stink, and I stood again and came towards her, came right up close, and again I smelled the sweet smell of doctors on her breath. With that there came a fog rolling through my head, and as it closed in, I felt my brain collapse.

- Did they find Mike? she asked me.

- How do you know he was missing?

- The police were here, she said.

- What did you tell them?

- What do you think? What I should have told them three years ago, if I'd had any sense. If they'd bothered to come and ask, which they never did.

- And what was that?

- I told them what happened to the baby. I told them you left her in some random place. But my hunch was she was already dead before you did.

I put my hands over my ears and tried to swallow, unshed tears blocking my throat. But through it all I could hear her voice:

- Oh, you were a mess, Katy, no denying it. That kid would have been better off...

- Better off with *who*? I whispered. With *you*? With *Mike*?

And the fog cleared, as if those last words had shone a beam through my brain, exposing every tiny hidden crack.

- It was so clear outside, that last night, I whispered. The moon streaming in, and Cara screaming, screaming, she just wouldn't stop...

I remembered feeling something snap inside of me, reaching out, putting the pillow over her...

- It was only for a few seconds, I whispered. And then he came back.

I remembered his shadow falling across the moon, making the whole room black.

My mother stood and thrust her face into mine. Triumph was writ large upon it - uneasy, uncertain, as if she didn't know yet what to do with it.

- And where did you take her that night? Do you remember that?

- He wouldn't let me leave, I said.

I shook my head.

But then he passed out.

I remembered the tiny room, Mike's body lying across the bed, his snores making the room pulsate.

- She was so heavy, I could barely lift her, I said.

Still the torch moved through my head, filling cracks with light…and I remembered another room, an even smaller one, and a tinier baby, screaming even harder, and I knew that scream, I'd heard it countless times through my dreams. Screaming, screaming, and a voice saying, yes, *my mother's voice* saying, God, will he never stop? Standing unnoticed in the little bedroom, as silent and dumb a witness as the moon - as a pillow, another pillow came out, and no one lifted it up, and at last, at last, the screaming stopped.

I caught my breath. In the room now I heard the silence, and through it all the ticking of the clock.

- Mother, I know. I *know* what you did. And I know why dad left.

It was my turn to move towards her, just as it was hers to shrink back.

- I had to make my daughter safe. From you, and Mike. I thought someone kind…and *sane*… might find her, if I did that.

I swallowed.

- But then afterwards, outside that inn, when he found me…he was going to kill me, I said. So I told him where I'd left her. He almost killed me anyway, I said.

It hurt to squeeze the words out.

- He told me he couldn't find her. But I know he took her, I know he did.

I looked around the room. The familiar objects stared back at me, not giving away a thing.

Where *is* she? I asked, speaking loudly this time, as if I'd finally found my voice.

- She isnae here, my mother said.

- *Yes*, I whispered. *She is.*

And I tore through my mother's house, searching everywhere I could think. In her bedroom the sickly fungal smell hit me again as I went through her things. Once I saw my dad's face swim out from an old photograph, and I heard him singing, laughing, just like he once did. I opened doors that hadn't been opened in years, forced light in and spiders out. I went down to the basement and turned my phone on every crack and crevice in that creepy space. Because hadn't I seen my daughter there, countless times, tied up and filthy, barely dressed, in my dreams, in the very worst of my dreams, when I couldn't sleep at night?

I must have ripped that whole house apart,

unravelled it at the seams, but still I couldn't find a thing.

In the end I sank against the damp and rotting walls down in the basement, my head slumped into my hands, trying to think. I picked up my phone, started to dial a number, and then thought better of it.

As I made my way up the stairs, I heard footsteps coming down.

She came straight at me then, nails out, making to scratch my face, but I grasped both her hands and forced them down. And then we grappled, and she collapsed and fell back, and I fell with her.

Her eyes were cloudy, and her breath was sharp and sour, coming out in gasps. She stood with difficulty, leaning on the handrail, and moved away from me. As I followed her along the hallway, I noticed the hair at the back of her head - it was pale and thin and wispy where once it had cascaded down her back in waves.

When we reached the kitchen, she turned to me.

- Come, she said. I want to show you something.

I held my breath. In my head the fog had taken over again, so thick now no voices could penetrate.

My mother beckoned at me.

- Come, she whispered again.

I looked past her, where the first light filtered

through the window at the back of the kitchen
- and on, to where I could make out the garden.
Most of it was covered in snow; but in one corner
there was a large magnolia tree. I remembered
that tree, swinging on the lowest of its branches
as a child, gathering fistfuls of petals that littered
the ground in the spring. And now the same
branches were weighted down with snow, and
underneath the tree there were no leaves but
a little patch of new, turned soil, where there
should have been snow, where the grass hadn't
quite grown back, and the earth showed, patchy,
dark and fresh.

My mother held up one finger and pointed at
the earth.

I imagined digging, the brown, sticky earth
clinging to my metal spade, digging a hole deep
enough to step into, deep enough to be buried in.

*A grave. Filled with bones, licked clean by years
in the ground.*

A face swam before my eyes, like a disembodied
moon in the darkness, the eyes empty sockets,
spilling over with worms...

I bent over, retching, and then stood and passed
one hand over my eyes. There was no magnolia
tree in this garden. There were no trees, nothing -
just clean, unmarked snow.

- Where's the tree? I asked her. Did you cut it
down? What did you do?

But she didn't answer; she just smiled at me again, saying nothing.

I was hot and feverish; my legs shook, buckled beneath me. I managed to back away from her, one hand clamped over my mouth to stop the scream coming out. And when I reached the hall I turned and ran, throwing open the front door, stumbling down the steps.

As I moved a blinding pain shot through my head, as though a bright knife were slicing clean through it, leaving a bloody trail behind. And I was conscious of a ringing; shrill, persistent; it wouldn't stop. But perhaps that wasn't in my head, perhaps it was my phone I heard ringing, on and on, until at last I answered it.

JAMIE

I left the hospital, shielding my eyes from the sun's glare on the ice, and started walking back to the inn. I shivered as I did so, wrapping my coat about me.

Back inside, I ordered a whisky and sat holding it in my hands. The fumes made my stomach curdle, and yet I finished it quickly, ordered another, drank that, and then put my head in my hands. I felt a pressure on my shoulder and the face of a kindly punter swam into my circle of vision.

"You alright, mate?" he asked solicitously. I nodded, and as I did so, my phone rang. I picked up straight away.

"Rachel."

"How's Peter?"

"Awake. OK, I think."

She breathed out with relief. "I'm leaving later today," she went on.

"Already? Don't. The snow..."

"Tell me to stay, Jamie."

"That's what I am doing," I told her.

I hesitated. I stood up, a little unsteadily, and, thanking the man in the bar, made my way heavily to my room. I started walking upstairs, treading carefully, in case one false step sent me hurtling backwards.

"Rachel-" my throat caught. It hurt to speak. I felt tired, stupid, guilty. "I'm glad you're pregnant - *so* glad. And I want to help with the baby, in whatever way I can."

"But...?"

"But-"

I stopped on the stairs, unable to move forward or back. I want certainty, I thought. I was desperate for it, as for the clarity that came after a long, cool drink. But beyond any rational thought, I knew I had to see Katy again, to be *free* to *see* her again. I couldn't give up on her, I could never give her up, even if she gave up on me. I had to see how her story ended. More than that, I had to help shape it for her. I felt a familiar craving consume me; every nerve end in my body ragged and pulsing, screaming out for her, as if for the most pure, most potent substance in the world.

"Jamie?"

I couldn't speak. I started moving again, reached the door to my room and opened it.

Rachel was talking. "You know, we might not choose whom we fall in love with, but staying married is a choice. Do you honestly think you can pass through life relying on the strength of your latent *connection*? That you can live by the blatant lies of the poets, and put no bloody effort in? That it'll all just be handed to you on a plate?"

The room had been cleaned and aired; a freezing

blast came from an open window. I sat down on the bed. "What will?"

"The Happily Ever After, Jamie."

"No, of course I don't."

"Then if I'm prepared to forgive you this *moment of insanity* and move forward...why don't you want to *try?*"

"I want to want to try," I told her, stumbling over the words.

"Then why don't you?" Rachel snapped back.

"I *can't.*"

"Won't, you mean."

I shook my head. "Trying wouldn't get me there. It wouldn't be *enough*," I said.

"What gives you the right to be so fucking greedy, Jamie? I'm two people now. Isn't that enough?"

"It's not you. It's *us* - what we were together."

"The thing you killed."

"It wasn't worth saving."

"That is a matter of opinion." She paused. "You know what, Jamie?"

I steeled myself. "What?"

"You continually underestimate yourself. You're a good man, but you're a fool. You know why? You confuse sex with love. You do it more than all the females on the planet put together. A whole word of pain is born out of that confusion, and your own is the most pitiable of all."

She cut me off then, but I continued sitting in the cold empty room, staring at my phone for a long time, until at last I moved over to the window. Tiny snowflakes bit into my ears as I leaned out.

My phone was ringing again as I put my head back inside.

"How are you?" I asked Peter.

"Terrible. Though Emmy makes a pretty good nurse. You missed your calling, Jamie."

"Have they found Mike?"

"Not yet."

"Have they found Katy?"

"They didn't say."

"I haven't found her either. I've tried her. No response."

"Then she doesn't want to be found."

"I'll keep trying anyway."

"I know you will. Anyhow, when am I going to see you?"

There was a vulnerability in his tone that was new.

"Soon," I told him.

I sank back on the bed. Though I buried my face in the pillows, all trace of Katy's scent had now vanished. I tried her number again several times but without success. Finally I managed to drift into a fitful, confused sleep.

My dreams sent me around wretched parts of Newcastle, a photograph in one hand, banging on doors, asking questions about my sister, as I'd once done years ago. But when I looked down at the photograph I was holding, it wasn't Sarah's face staring up at me, but another, heart-shaped, beyond beautiful, eerily familiar…

At last I came to an old house, its front garden overrun with heather and bracken, ferns crawling like spiders up its walls and coating the cracks in the render. As I walked up the front stoop, I could smell river water mixed with something sweet and synthetic. I banged at the door, louder and louder. Eventually it opened, and there was Katy, wearing a lurid green dress that shone in the overhead light.

"Why are you wearing that dress?" I asked her.

"It was my mother's," she said.

"I wasn't looking for you," I told her.

"Oh, but I think you were," she said. Her voice was soft and undulating, glowing and trembling. I felt her hands on mine, pulling me into the house.

"I'm trying to find my sister," I said.

"I'll help you find her."

"But I don't trust you," I told her.

"It doesn't matter," she said.

Her heart-shaped face tipped up towards mine, and I took in her luminous grey-gold eyes, the slightly crooked nose. Then I was kissing her, drawing her hair back, breathing her in. My fingers shook as they explored her, lifting her dress, tracing the familiar path upwards from her thighs. I felt her shift her legs further apart, and then she bent my head towards her and stroked my hair. I could feel the pressure of her hands on my scalp, gentle at first and then harder.

Now, I thought, *Now at last she is here, with me. She is mine. Nothing else matters.* Very carefully I entered her, felt her contract around me and contract again. And then I thought no more, my mind, my senses imploded, and I came.

I woke with a start, my heart racing, my mind closing up, as adrenalin flooded my body with nervy heat, fuelled by fear or desire - I wasn't sure which. I couldn't tell the difference between them. The fog of booze and sleep had at least been driven from my head.

The room seemed full of Katy's scent now. I lay there confused, imagining the soft tread of a footfall by the bed. The shadows in the room seemed to listen with me. It was so dark in the room now I couldn't see a thing. "Katy?" my voice wavered.

I sat up, stretching out into the dark room before me, finding only empty space. I fumbled around for the switch by the bed, found it and flooded the room with light.

The room was empty, but it was no longer cold - someone had closed the window. And there was a glass of water by my bed. The glass was full to the brim before I slept, but there it was - half-empty, with the faintest trace of lipstick around its rim.

KATY

- Katy?

The voice was familiar, if a little rough around the edges, more tentative than I remembered it.

I stopped walking and tried to catch my breath, taking in lungfuls of freezing air.

- Caitlin.

- Where are you, Katy?

I looked up, clocked the name of the nearest street.

- Edie Street, near mum's, I said. Why?

- I want to talk.

- What about?

- Mike. Mike was here, she said.

I felt my heart take a leap.

- He'd been in a fight, by the looks of it.

- What did he want? I paused. What do *you* want, Caitlin?

- That's not a nice way to greet a friend now, is it?

- We're not friends, I said.

- I sent a card, after the baby.

- I didn't see it.

- I tried to contact you, before you left.

- Not that I knew of.

- Well, you were pretty out of it.

- Yeah, and I bet you picked up with Mike where I left off.

She was silent for a bit, and I remembered this about her, how she never came straight out with stuff - made you work for it.

- What do you want, Caitlin? I said. My friend Donna told me you wanted to talk to me. What is it?

She dropped her voice.

- I cannae tell you like this. Come see me instead. I'll send you my address.

I hesitated.

- I want to see Jamie first.

- Who's he?

- You don't know him.

- Somebody new?

- Sort of, I said.

- What's he like? Is he hot?

I looked around me, at the street, as if expecting Jamie to appear any second.

- He...he makes me feel safe.

I'd never said it before, but now I did, and it was the truest thing I ever said.

She laughed, a coarse sound, with no happiness in it.

- Well, I wouldn't get him mixed up in this. Not if you want to keep him safe.

- Mixed up in what?

- Give us a chance, and I'll tell you all of it.

- And what about Jamie?

- I told you. Keep him out of it. You and yer posh London friends, Katy. You forget, aboot the old ones who once helped you out.

- I didn't see much help coming, I said.

- Where you staying?

I hesitated, then came out with it.

- I'll pick you up in ten minutes, she said.

The man at the reception was fortunately fast asleep, so he didn't give me any grief. I walked up the stairs, hesitating at the door to the room where we had stayed, listening, but I couldn't hear a thing. In the end I opened the door and crept in.

He was fast asleep. I came up to him, sat by him on the bed. His face looked relaxed and innocent, and I longed more than anything to creep under the covers with him, draw the sheet over my head and hide from all of it: my mum, Mike, Caitlin, and the rest.

I heard a horn sound in the street, and I ran over to the open window, saw the car beneath and one arm waving from it.

I shut the window up and turned again to the bed, picked up the glass of water next to it, and drank a bit.

Then I stood by the bed, hesitating. There was no knowing what Caitlin had planned. After what

had happened to Peter, I just couldn't drag him
into it.

I bent over him, and I whispered

- This time, I'm going to deal with my own shit.

I settled in the car next to Caitlin, careful to
fasten my seat belt. She was a crazy driver,
usually high, though whenever we were stopped I
was always the one that got a hard time about it.

- Where's Jamie?
- I left him, like you said.

She gave me a long hard look.

- You sure he even exists? She laughed. But
why would I doubt it? she added. You always did
collect men like they were sweets.

She started to drive. It had stopped snowing
and a pale moon was washing the streets with
silver.

- Where we going?
- To my place.
- How do I know you're not harbouring Mike?

She looked straight at me.

- You really don't trust me one bit.
- Like I ever did.
- We were friends once.

And the memories from that time, they came
at me now. Talking and laughing constantly we
were, exchanging secrets and hairstyles, even
before drugs and cigarettes.

- I hit rock bottom in London, I told her.
- What changed?
- I did.
- How's your mum?
- The same. And yourself?
- Ah'm not so good, she said.

And she did seem a bit of a mess - hair not as shiny and blonde as it used to be, and shaved round the sides, a fair few new piercings on the ears, the skin swollen and bruised around pins on her lips.

She was driving through a part of town I wasn't familiar with, in an altogether different direction from my mum's or from Mike's.

- You said you wanted to talk, I said.
- Not here, not now, she said.
- Did Mike tell you what happened? To Jamie's brother?
- Yes, he did.
- I thought you said you didn't let him in.
- I didn't. I talked to him through the window. He was in such a mess.

Her voice was suddenly soft.

- You feel sorry for him? I asked her, suddenly furious, my heart bursting in over the sound of the engine, the blood thudding in my ears so I could barely hear what she said.
- Katy, at one time I would have defended everything he did. I'd have done anything for

him, she said.

We had stopped driving, were parked now outside a house, a small scruffy one, jammed next to its neighbours on a quiet stretch of road.

- And now? I asked her.

She looked down, lit a cigarette. Now he's gone too far, she said.

- Were you together?

- Yes.

I was expecting that, and I thought I'd be mad about it, but in fact I didn't give a shit.

- I don't care. We're over, I said.

I looked over at the house. Where are we? I asked.

- This is my place.

- How long you been here?

- Three years. A bit over, she said. She got out of the car. Come inside, she said.

- What about Mike?

- I told you - I told him to fuck off.

- As if that would ever be enough.

As I stepped out of the car, I looked left and right at the shadows on the street.

- You sure he won't come after us?

Caitlin took my arm.

- You'll feel safer once we get inside.

We walked into the place and then she bolted and double-locked the door behind.

- He has no idea you're here, she said. I think

now that we're safe.

She turned to me, a trace of her old smile clinging to her face.

- Do you want a drink?

She took out a dirty glass from a cupboard over the sink, unscrewed a nearly empty bottle of wine on the side and emptied its contents into it.

- Drink, she said.

She took the glass and tipped it towards me. I shook my head, and she took a sip instead, lit a cigarette.

- Don't you care? That I was with Mike after you left?

I flinched.

- You were always competing with me, for as long as I can remember, Caitlin. Well, you win. Take him. If the police don't lock him up first. I couldn't give a shit, not now, I said.

My palms were sweating, and I jumped nervously at any sound I heard outside.

Caitlin gestured to a broken chair in the kitchen.

- Sit, she said.

- You know I've been looking for my kid?

- I know that, she said.

She took a last drag of her cigarette, then got a plate and tipped the ash into it.

- There's no need though, she said.

- What do you mean? My voice was rising. I'll tell the polis now who hid her. Even if he kicks the shit out of me again. Even if he kills me, I said. All of you, covering up for him. Whatever I did, it was worse what he did. He hid her, and my mum... I shivered, thinking of my mum. I know about my baby brother, I said.

- Aye, that. Everyone knows that and all, she said.

I hid my face in my hands.

- What the fuck do you mean about Cara? I don't need to look for her. Is she dead too? Is that it?

- You don't need to look because *I* know where she is, Caitlin said.

The walls of the room seemed to move closer, as if to listen to what she said. I was silent, scarcely dared breathe.

Caitlin got up, turned her back to me, went over to the sink and then leant over it, both hands clutching on tight. When she turned to me again, all the colour had drained from her face.

- I know where she is, she whispered.

I stood up, took a step towards her.

- You do? And you never called me to tell me that? You never said?

Caitlin bent her head.

- I took her, she told me. Mike asked me to. I'd have done anything he said. I tried to call you to tell you, she said.

- Like fuck.

- And now - I've been trying to get in touch.

I wanted to kill her. Right in that moment, if I'd only had my knife, I would have plunged it right into her.

She was still talking.

- I always wanted a kid. I always wanted Mike's kid…

- And what did you do with her?

The room was moving now, not just the walls, the whole floor was shifting, pulsating with a strange energy. I took another step towards her.

- He came for her. He might come again…

I don't know what I would have done to her if I hadn't heard this ringing in my head, or perhaps it wasn't in my head, it was outside, perhaps it was the doorbell I heard ringing, ringing furiously, and a loud knocking, and a voice on the other side, yelling "Open up!"

I didn't care if Mike was outside. I was too mad with her. I continued to move towards her, until I felt my legs give way beneath me and I sank to the ground. I remember a sharp pain to the side of my head as I did so, and after that I remember nothing at all.

JAMIE

Ahead of me a bright dawn burned in the sky, and yet I felt none of the hope it seemed to signify. Worry weaved through me as I moved, groggy with sleep, through the streets of Kolcan, using my phone to guide me to the address I'd been given by the strange girl who had picked up Katy's phone. She hadn't given anything away, only told me to come and come quick. Now I stumbled through the freezing streets, cursing, passing rows of secretive houses as I did so, doors closed, windows staring out at the streets like a sea of dark eyes, jagged roofs cutting into the grey skies like the serrated edges of a thousand knives.

Eventually, I stopped outside a small house near a smooth stream that slid, silent and watchful, through the cool blue air.

I rang the doorbell, hearing voices on the other side of the door. Impatiently, I rang again. After what felt like hours, I heard footsteps approaching.

Yellow light streamed out through the door. A policeman stood on the threshold, blinking at me.

"Where's Katy?"

"Who are you?"

"Her boyfriend."

"Hold on." He put out a hand to stop me as I tried to move past him. "I need some proof of identity please."

He took a card from me and left, leaving me lingering on the doorstep, listening to urgent voices that came from deep inside the house. At last he returned.

"It's ok. You can go in."

In the kitchen there was a girl around Katy's age, with dirty blond hair and piercings on her brows and lips. A young child was sitting on her lap, a child with dark curls and colour in her cheeks, clutching what looked like a toy rabbit. With a shock, I registered the girl's heart-shaped face, her luminous eyes.

A policewoman was sitting at the table, taking notes.

"Where's Katy?" I asked her.

"You must be Jamie," the pierced girl said.

"Where is she?" I repeated.

"I took her upstairs," the girl said. "She collapsed."

"Wait," the policewoman said, as I moved to run upstairs.

"She knows him," the girl told her. "He was helping her. She said…" her curious eyes assessed me for a few seconds and then flicked back to the child on her lap. "She said he was the only person who made her feel safe."

I ran upstairs, taking the steps three at a time.

Katy was lying on a single bed, in the middle of a bedroom painted a bright yellow. There was a cot by the side of the bed, filled with soft toys. A mobile was turning over the cot, playing the same simple melancholic tune over and over.

She raised her head when I came in, the yellow room making her pale face seem even paler. She didn't even seem to recognise me. Her eyes were blank, glazed over, the lids heavy. "I found Cara," she said.

"Why didn't you come find me, before you came here?"

She didn't seem to have heard me, then finally, she whispered

"I didn't want to drag you into it."

I heard footsteps heading up the stairs and turned to find the girl behind me.

"You seem nice," she told me.

"Who are you?"

"An old friend," she said.

"How come you have her daughter?"

"That's a long story," she said. "Are you happy to be named as her next of kin?"

"Yes," I told her, without hesitation. I turned back to Katy, picked up one of her hands.

"It'll be OK," I told her. She didn't respond and I turned back to the strange girl. "What's the matter with her?"

"She's psychotic."

"She's *what*?"

"Or rather," the girl corrected herself "She's bipolar with psychotic features. Came to a head after her baby and now again." She moved closer to me. "She sees and hears things that aren't there, just like her mum did."

I turned back to Katy. Of course. It all made sense now: the mania, the mood changes, the paranoid conviction that people were after her.

"Of course the drugs didn't help. And now she seems to have had an episode of some kind. The ambulance should be coming soon," she said.

"Did they find Mike?"

"Yes."

"Where?"

"On the moors."

Of course.

"He was only a few miles from here. They needed a helicopter to spot him. The snow helped, but it hindered too. He was near death when they found him."

"And what did he say?"

"Eventually, after a lot of questions, he led the police here. To my place."

I looked around the house. The bedroom I was in was nice, the rest of the place rather dreary and shabby - in need of a complete makeover.

"It's a bit of a mess," she said apologetically. "Mike's mate was going to help fix it up, but he and Mike fell out."

"What's your connection to Mike?" I asked her.

But she had already left. I turned back to the bed. Katy's face scared me; she looked like a corpse - hollow-eyed, sunken-cheeked, deathly pale. In the distance now I could hear the faint sound of an approaching siren. I continued to sit by her side, holding her hand, waiting for answers, picturing the ambulance moving through the silent streets towards us.

A couple hours later, and I was sitting with Peter in his new room at the hospital, this one slightly more spacious than its predecessor, with thicker curtains, through which could be seen a distant slither of glowing moon.

"Bipolar? With what..?" my brother grumbled at me.

I sighed. "With psychotic features. A severe mental disorder, which may be characterised by hallucinations, as well as…" I leaned over, holding my head in my hands. "Look it up, Peter."

"Well I can't bloody well do that, can I? I'm still in this wretched place, in case you hadn't noticed. With non-existent network coverage, just to compound the pain."

"Doesn't seem so bad to me."

I raised my head to examine for the first time the room I was now in. There was a large TV hanging over the bed, a stack of Country Life magazines beneath it. Every spare surface was covered in gifts: an orchid trailing exotic blossom over the plywood surface of his bedside cabinet, a rather fine bottle of vintage Glenfiddich, a box of expensive Belgian chocolates. I couldn't help but notice the note on the box:

"Save these to enjoy with me. J x"

"Who is J?"

"What do you mean?"

"The chocolates." I gestured in their direction. "What if your wife sees them?"

"Jamie, I cannot believe you question the integrity of any person I am involved with, when you-" Peter waved his good arm in the air in a rather feeble imitation of a once grandiose gesture.

"Go on, say it."

"Say what?"

"You think she's a lunatic."

"No, Jamie, I believe you were enlightening me as to the correct term. So, tell me more. What causes this…her symptoms?"

"Prolonged drug use, genetic predisposition. Sometimes - trauma. In Katy's case, a mixture of all three."

"And how does it manifest itself?"

"She…she hears and sees things sometimes that aren't there. She can't sleep for long periods. Sometimes she's animated, excited, sometimes…"

"Volatile, violent, unstable."

I sighed. "I've been made her next of kin. So they've told me what Mike told them, how he finally admitted he'd found the baby Katy had left…" I swallowed. "The baby she'd…abandoned…and he gave it to her friend, Caitlin. Her mother knew all about it."

"So, where is the kid now?"

"In care."

"Will Katy be allowed to see her?"

"In time, of course. If…she gets diagnosed and then treated properly. If she makes progress."

"Will she get her back?"

"I don't know that."

"Surely there was no legal adoption?"

"No…no."

"Is this friend after proper custody?"

"I…I don't think so."

"So, Katy's in with a chance then, if she can present some sort of normal."

"I guess so."

"And the police cocked up. Never twigged the kid was gone. Never launched some sort of formal investigation."

"There was some inexperienced social worker on the case. She let it go, apparently. Never followed up on those initial visits. Made a mistake. Signed off too early."

"She should be struck off. So, she's in with a chance, psycho-girl."

"Don't call her that."

"What's the matter with you, Jamie? You look so glum. I thought you were a sucker for happy endings."

"I'm just tired." I looked over at my brother miserably, hating him. The hate passed in a few seconds.

"How are you sleeping?" I asked solicitously.

"You know me, Jamie. Nothing affects my sleep. Though the pace of this place drives me bonkers. I'm raring to go."

Indeed he looked so wired, as if ready to bounce of his bed any minute.

"I envy you."

"So you've said before. Several times." Peter smiled. "So, how is she?"

"She needs to rest. Her doctor is confident the right drugs can help her, but they won't kick in properly for a couple of weeks."

"And you?" Peter smiled, not unkindly.

What could I tell him? I should have felt relieved - Katy was in a safe place, her child had been found, but I felt as if the ice I'd been walking on for some time now was finally breaking up beneath my feet. Huge fissures were appearing, giving me glimpses of the freezing water below. It was an inky blue, impenetrable, and it was impossible to see myself in its reflection.

"You need to go home, Jamie."

"Where's home?"

"London, you idiot. Go and stay in my flat. You need to go back to work. You'll get the sack at this rate."

"I'm working remotely."

"You can't do that forever."

"This won't take long."

A silence fell between us, and each of us looked at

the other as if understanding him properly for the first time.

"I'm not telling you to go back to Rachel," Peter said.

The name sounded like a false note in the room. I started on hearing it.

"I'll be there for the baby though, every step of the way."

"She won't need you to pay for it, knowing Rachel."

"Well, I will anyway."

"Hmm, you'll probably get on better than most married couples, once she forgives you. Which she will do eventually, I suppose. She's too rational not to." Peter paused. "God, I'm desperate for a cigarette. Your colourful personal life is going to kill me, Jamie - let alone any further encounters with any maniacs you might send my way."

"You should quit."

"Being in here has left me little choice." Peter paused again and then spoke in a rush. "Go back to London, Jamie."

"No."

"Go back to work."

"Not yet."

"Leave that crazy girl alone."

"I can't."

"Won't."

"*Can't.*"

"For fuck's sake, you're going to be a dad!"

I blinked, startled by his sudden fury. "So what?"

"You really have no idea, do you? Being a parent changes *everything*."

"Does it?"

"You idiot," Peter said, not without affection. "Romantic love? Ha! Save it for the poets! The moment your first kid draws breath, it's dead in the water. Life changes, Jamie. And being a parent is an incredible thing."

"I thought you didn't like fatherhood."

"I never said that."

"You complain about it all the time."

"What parent doesn't? The birth of a child - it changes you. Your former self - romantic, selfish, fickle - it dies. You'll see."

"But Katy…"

"Forget Katy. What kind of a mother would she make, Jamie? Seriously - look what a cock-up she's made of it already. And how's she going to feel when she knows you've fathered a child with your wife, hmm? She might not be so keen on you then. *If* she even loves you now."

"She does, you git!" I stood up. "I'm going for a walk." I turned and began moving away.

"Jamie! Come back!" I heard Peter call after me. "I still want to be friends!"

I didn't answer him. I carried on walking away, but not fast enough or far enough to drown out the sound of his fine laughter that followed me out of the room, like a clarion call to my saner self.

I stood under a streetlamp outside the hospital and lit up, sheltering the tiny flame from the wind that rounded on me, making my ears and cheeks burn with its stinging breath.

The cigarette helped clear my head. In a black sky stars swarmed; all was still and cold and quiet.

I could manage this, I thought. Whatever happened, whatever Peter said, I could manage this. I finished the cigarette and made my way back to the inn.

I called Katy from my room. There was no response and so I left a message.

"Katy, I love you. Whatever you did, I don't care. Whatever happens with your daughter, you know I love you, right? You have to know that. I *love* you..."

I lay back upon the bed, my head spinning. My eyes closed. As I slipped very slowly into unconsciousness, I felt Katy with me in the room. She was kissing me, and I was kissing back, reaching out to bring her closer, desperate to feel her around me, to bury any guilt, impotence, pain, in the sweetness of her flesh, then to drink at that sweetness until there was nothing left.

KATY

When I woke again I was blinded by brightness, whiteness, space. There was a woman pressing a damp towel to my head; she was dressed in white; the bowl she was carrying was white; and the towel she was holding. And the windows, and the walls and sky outside.

- Where am I? I asked her.

- The ambulance brought you here, she told me. You were delirious for quite some time. How are you feeling now?

I tried to move my arm but there were a million wires attached to it and on my hand there were two plasters from which wires and little points of pain fanned out.

- Where am I? I asked again, as she handed me two white plastic pots full of pills.

- You're in the hospital, she told me. You're not well, she said. So we're going to look after you for a bit.

I tried to sit up in bed when I heard that.

- But I've got to see Caitlin. She's with Caitlin, I said. I thought she was at my mother's house…I thought she'd buried her in the garden. I turned a glowing face to the nurse. But I was wrong. She didn't do that. My little brother she buried, but not Cara. So she's alive! I'm so happy she's alive. Even after what I did. I have to go to her!

I was trying to lift the covers off the bed, now, struggling and trying to cry out Jamie's name - but he didn't come, only a second nurse, and then a doctor and a needle that flashed in the light.

And then nothing after that.

When I woke again, the blinding pain had gone, but the fog had returned, and with it an eerie calm and a torpor, such that I could not move my limbs. A woman came in a white coat, and then a man, and they talked to each other in low voices. Then another woman came, bringing water, and after I'd drunk a little I asked where Jamie was.

- There's someone waiting for you outside, answers to that name, the man said. He helped bring you here, in fact.

- Let him in, I begged.

- Not until you've had a bit of a rest.

And so I had no choice but to lie back, to take the pills that were offered, to sleep and wait again until the fog lifted a bit. But when it did, I saw the night sky through the high windows, and outside, the silver moon and stars surrounding it, and inside, every other little detail, each line and edge, and Jamie sitting by my bed, with faraway eyes and the hair that was so desperate for a cut and

the face that I was now so grateful for, it could
have been a god's, and the voice, so soft, and
the touch of a hand on mine so gentle that tears
coursed silent down my cheeks.

- How did you sleep?
- Did you see Cara, at Caitlin's house?
- Yes.
- She's alive! And is she lovely? Just as I said? I
asked.
- She is.
- And Mike?
- He's with the police.

He leant over me, and his lips brushed my
cheek.

- And Caitlin? Can I talk to her?
- Not now, he murmured. The doctors say you
need to rest. When you're better, when you're
rested, he said.

He closed his hand over mine, turning the palm
up to face his and pressing his own into it.

And so again, and against my will, there came
sleep.

I felt my hand pressed, a warm pressure, and
the warmth spreading like sunshine, moving up
my arm to my chest. I smiled down at the child
I saw sleeping on my chest, the child with the
heart-shaped face and dark curls, and when I
smiled I heard a familiar voice murmur at me,

though I couldn't make out what it said.

I opened my eyes and they met Donna's face and then the little silver cross she wore around her neck.

- You're here.

- Yes.

I looked over at her.

- Where's your stomach gone? I said.

I was used to the belly that swelled and stretched her dress.

- I had the baby, she told me.

- Where is she?

- You're holding her. You asked to hold her, she said.

I looked down. I was holding a new born, a tiny red wrinkled thing with no hair.

- Oh, I said.

- Don't you like him?

- He's a bonnie little thing. But where's Cara? I said. Will I get to see her?

Donna flushed as she took the baby back.

- You'll have to get better first, she told me.

- But I don't feel ill one bit. How did you know I was here? I asked her, when I'd watched her feeding her son for a bit.

She looked up from her breast.

- I kept calling. In the end Jamie picked up. And I came here, to see you.

- Oh, Donna, that was kind. It's a long way to

Scotland. You're a good friend to do that.

She smiled.

- I wanted to check everything was OK, she said.

- And is it? I murmured.

- Yes.

I smiled and closed my eyes and drifted back to sleep, and when I woke again Jamie was there.

- Where am I? I asked him.

- You're in hospital.

- With Peter?

He shook his head.

- No - this is a different hospital, he said.

- How's Peter?

- Getting a little better every day.

- I'm glad, I said. Where's Caitlin?

- Wanting to see you.

- I can't. I can't forgive her...

- She feels terrible.

- Whose side are you on?

Suddenly I felt so tired, half dead. I turned away from him.

- I need to sleep.

- I love you, he said.

When I turned from him, his voice became so faint I couldn't hear it and I think then he must have left. I was alone, but I didn't mind it, because everything was different. All sound had been smothered, all demons vanquished. There were no dark corners in this bright room where they could hide, no shadows lurking there, and in my head and outside a strange sort of peace. I curled myself in, like a tiny foetus, limbs wound over and around themselves, like they were a puzzle that I made fit, and I listened to my heart's unruly dance beneath the thin cold sheet.

The police came and I was trying to hear what they said, but the words seemed to come from a faraway place, and no matter how hard I tried to catch them, they'd slip between my fingers like tiny fish. When they left I closed my eyes, and all I could see were these flashing fish, their silver scales so bright they'd blind.

There was a question, someone was asking me a question, but I couldn't hear the words themselves, only their tone, and I couldn't do anything but nod and stare at the blank white wall ahead.

There wasn't a spot of dirt on that wall, and I stared at it for a while, as if it were a blank piece of paper and I was picking up my pen to write. Except I couldn't have written a word. I couldn't even speak - but almost against my will, my voice, the only voice now I heard, pushed out a single word.

"Jamie," I said.

And then I brought my knees in close and listened to the roar of silence in my head.

I felt his shadow fall over me as he stood against the wall, felt his hand resting on me, and I turned and turned again, but his hand didn't leave, so I stayed very still and concentrated on breathing in and out.

- I have some photographs, he said.

And he showed me the photos: of Cara as a baby, in her cot, then sitting in her highchair, then on a swing, in the park. A toothless grin, and then a smile, with two tiny teeth in the mouth, and then some hair and a single candle on a cake. And finally more hair, proper curls, behind a balloon, a shiny silver balloon with the number two on it.

- How did you get these?

- Caitlin gave them to me to give to you.

- I still hate her, I said.

- Cara will be three in one month, she says.

- I want to see her, I said.

- Your mother wants to see you, he told me.

- I'll never see her again, as long as I live.

- Katy…

But I shook my head.

- What about Caitlin? I asked him.

- She wants to see you too. She's been waiting, he said.

I wound a single strand of hair around my finger, twisting it round and round until I could feel the tingle of blood in my finger.

- Can I see her now?
- Yes.

Caitlin looked better, I had to admit - like she'd had a good rest. Her skin wasn't so lined and thin, and she'd taken some of the piercings out.

- Where's Cara? I asked her.
- She's in a safe place.
- How is she?
- She's doing well, she told me.
- Are you going to keep her?
- I can't keep her, Katy. Even if I wanted to, she said.

She put her head in her hands and started to weep. Then she lifted her head up and her face was wet.

- You shouldn't have helped Mike, I told her.
- He can't hurt us now. He's locked up.
- He's already done enough.

That truth was like a single light bulb swinging before my eyes, and when I blinked a single tear fell out.

After she left, I told Jamie
- I have to get out. I have to leave this room, I said.

With difficulty I got up and wrapped a blanket about myself.

He didn't try to stop me, only held his arm out and I took it. He walked with me along the white and empty corridors towards the exit to that place, and then towards a small green space that was sectioned off.

Pale, wintry sunshine spilled onto the trees and onto the snow that lay upon them, so that all around I could hear the drip, drip, drip of melting water. Through the snow I could see patches of earth showing, and each blade of grass and each twig on each tree I could see with almost painful clarity.

I went across to a bench on a raised mound in the centre of the small garden. I was blinded by the light, as if taking my first steps; not thinking at all, just feeling, and all I could feel was light.

In the distance I could hear the wail of an approaching ambulance. From where I was standing, I could just make out the blue hills, but their aspect seemed different.

- Am I no longer in Kolcan? I asked him.

- You're around eight miles away, he said.

- No matter how hard I try, I told him, or how fast I run, I always end up right back at the beginning. Right where I began.

Jamie put his coat on the bench.

- Sit, he said.

I sat and looked up at him.

- I got your message, I said. The one you left on my phone. And I think one thing at least is clearer now.

He sat down on the bench next to me, sitting close, but not a single part of his touching mine.

- What is that? he asked.

- You and me, I said.

He smiled, just with his mouth at first, and then the smile crept into every corner of his face, until at last it reached his eyes. And I smiled back, but I was tired, so tired, I could barely stand.

- I need to go back, I said. I need to rest.

I let him lead me back into my room. There, I lay on the bed, and he lay next to me. It was a narrow bed, but we lay side by side, his back facing the wall and the whole of my back pressed up against him.

I sighed with relief, feeling Jamie's breathing at my neck, his heart beating into my back. It wasn't safe to move, I thought, not yet. I would have to lie still, and wait…

I couldn't see the whole road ahead. Not all of it. But one thing was clear: just for a while, for a wee while, this was a good place to stop.

JAMIE

Two years later

London to Kolcan, Kolcan back to London.

It was a hard slog, but I was determined to do it, to prove to Katy that I could.

It had taken a while to win her trust back, after she'd heard about Rachel's pregnancy.

"You left Scotland, having met me, and then you were with her again. It must have been at that time."

"But she was still my wife. And I did leave. And I came back to you. And I haven't been with her since."

"And you'll leave me in time."

"No, Katy. I won't. But I can't leave my son. Even if I'm not with Rachel," I said.

That was before Max was born. He was almost two now and he and Katy had met twice, no, three times, and I think she understood, or at least she accepted that this had happened, and that my failure to step away from Rachel at a particular point in time hadn't necessarily led us in the wrong direction. I'd come to Katy eventually, as I'd wanted to in the very beginning (though I hadn't wanted to admit it), as I'd promised to do, but it had been by a more circuitous route than I'd initially imagined.

And Peter was right of course, though I would never tell him so. Max changed everything.

For now, any togetherness for Katy and me was still tentative, more of a coming together than any formal coupling. Sometimes it worked, sometimes not.

She was like new terrain I was travelling, and sometimes I was comfortable, sometimes I was lost, bewildered, and it seemed as if all the elements were against me. But I'd grown used to the struggle - I'd normalised it. I told myself that one day it would subside, and with each day that passed I hated myself a little less for wanting her.

Katy had decided to settle near Kolcan (she couldn't quite face being in it), as long as Mike was still locked up. It looked as if he would be locked up for a while. He got ten years for intent to cause grievous bodily harm. She was implacable about her mother - refusing to ever see her. She once insisted that anyone who cared to look for it would find a tiny grave in the back garden of her mother's house, in grass once shadowed by a leafy magnolia tree. When I suggested we should pass on that information to the police, she shook her head. "Leave her alone. Let her just stew in her own guilt."

Marcus had helped Katy get a job through some contact of his who'd materialised up North and who owed him a favour. She'd learnt to drive in order to get to work (her office was some thirty miles from Kolcan). She was determined to do everything she could to prove to the authorities that she was worthy of looking after her own kid.

It was a struggle for her too - any outcome as to Cara as yet undecided, but as long as she took the medication she needed daily, she might be in with a chance, she'd been told.

She was a lot calmer now, even at times contented.

Sometimes I missed the restless energy of the old Katy, who didn't stop moving or playing with her hair. I hated to admit that, even to myself. But after all, that was the Katy I fell in love with, the girl who needed me.

I was never anything but upbeat about her to my brother though. Peter had made a full recovery physically from Mike's attack, if not mentally (he wasn't quite his old recalcitrant self). I never confided in him, but I suspected he could read me as easily a book, if he cared to try.

A year ago now, Peter had called me up in a state. They'd pulled a body up that had been buried in wasteland just outside of Newcastle. The body had suffered lacerations in line with a vicious attack.

Peter and Emmeline had made a desperate trip to Newcastle to see the body.

It had turned out to be a false alarm.

"The body wasn't hers," Peter rang to tell me, twenty-four hours later.

He sounded euphoric, drunk with relief.

Two days ago we received another call about another body. This one had been found in a disused, flooded quarry pit near Hull.

My brother was playing golf with mates in Malaga so he couldn't make the trip.

"It's my turn anyway," I told him.

As I drove North, I imagined silver water, unbroken by wind, and the ripples the body would make as it exited, dripping, spinning in the sunshine.

It would likely be a bloater, I thought. I'd seen pictures of them before: bodies that had been submerged under water for an age - blackened extremities, skin puckered, rubberised. Grotesque.

I drove on, remembering my long drive with Katy up to the Highlands that first time we met. The way she'd pulled her skirt down to cover her bare knees, the raindrops at the base of her throat, the cigarettes she'd smoked at the service station.

The dead hare on the road.

The cut of her knife on my skin, the bitter wind against my cheeks.

It was summer - the day was windless, cloudless, empty.

For some reason I felt as if I were returning home.

As it happened, they'd already removed the body, and I had to go into a morgue to see it. They showed me pictures of the water though. It was nothing like I'd imagined it: clogged with rubbish, with dirty plastic bags that floated amid the scum on its surface.

It was surprisingly deep, though, which is why the body hadn't been found for a while.

I wouldn't have been able to recognise my sister from her face in any event. It was her fingerprints and her dental records which were an exact match.

"Sarah," I said.

It was as if a door had closed in my mind, a door that led to waters deeper and darker than the lake in which she had been found.

"Why Hull?" I wondered, having called Peter to tell him.

"I guess we'll never know. Life is full of mysteries," he told me, his voice breaking slightly.

I felt a prickling at the back of my eyes.

"Yes, it is."

I called Katy to tell her, and she came.

I didn't ask her to come. But she came anyway.

We stayed in a hotel, some handsome red brick piece in the centre of Hull.

I could grieve properly now Sarah had been found,

and I did, starting that night. And Katy held me, for a long time, while I did it.

It was the first time she'd helped me, she said. And not the other way round.

But she *had* helped me, I told her. She'd brought love back into my life, and it had spread from there to Peter, and from Rachel and I to our son. There was love, and it came in waves, and sometimes it brought turbulence, but always, like now, it carried me along with it, if I was able to let it, washing me clean - leaving me lighter, freer, more alive.

THE END

ACKNOWLEDGEMENTS

This novel has been crafted with blood, sweat, toil and tears. In some ways it has been my bête noir. I've also described it as my baby. It's the story I refused to give up on, and I am indebted to all those who worked on it with me and helped me to improve it: to my friends Philippa Ackland, Siward Atkins, Suzana Urlich and Kate Mitchell, to my mother, Doris Urquhart, to Imogen Russell Williams and Alanna Jones for their fine editing skills, and finally to Graham Rees for his brilliant book design. I appreciate your help and encouragement.

Thank you to those in the literary world who read earlier versions of *Loss* and urged me not to give up on it. Most notably, Jonny Geller, whose email with constructive criticism was in retrospect one of the most encouraging I have ever received, making me more determined to make this novel and my writing generally the best it could possibly be. Thank you, too, to Diana Beaumont for her wise words. Lastly, I must thank the many fine poets, whom I know through Twitter, whose work I've admired so over time, and who have fuelled my darker side. The poetry I wrote in recent years was inspired by this novel, or was it the other way around? Anyway, you know who you are!

I do hope my readers enjoy the culmination of my creative efforts, combined with these individuals' support, their time and their patience.

Jane Lightbourne
Nevada Street Press
October 2021

ABOUT THE AUTHOR

Loss is Jane's first novel for adults, published by Nevada Street Press. Jane is also the author of *My Cat Called Red*, a story for children aged 8 to 12, which features the magical cat, Red, and the purr that transforms children's lives. As well as writing fiction, Jane worked as a lawyer, as a barrister initially, and in the City after that. She lives in London with her three children. Jane is currently working on a new book for adults and will be releasing a second story for children later this year.

Jane can be contacted through her website
www.janelightbourne.co.uk
or by email at
books@janelightbourne.co.uk
Her Twitter handle is
@JaneLightbourne